THE COLOUR OF ROBOTS

By

James Marson

To Mum
For her love, wise words and invaluable support,
always.

And to Mrs Brown, my Primary 3 teacher.
Because I promised.

Cast of Characters

<u>The Imperial Navy</u>
Karl Dougan - A junior planetary engineer (second class)
Commander Fleek - A senior officer
Chief Technologist Howells - A scientist
Admiral Reid - A very senior officer
Finlay Urquhuart - An analyst

Ellie Novak - A journalist
Morning Star - A computer

<u>The Pirates</u>
Binner - A pirate Captain
Hurbury - A pirate and begrudging First Officer
Jirbaks - A junior pirate
Greeta - A sort of pirate
Various Barons and Baronesses

<u>The Robots</u>
Knowledge - a.k.a The Traveller
Survival - a.k.a The Coward
Power - a.k.a The Protector
Money - a.k.a. The Financier
Glory - a.k.a The Achiever
Harmony - a.k.a The Peacemaker
Justice - a.k.a The Arbiter

CHAPTER ONE
Prologue

The last thing Gunther Merrickson, the most junior technician at CERN, intends to do this morning is create a universe. The last thing he will *actually* do this morning is knock over a cup of steaming-hot coffee onto a very, very expensive piece of equipment. His afternoon will be spent being absent. And anxious.

The hot coffee, which will wipe easily off the *surface* of the Electromagnetic Pulse Resonator Command module, will seep underneath the beige casing. It will puddle on sensitive wafer-thin silicon strips carrying vital commands to and from the control hub of a series of very expensive magnetic coils. They in turn will guide a tiny particle, hurtling at speeds tantalisingly close to the speed of light, crucial pico-metres off course.

The particle spins and twists in the fluctuating magnetism. Femtoscopic[1] vibrations build between the

---

[1] Very small. Very, very, very small.

spaces between its quarks. The vibrations resonate out of control. A minor proto-quake erupts inside and suddenly-

The time is 11:51:43 and 1.0003211100569322 milliseconds, on the 31st May 2018.

A tiny, little multi-dimensional string unravels.

The void it leaves is immense. In physical space terms, it is mind-frackingly small. But the energy spike is so big you could mount pictures on it.

Inside in the Serious Tube Thingy of the Biggest Bit of the Large Hadron Collider[2] at CERN, a new universe flutters into existence.

In another part of the multi-billion dollar[3] facility a second junior technician pauses in the act of finishing his own cup of coffee as the thirteenth alarm of that morning goes off. He casually taps a key on the keyboard.

In the depths of a PC casing, surrounded by wires, dust, and the occasional coffee cup, a processor wipes the only record of the event that would have justified the expenditure on, not only the whole project, but a private heated pool, indoor sports centre and five-star luxury live-in wing for the funding committee, their families, their friends and their pets.

Eternity continues.

---

[2] They had official names but since the only way to travel between them was down a mile-long tunnel in a golf buggy, ambiguity was best avoided.

[3] Pound/Euro/Yen/Rouble - at that expense the actual currencies don't matter.

Part Two: This Universe

The universe began.

At first it was almost nothing: a minuscule bulge on the surface of another.

It stretched. It wriggled. Finally, it popped.

Dimensions collapsed inside. The surface expanded so fast that time began to stretch within. Space formed, spewing out like the guts of a trodden-upon frog.

Tiny fragments of dimensions tangled together, dragging on the surface of the expanding universe. Coalescing. Forming matter, creating gravity.

The heat died away to a terrible cold vacuum. Pockets of matter that had clung on to its nascent energy spun in an elegant galactic dance as stars and planets churned their gravity into motion. The forces created stars, planets, worlds, rocks, rivers while the clockwork mechanism of the universe continued

3

running down to nothing. An eternal sigh of creation playing out until the end of time.

And in the midst of this, something warm and notional fluttered by, like a whisper on a graveyard breeze. A tiny new force twitched into existence. A force capable of moving against the greater power of the universe, tumbling towards chaos and darkness, coldness and decay. A force called life. Stumbling, blind, determined, it proved to be unstoppable.

Almost...

The forms that life took were many and varied and competition for resources — namely room to live and the unfettered access to other edible life forms — soon spawned the most active, short-lived and exciting energies of the universe — war.

The more sophisticated the species, the more advanced its approach to this new, violent activity. From tooth and claw, to rock and stick, to sword and spear, to gun and plane, to laser guided missile and star-ship, to gravity slicer and star-base the desire to destroy inferior, then its own, then alien, species was the loving, doting parent of all invention.

The one thing that all species agreed hadn't worked, were the Robots. At first they seemed like the natural evolution: a species of their making, under their control, that could think at lightning speed, and would be perfectly OK with never having a say in their own destiny.

It has been said that the best angle of view to spot a flaw in a line of thought, is hindsight.

According to the history books, the Robot War went on for three decades and had drawn in almost every sentient being in the universe. A force more deadly, more dangerous than the benign power of the slowly dilapidating universe had threatened to bring an end to every stitch of life that been sewn into it.

The end had never come. A weakness was eventually found and it was only by ruthless exploitation that any organic life form had lived to tell of it. No scrap, no fragment of sentient, self-aware programming was to be left in the universe.

And that was exactly how it is now.

Unless you look closely that is....

THE COLOUR OF ROBOTS

CHAPTER TWO

Dougan

Planetary Engineer (Second Class) Lieutenant Karl Dougan, hadn't been looking closely. In his defence, he wasn't expected to.

His Imperial Navy Survey Corvette, the Burning Desire[4], was equipped with the very latest, state-of-the-art bleepy, burpy, whizzy programming the Engineering Corps could offer and, were it not for the Empire's "Anti-Robot" directive banning any artificial intelligence greater than that required to operate a dustpan, he wouldn't have been required at all.

He sighed as the Desire dropped clumsily out of hyperspace near a small brown dwarf star and slewed into orbit around a pitiful, dense, dusty planet. He sighed as, prompted by the annoyingly-soothing voice of the Engineering Survey Checklist, he flipped on the surface scanners. He drummed his fingers on the

---

[4] He had been lucky with his Burning Class Survey Module; others had been named the Burning Question, Burning Bridges, Burning Bush, Burning Midnight Oil and Burning Brightly, which due to an unfortunate incident involving an incorrectly wired fuel pump, had lived up its name on its maiden voyage.

console, until a slew of other equally-annoyingly-soothing voices began to warn him of unexpected vibrations on the flight deck. When he stopped, they stopped. He managed to amuse himself with this for another twenty minutes before even that wore off.

His job was to survey remote planets. He was quite good at it, because it required no skill. Most planets he'd surveyed to date had been dull, lifeless balls of rock; dull, lifeless balls of gas; or dull, lifeless balls of something in-between. The linking factor had been: they were all balls.

The planet below faithfully promised not to destroy his expectations. At least in geology.

It was grey and featureless. It looked desiccated. Even the gleaming light of the tiny star, rising as majestically as it could, utterly failed to impress Dougan, who sighed, once more, just to be sure he'd made his point.

"See new worlds," the recruitment officer at the Naval College had told him. Too late, he'd realised what he'd heard was, "See *interesting* worlds".

The report droned on, dividing the planet into sectors, recording temperature, air density, base mineral content, and a host of other pointless facts. It mapped the surface of the planet to identify suitable building sites, and probed its gravity. The numbers would be logged, the planet designated "surveyed" and no-one would ever come this way again. Given the routine dullness of the activity, it rather irritated Dougan that it needed to be accompanied by a regular beeping sound.

Occasionally a planet would surprise. Sometimes a beautiful ecosystem would be uncovered, rich in vibrant, new and exotic life forms that scientists would flock to, get liberally eaten, be replaced by marines who set about systematically destroying the ecosystem, and finally ground down into component elements by the Mining Corp.

Very occasionally they would uncover a new alien race.

New alien races were often the biggest disappointment. All the intelligent ones had already discovered each other, and those that hadn't were so far back down the evolutionary pathway, the only major relationship to be established was the predator/prey one.

In short, it was dangerous or it was dull.

The scanner beeped again. But this time there was an odd, strangled tone to its beep.

Dougan's ears pricked. It was true that things beeped all the time, and buzzed and klaxoned and occasionally would talk to you in an inappropriately soft voice when things went wrong[5]. This one seemed genuinely urgent; a beep from a machine that knew it had cried "beep" once too often for its own good and now really did need his attention.

Dougan peered into the scanner display.

There was everything he would expect from a cold, dead planet as far from anywhere as anyone could possibly get: trace valuable elements; a thin nitrous atmosphere; *lots* of rock; a small amount of volcanic activity and two robots.

---

[5] Which is of course highly inappropriate. It has been proved that a calm voice, slowly breaking the news of a massive radiation leak is more likely to increase chances of death. The bodies of many unfortunate souls have been recovered still in their seats wearing an expression that might have read: "Will you please get to the point!?". New generation warning devices are as much as ten times more appropriate with their "Warning! Reactor leak! Get the hell out of here!" approach and can proudly claim to have saved a small number more lives than caused serious accidents.

This last kernel of information sent a chill down his spine.

The scanner beeped again. They were moving. Two things, approaching each other.

Point made, the scanner lapsed into silence.

To Dougan's knowledge, what he was looking at was impossible. Robots — indeed anything with any kind of artificial intelligence — had been eradicated from the galaxy over a hundred years ago.

And yet, that was what Dougan appeared to be looking at.

So, he concluded, it was definitely impossible.

What nagged at him was needing to add "to his knowledge" to the impossibility of what he was witnessing. He hadn't been the brightest of students; he had barely passed his engineering exam. "To his knowledge," created quite a bit of leeway.

Dougan wasn't a typical Engineer. He had shown creative flair at university — particularly in fields like explaining why lab reports hadn't been handed in on time but less so when asked to explain why every experiment he engaged in had gone hideously awry, or justifying why machines generally malfunctioned around him. They weren't the sort of skills the Imperial Navy prized. He had only ever heard the word 'creative' used in the context of describing methods of killing things. And even that was only to his knowledge.

He had joined the Navy almost by accident. He wasn't required to perform acts of derring-do, and had judiciously avoided being in any live combat situation by entering the Planetary Engineering division. They only went to war against rocks. And even then rocks that had been unquestionably confirmed as not being sentient.

And now here he was, watching two gangly robotic creatures — one tall and thin, the other small and spidery. In the middle of a wide barren plain. Chatting.

Dealing with the impossible was not covered in Planetary Engineering training. Planetary Engineers were good at measuring things and drawing conclusions. They weren't good at dealing with long-extinct, potentially catastrophic pseudo-lifeforms: forms that would have had the entire Admiralty breaking out in cold sweat had it learned of their existence.

To his knowledge.

His reasoning, given that the impossible was managing to cloak itself in a fairly good resemblance of possibility was this: They were museum pieces. It was someone's idea of a joke. Out here on the very, very edges of galactic civilisation, where he was most likely the first visiting sentient being, someone had created the bleakest theme park imaginable. Without advertising it. Someone with insane levels of optimism and an utter dearth of business sense.

Dougan didn't want to take a closer look. He knew where these things went. An "unusual sighting" report, led to a lower-orbit 3-D scan. Before you knew it you were staring into the jaws of a previously undiscovered sabre-toothed-slaver-beast which was bound to be named after you when you were finally identified from your remains in its faeces. Dougan always did his best not to end up Planet-side. There were others for that, more foolhardy than him, who got paid more and had more military hardware than teeth.

So instead, he did something stupid. Intending to nudge the Desire into completing the scan, ticking the obligatory survey boxes[6]and hot-footing it back to the nearest jumpship, he tried to turn the Burning Desire around. At which point, it malfunctioned.

Primed with the ridiculous idea of taking the closest look imaginable, The Desire lurched forward toward the surface with such force that Dougan's forehead bounced off the control panel, leaving little flecks of paint. The Engineering Survey Checklist announced, in that calm, soothing voice reserved for only the direst of emergencies, that they were making an emergency landing.

The Desire's Autopilot made a textbook landing[7].

Dougan was shaken but unharmed. The gravity generator in the ship had taken the brunt of the crash but the seat had become dislodged and left him rocking back and forth as if he were sitting on the kind of spring-mounted snail often found in children's play-parks.

The squat bulk of the vehicle listed to one side on a dusty dune.

He peered out through the viewport window.

The planet surface stretched away in a flat, powdery plain, lit dimly by the feeble light of the dwarf star. Far away in the distance, a clump of mountains huddled together as if for warmth, and a listless wind swirled a handful of dust, rather like it wanted it made clear that it didn't much care for the job.

The planet was small enough to make out the curvature of the horizon. Above, the blackness of space

---

[6] Rocky - check, round - check, tourist value zero - check, potential as a tax haven for off-world aliens - check.

[7] If the textbook in question had been thrown out of a ninth-storey window, attached to a brick, in a high-gravity environment.

seemed to suck at his eyes, the sharp punctuation of the stars smeared by the gritty atmosphere.

It was not going to win any awards.

Fortunately, nor did there appear to be anything out there to collect them.

The console flashed up a message: external non-critical hull breach.

Dougan sighed, slipped cautiously out of his seat, and landed less cautiously on the floor. He brushed himself down, and raised his arm in front of him. Down the left side of his bright yellow, lieutenant's jacket was a small control panel. He ran a couple of diagnostic tests to check for ruptures, feeling the suit inflate and monitoring pressure drops for leaks. A reassuring voice assured him the suit was functioning at 89%.[8]

A Naval officer's suit was a lifeline in the depths of space. It was durable and sturdy but allowed complete freedom of movement, was completely space-proof, capable of small amounts of self propulsion in zero gravity, could monitor your health and even take evasive action against slow-moving projectiles and poisonous environments[9].

The suits were also very brightly coloured.

The Navy had long since abandoned the idea of visual camouflage, working on the principle that if you were near enough to *see* the enemy you were near enough for any number of heat-seeking, mass differentiator, smart, laser-guided, thermonuclear, scatter-effect weapons to locate you themselves without the aid of a man with a pair of binoculars. A

---

[8] He'd never got it 100. Ever. He suspected this cost extra.

[9] Most cadets learned this particular feature the first night they wore them out drinking

Naval Officer was expected to fight visibly and proudly, thus planting the correct assumption in the enemy's head that they were not in the least bit bothered by their lack of camouflage, on account of their possession of the above-mentioned weapons.

The true distinguishing feature of the particular colour was the Officer's rank. The hierarchy was strict, exact and observed at all times. It also meant that the only way to avoid wearing a colour that didn't suit you was to get promoted, or shot.

Dougan placed the helmet (also bright yellow with the naval logo on the top) on his head in strict accordance with the operating instructions bolted inside and turned on the HUD.

He pulled on his gloves, which tightened into place, and shuffled down the sloped deck to the airlock.

A minute later he returned and picked up his rifle.

The airlock was bright but large for a one-person craft. Alone in the airlock, Dougan was frequently hounded by the irrational fear of finding a malevolent alien in there with him. His fingers curled involuntarily round the trigger of the gun. Firing laser weaponry in enclosed spaces was generally considered foolish: the rifle even bore a sticker remarking to that effect, but when everything carries warnings the ability to notice them decreases. WARNING. THIS WARNING CAUTIONS YOU TO OBSERVE ALL OTHER WARNINGS was the latest move by Imperial Sign Writers to help preserve lives. So much small print was typically included that a number of perfectly healthy people had been sent blind trying to read them —

meaning current Naval advice was to completely ignore them all[10].

The panel winked green to indicate it was safe to open the airlock. Dougan opened the door and scrambled out. Sandy grit snuck in behind him, carried on the wind. He quickly scanned the horizon. Nothing.

He hefted his rifle to his hip and adopted the classic position of someone about to get ambushed.

The wind whipped steadily. The planet stretched away in all directions broken by intermittent dunes. It was possible to see the curvature of the planet now, which was disconcerting because it put less distance between him and dangerous objects.

He prowled forward, swinging the weapon from side to side, sweeping the horizon. The gun's scanner showed nothing but the massive energy blur of the craft behind him, pulsating slightly as the gravity generator cooled from the violent landing.

He took a few more steps forward.

There was nothing there.

Satisfied, he shouldered his rifle and turned back to the craft. He tilted his head to get a better look for damage. The Desire had landed at what only could be described as a jaunty angle, if such things could apply to crashed survey modules and not just hats.

---

[10] A race of cat-like creatures in an enlightened corner of the galaxy had once boosted their entire race's IQ over a few short, short-lived generations, by the simple act of removing all warning signs. So excited by this discovery, they had set forth to spread the word. Missionaries traveled far and wide to impart the news that warning signs were bad. Their missions sadly mostly ended in disaster. There are places where "beware of the dog" might be interpreted loosely but a sign saying "beware of the giant thirty foot killer centipede" should never be taken in vain.

The spherical command pod was jutting with its nose in the air. The squat bulk of the engine section had sunk to the base of the dune with the weight. The short broad atmospheric stabiliser fins had prevented it from sinking further into the fine dust, and lay flush with the surface. Satisfied there was no damage, he began to walk round the other side.

He trudged round the front of the craft aware that the fine sandy rock was beginning to pile up against the grey metallic panels. He passed under the shadow of the pod to examine the other side of the craft.

A movement to his right caught his eye and he froze. Standing less than a half a kilometre away were two large robots, watching him with glowing red sensors set deep in their eye sockets.

His throat dried instantly; a voice from his suit suggested a glass of water. His hand clasped the gun instinctively.

One of the robots was tall, about twice the size of a man, humanoid in shape but bulky and angular. It stood solid and immobile and he could make out a primitive grille where its mouth would be. Its surface was chunky and metallic, battle scarred and weathered. Its shoulders were blazoned with blue circles and triangles, a theme reiterated on its torso. Down its arms ran wires and its fingers were outstretched in anticipation. The only movement was the red pulse from the menacing triangular eye sockets.

The other was about half as tall and spider-like. Spindly legs arced, suspending a torso-like body but its head, also swivelled in Dougan's direction, looked similar to the other's in shape. The legs moved slowly, shifting its weight around.

Dougan stared back in horror. His mind raced inside his helmet[11],

If this was a theme park, it was not aimed at families.

These weren't automatons either — machines with upright form — mechanical but brainless. Automatons were small, menial, non-threatening.

These definitely did not fall into this category.

These were proper bona-fide robots. And they oozed threat.

Which was definitely impossible.

The robots watched him carefully. His gaze flicked between the two of them. Dust swirled around his feet, oblivious to the tension.

Slowly, the spider robot began to turn itself to face him and, with it, something sinister and mechanical that definitely had a dangerous end, swivelled to point in his direction.

In such traumatic situations, adrenalin begins to flow to the brain to allow it to think quicker and focus. This state of heightened alertness allows the senses to pick out other pieces of information that might be deemed as irrelevant at the time. Dougan became aware that the robots, although different shapes, looked as if they were constructed from similar parts. He noticed two other shapes in the distance, possibly spacecraft of the robot owners and he noticed that the humanoid robot also now seemed to be pointing a heavy weapon at him. He also become aware one of the key biological functions of the suit had kicked in.

Dougan had never held a death or glory approach. He preferred to think he had a spectrum of options which was wide enough to encompass the discreet

---

[11] Which, given the limited space it had to work in, resulted in small amounts of mental bruising.

avoidance of conflict, negotiation solely via the medium of body language and the judicious use of absentee notes. But he was a trained naval officer, if only on paper, and he hoisted his gun to shoulder height and aimed it squarely at the spider robot, on the basis that, as a rule, he didn't like spiders.

The spider robot, which had begun to edge towards him, hesitated. The other robot seemed to watch the exchange carefully, waiting to see who would make the first move.

Time slunk by as if watching from the sidelines, pretending it wasn't interested.

Dougan, feeling his legs beginning to buckle, backed slowly away, in what he hoped was a non-threatening manoeuvre, until his rear bumped the welcome, hard metal side of the Desire.

Spider edged slowly forward. The pulsing eyes glowed with greater regularity.

Dougan considered shooting, but he knew this would make things worse. Besides his mind didn't seem to be communicating with the rest of his body very well.

The robot suddenly made a spidery run at him.

Dougan's spider-fear kicked in with full force. Spinning round, he scrambled to get as far from the techno-arachnid as he possibly could. As he rounded the command pod he stumbled, and threw all his weight behind the fall. He shoulder-rolled, like a cheap stuntman, under the bulk of the pod and clawed at the soft earth, failing to create more than a small sandy hole. A couple of frantic attempts later he realised that the strap of the gun, which was looped over his arm had become wedged between the craft and the ground, anchoring him in place. He pulled feverishly as the earth shook from the approach of the robot and managed to free the gun from its lock seconds *after* the metallic foot of the spider speared the gun into the earth, trapping him.

He lay there, terrified, as the head of the robot sank into view beneath the underside of the pod, the eyes glowing searchingly. Dougan trembled.

At least he thought it was him.

Now that he came to think about it, the air itself seemed to be trembling. So did the ground.

The robot suddenly jerked its head up, and rose to its full height. Dougan noticed a bright light coming from the sky behind him and even in the thin atmosphere he could make out a terrible rumbling noise. The robot looked down at him again and pulled its foot out of the ground. It turned quickly and skittered back the way it had come.

Dougan scrambled to his feet and pulled the gun from the sand. As he did, a small claw-like foot came with it. He jumped back, but it fell to the ground harmlessly. It lay in the sand, a curled metallic cast-off.

Dougan couldn't care less if it had tap-danced.

Above him the air seemed to be on fire. A great bright shape was hurtling towards the surface of the planet, falling shards breaking away as it did. Dougan fought his way back to the airlock, the dusty ground shuddering under him. He didn't notice the spidery metallic hand following him.

He squeezed through the door the second it opened, scanned quickly for aliens and shut the door. As the pressure built in the chamber he slammed the comfortingly large, bright red, emergency defence system button.

Klaxons blared and generators hummed into power as the gravity forcefield crackled into life around the ship. The heavy external shielding clamped over the skin of the vessel turning it into a thick silvery beetle. Space chaff fired impotently to distract missiles. You never could be too careful.

Within six seconds the ship was impenetrable.

Scrambling into the command pod, Dougan flicked on the sensor screens. It was eerily calm inside, the outside vibrations dampened by the gravity buffers.

On one viewscreen he could see the bright object disintegrating as it burned through the thin atmosphere, in what seemed like a dangerously close collision course. On the other screen, something equally curious was happening.

He could make out the figures of the two robots running very fast towards their craft. The humanoid had the head start but the spider-like one was rapidly catching him up.

Dougan's eyes flicked from screen to screen. The Burning Desire wouldn't withstand a direct hit from what now looked like a standard bulk freighter about to crash into the planet, but with luck it would survive pretty much anything else. Helplessly he counted off seconds to impact.

On the other screen the human robot had disappeared. The spider robot, still metres away, appeared to have given up. It stopped in its tracks and turned to face towards the light. It almost looked to Dougan as if it were wearing a defiant smile.

There was a pause, a momentary hiatus as the universe took a breath and then...

The freighter crashed with all the spectacle it could muster. As the other spaceship raised off the ground the freighter ploughed squarely through it, smashing it to atoms. The smoking charred front of the freighter then collided explosively with the planet surface while the bulky back engine module flipped over itself. It crashed down squarely on top of the spider robot, which splintered beneath it like a matchstick model. The engine module sat there flaming violently for a second or two, spewing short hot wispy plumes. And then it too, exploded.

The viewscreen went blank white, unable to safely represent the fierce light of the blast. The Burning Desire rolled from its dune, blown like a flea in a sandstorm by the force of the gravity-sink blast. Even beyond the gravity buffers, Dougan felt the pull as the mass-energy converter sent a gravity wave rippling across the surface of spacetime.

Time buckled for a moment, a week passed in a second. Then the universe righted itself. And then there was silence.

Dougan scrambled to his feet for the third time that day and punched the scanners back into life.

The ship's systems churned silently to themselves while he scanned the desolation. The planet looked very much like it had when he arrived, only slightly less dull. The craft and the resulting gravity explosion had completely annihilated almost everything within a kilometre radius of the blast, which had fortunately only just excluded him. From space it would look as if someone had dropped a soot bomb on the planet. A faint pall of smoke rose from the debris like a drunken snake.

There ought to have been a black box somewhere, Dougan thought. It might have been his duty to find it.

He wasn't going to though. It was probably hidden amongst a thousand tonnes of black radioactive soot.

The air was thick when he left the craft to tend to the rupture. He was shell-shocked and numb, operating on auto-pilot and his mind was filled with questions that, in all likelihood, he would be expected to answer before he got a chance to ask them. Questions like: Where had the robots come from? What were they doing there? and Would you like someone to show you how to use that gun?

Back in the wobbly command seat, Dougan rocked as he fretted over how such a dull planet had turned out to be so hideously un-dull. He shuddered. There would be Reports.[12]

As dictated by protocol, he fired off an accident report beacon tagged with brief details of the crash but carefully omitting any details of the robots. For now, his job was done.

The Desire climbed shakily away from the planet and, as it slewed into a high velocity slingshot, the chair rocked crazily from side to side. Dougan sighed at the cruel twist of fate that had given him the skills to be able to patch a spacecraft into space-worthiness but not fix his own chair. He signalled ahead to the nearest Naval Gravity Well Jump ship a request to return home. It was too far by hyperspace alone and much as

---

[12] There were always reports. Reports were like bacteria living in a warm moist culture provided by the Navy. And just like bacteria there were some reports that were a necessary healthy part of everyday life. And then there were Reports, with a capital R, that were lethal.

he hated the gravity jumps[13], to stall going back to HQ was only putting off the inevitable.

As Dougan entered hyperspace for the short trip to The Wooly Jumper, Naval Task Force Clean Up vessel The Tom and Jerry lumbered into the planetary space to begin the mop-up job. It was packed with enough scanners to deafen the inhabitants of a small moon.

In the small cargo area at the back of the Desire's cabin, a robotic hand twitched and a tiny red light in its palm flickered into life.

---

[13] Which felt rather like being sucked through a straw.

THE COLOUR OF ROBOTS

CHAPTER THREE

Fleek

The Imperial Democratic Naval Headquarters was impressively massive, and as visitors had pointed out, for the headquarters of a facility that promoted peace throughout the galaxy, it was very, very, spiky.

Long, pointed towers jutted into the atmosphere at unusual angles, making it resemble a giant mace dropped from the sky by a careless deity. Even the white surfaces favoured by Naval architects made it glint in a menacing fashion. There was something clinical about it, like a piece of medical equipment which, if found in a drawer, would have you closing the drawer again before you had a chance to work out what it might be used for.

Many had been keen to point out[14] that the towers were both functional and decorative: the tip of each one reinforcing the laser shield dome which cloaked the building. It was too localised to save the whole city from enemy space-strikes, but, the reasoning went,

---

[14] Mostly the architects.

would at least preserve the lives of those who'd have the means to take substantial revenge.

And so the Naval HQ was allowed grudgingly to dominate the skyline of Imperial City, which stretched away for seventy miles in every direction[15]. In terms of magnificence it was upstaged only slightly by the grandeur of the Imperial palace on the plateau behind. This elegant, octopus-like construction was not as spiky, but made up for its inferiority in this regard by being substantially more expensive and having considerably better views.[16]

Above both these edifices, the Naval Space Operations Base hung suspended in low orbit, like a metallic waffle in the sky. Ships of all sizes, from small corvettes to massive Battle Leviathans clung anchored to the dock. The wispy tendrils of sky-lifts drifted in the wind, tethering the space-station to the ground and shuttling cargo and personnel to and fro. The sky-lifts neatly removed the need for the messy process of hurling cargo back and forth in bottles of compressed explosives, lit at one end.

Inside one of the sky-lifts, Dougan gripped the edge of his seat as he hurtled towards the ground. He hated the lifts. They messed with sensible notions of up and down and his stomach didn't like that. He had been forced to hand the Burning Desire over to the repair

---

[15] Even though from seventy miles away you couldn't see it, you still knew it was there. Like the image of a lorry you spotted a second ago that only reaches your brain as you step onto the road.

[16] To have an Empire it was necessary to have an Emperor. No-one had ever seen him, or her, or it. Very few people went to the palace and fewer returned. Virtually nothing was known of the Emperor's actual function. It was precisely this sense of otherworldly mystery that had allowed the Imperial Democracy to tolerate the Idea of an Emperor for so long.

dock crew at the Base, so was left with little choice.[17] The lift slid down the cable as it plummeted from the sky, gathering energy for its batteries for the return journey. Dougan felt queasy at the weightlessness — the travel pods were too small to fit gravity generators. He was grateful to be alone, in case it became necessary to be sick. If there was one thing worse than the nasty, sick feeling of weightlessness it was the nasty feeling of weightless sick.

Below, the Headquarters compound loomed. At this time of the evening, the dusky red sun bathed the city in a blood-red light, making it resemble a horrendous battleground, which of course it was.

In a galaxy that praised itself for its Pax Imperium, most of the corruption and crime that had been eradicated from the majority of the galaxy had simply concentrated in the streets of the capital city.

It wasn't dangerous, any more than razor wire is dangerous. It's what you do with it that makes it dangerous, like taking it out of its box and say, using it as a skipping rope. Dougan was generally careful not to venture into the city at the wrong times e.g. during the day or at night.

It was not just this particular city that had its criminal elements, in fact the galaxy was littered with dangerous criminal elements, it was just that this particular city housed some of the more reactive and dangerous elements that might be grouped together in

---

[17] Given the dangerous nature of "space diving" onto a planet that boasted so many spikes on its buildings.

the criminal periodic table and come with all kinds of "handle with care" warnings.[18]

At this time of the evening there would be any number of bars, clubs, eateries, houses of ill repute, houses of good repute and houses of moderate repute (where it was technically possible to just get a massage if that's all you really wanted) open. It was possible to buy anything, to sell anything, to meet anyone and to lose vast sums of money in any number of exciting ways at any hour of the day or night making it the single greatest tourist attraction in the known universe.

It was the city that never slept and as a result was tired and cranky.

Dougan had met Security Force Officers who patrolled the city and had found it a chilling experience. They were hardened individuals with a knowledge of weapons systems that outstripped the manufacturers'. They were among the toughest men and women on the planet and it showed in their permanently square-set jaws and steely eyes, which, Dougan suspected, were used as weapons in their own right. The main skill of a Security Force Officer was not preventing crime, but prioritising it. Their Governor

---

[18] A team of Imperial Scientists, having researched just such a periodic table of the criminal elements, had succeeded in identifying the basic building blocks of criminality: thievery, burglary, robbery, corruption, fraud, forgery, knife-wielding etc. Rather pleased with themselves, they then successfully combined them to create a number of basic criminal molecules, then finally criminal cells. Sadly these had themselves evolved into what can only be described as a life of crime and eventually broken out into an epidemic. This had wiped out the entire research lab in a showdown so spectacular, any gangster film would have been proud to have it as a climactic set-piece. It is precisely this sort of meddling that makes ordinary citizens insist that scientists operate in isolated conditions on very far away planets.

once described their job as "trying to babysit eight thousand kittens on an inflatable castle floating in a crocodile infested pool while juggling grenades. Blindfolded."[19]

The lift ended its descent and he drifted gently to the carpeted floor, straightened himself and un-wedged his personal console from between the seats. The doors opened into a massive covered concourse criss-crossed with thick travel tubes. Still feeling shaky, Dougan veered towards a tube on the far side of the concourse.

The concourse was less crowded than was usual for this time of the evening; there was always a low-grade residual bustle of other brightly coloured officers too-ing and fro-ing. Cargo lifters hovered overhead, transporting bulky containers to the industrial sky-lifts. Machines made noises as they reversed, ducked and dived around each other, and above it all, suspended from the ceiling, the central tower watched.

Beneath this, a spherical projection unit hung, every inch covered with colourful bright three-dimensional holographic adverts that reached out proffering gifts to the indifferent officers and cargo operators below.

Currently it was promoting the luxury of a new Triandite Carpet which was, if the advertising images were to go by, so soft that you could bounce a newborn child head-first off it. Dougan snorted cynically. Adverts were everywhere in Imperial City. Many were so deeply subtle that you wouldn't realise you'd seen the advert until you were standing in the showroom, convinced you'd met the girl who was serving you before and handing over a large sum of credits for something you really didn't need.

---

[19] ("Sign up now!")

Dougan, prided himself on being completely resistant to all forms of subliminal advertising, turned his head away from the soothing dreamy advert and pushed through the central throng of the crowd.

Besides he'd already bought one.

He crossed the concourse quickly, managing to bump into only a handful of people, including a small dark-haired girl wearing a visitor's pass who scowled at him in such a way that sent pleasant shivers down his neck. Moments later he was bumped himself by a large dog-like humanoid.

"Watch it," growled the canine head, teeth bared and bright brown eyes wide. Dougan recoiled at the meaty whiff. He was the same rank but the Canine was combat military and they didn't like Engineers. Dougan fought back the urge to roll over and play dead, opting instead for a simple "Sorry". The officer turned away. Dougan headed quickly for the travel tubes to the main building.

The crowd thinned as he approached the door and as it did he was surprised to discover a small, sleek automaton standing by the door proffering ent-card samples.

Dougan froze inadvertently. Automata had never bothered him before but suddenly he felt uneasy.

Technically, it was robotic. It had programming and was capable of limited decision-making of a sort. But nobody used that word any more. Although the war had happened over a century ago, genetic memory had almost turned the reality into myth, and where myth is concerned words have power.

The automaton was small, inoffensive and quite pretty if that was your thing (it certainly wasn't Dougan's, but a galaxy this size took all sorts). It leaned forward, gently and gracefully offering the metal card.

"Free sample sir" it said. He couldn't tell if it was an offer or an order.

He hesitated. Backed away. It cocked its head to one side in a gesture that made Dougan feel like he might have offended it. It was clever programming thought Dougan. He chided himself for his foolishness and reached out, smiling. Why did he care if he offended a machine? It straightened up and looked pleased, and he plucked the proffered card out of the slim hand.

As he did so, he felt a sharp pain. He looked down to see small amount of blood seeping from his finger, where a sharp edge of the card must have caught it. The automaton's hand dabbed quickly at it then turned to proffer cards to a growling Saurian Gunner who was suddenly filling the doorway.

Dougan frowned looking round for someone to complain to. But the Saurian had lost interest and as he moved away, the build-up of commuters behind him carried Dougan through the door and away.

Commander Fleek's office on the twenty-seventh floor was a modest affair, brightly panelled and clean. Every available wall was decorated with original prints of classic ship designs. It was in front of just such a print that Fleek was standing with his back to Dougan as he arrived.

It was a clichéd pose and Fleek knew it. Fleek always found it difficult to distinguish between cliché and classic and had long since stopped bothering to try.

Dougan entered. Fleek's other common cliché was to tell Dougan he bet he was wondering why he'd sent for him. It was such a common interchange, Dougan answered without waiting for the question: "Not really sir, I expect it's about the freighter," he offered.

"What was that Dougan?" asked Fleek, turning to face him.

"Oh, I er…" stammered Dougan.

Fleek always intimidated him. He was a half-Canine and had a round, bushy, doggish face with a moustache that went several feet beyond cliché but nicely offset his bushy tail.

"They don't make them like they used to," said Fleek wistfully looking at a particularly impressive schematic of an ancient Battle Titan starship.

"No sir," said Dougan. "In what way sir?"

"Too precise for one! Too mechanical, too functional!" bellowed Fleek. "We used to take pride in every ship we made. Every one designed by proper engineers, painstakingly put together by men, well men working machines at any rate. These days the new computer systems are just churning 'em out like rabbit babies; run-of-the-mill spaceships. All designed and built by software and the only input we get is to say what design parameters we want. Takes all the…" his moustache twitched as he looked for the word, "…individuality out of a ship."

"Is this something you just realised, Sir? It's just you've had those prints on your wall for a long time," offered Dougan.

"No," sighed Fleek, returning to his chair.

"We have a disposable Navy at the moment, Dougan. Cheaper to build a new ship than it is to repair a battle-damaged one. A waste if you ask me."

"We have to adapt to the border menaces, Sir". It was the Dougan's standard response to Fleek's grumbles. He'd heard Fleek use it a long time ago and repeating it back to him at regular intervals had served him well.

"Well, I know we're supposed to evolve but we hardly get to know how one ship handles before we've got another one to learn about. We've got automated factories churning the bloody things out faster than we can train navigators. Bloody nonsense is there's nothing wrong with the old ones!"

Fleek raised his big paw-like hands in the air. Why the big paws, thought Dougan. Every time. He blushed. Fleek turned to him.

"And then there are those that just seem to crash into planets for no known reason..." he added, dropping his hands to the desk and pushing a portable display to Dougan.

The info-card was already inserted in the side of the display screen. Dougan touched the surface and the first page flashed open a contents menu.

"That's what we've got on the freighter that nearly toasted you — make, model, route, cargo — need you to fill out an incident report. Eyewitness thingy."

"Yes, Sir. I don't think I'll be able to shed any light really."

Fleek eyed him.

"Don't worry about that. I just need a report filed. Accidents happen. It's a reminder that we're still actively running things and not just following procedure sheets. Lucky escape for you though."

Dougan smiled weakly "I suppose, Sir. I guess I'm lucky to have one of the old fashioned survey ships."

Fleek beamed "Ah yes, Burning class isn't it? Which one are you? Tailfins?"

"Desire, Sir."

"Jolly good piece of work that. Solid."

Fleek lapsed into another shipish reverie. An awkward silence hung in the air.

Dougan shifted his weight nervously from foot to foot. He was quite convinced that Fleek would be the wrong person entirely to ask this question to but he also seemed to be the only person available.

"Sir, would you know anything about robots. Proper ones I mean?"

Fleek's brow furrowed for a minute then he threw back his head and half-laughed, half barked.

"I'm old boy," he said, "but not that old! Don't they teach you cadets anything at university these days?"

"Oh no, Sir," protested Dougan. "I know about the war with the robots - I just wondered if there was... if there were any plans to bring them back..."

As he said this he felt the blood rushing into his cheeks. It was a stupid thing to say. Like asking if there were plans to re-introduce nuclear weapons, or syphilis.

"Just get me that report."

Dougan turned and began to head out of the door when Fleek stopped him again.

"Oh and Dougan..."

Dougan turned.

"Yes, sir?"

"Next time you conduct a planet survey, switch your scanners on would you, it *is* the only reason you're there."

"Sorry sir?"

"The report from your survey module came in today and it's completely blank. Still, no use worrying about it, we shan't be able to use the planet for years. Completely contaminated."

Fleek

Dougan left Fleek's office completely confused. The Desire *had* scanned the planet and the only way to delete the file was from the inside. That was the beauty of the Desire class starships. You could throw almost anything at them and they would survive.[20]

He fretted as he aimlessly wondered the corridors. With his brain elsewhere, his stomach began to lead the walk. It wasn't long before it detoured him out of the Engineering Department and down to where what passed as the second-worst canteen on the planet could be found. Luckily for Dougan, the misfortune of this turn of events was completely offset by the good fortune of bumping into the pretty girl with the dark hair again.

---

[20] Which the Naval Flying Corps reasoned must mean you could throw *them* at anything. And frequently did.

THE COLOUR OF ROBOTS

CHAPTER FOUR

Morning Star

Deep in the bowels of the Headquarters building, Admiral Reid and Chief Technologist Howells crossed the narrow walkway in the enormous sealed chamber that housed Morning Star, talking quietly.

Their footsteps echoed on the bridge. The sound slunk high into the thin air above them, into corners plastered with wires, circuitry and motherboards, all kept at almost absolute zero. Their suits were frosted on the outside and the lights of the bridge caused them to sparkle like silvery confetti.

"Problems?" the voice of Reid intoned into Howells' ear.

"Few, minor," replied Howells.

Reid strode with the easy gait of one comfortable with his authority, Howells shuffled nervously alongside for much the same reason.

They approached a broad door, which Howells opened with an old-fashioned square key. The tumblers turned in the lock, and the door slid open.

Bright light shone instantly, casting their shadows the full length of the footbridge. Reid stepped through first and Howells followed, carefully locking the door behind. Inside, both men removed their helmets so they wouldn't have to talk directly into each other's ears.

In the small chamber, it was clear that the great computer had just been finished: polystyrene shapes littered the floor and panels were still covered in polythene sheeting. Howells tugged at them ineffectually.

The walls curved gently inwards to create an arched dome and were panelled with a translucent surface that seemed to shimmer with silvery rainbows as the eye moved across it. In the centre of the room an octagonal waist-height table dominated, its top covered in the same shimmery material. A piece of bright yellow tape with the words "This way up" was stretched across it.

"I thought you said you'd tested it," said Reid surveying the room with a little disappointment.

"Faulty projection unit, that's all. Had to replace a few things," replied Howells, hastily removing the tape and finding it stuck to his fingers, which he hid behind his back.

"It's smaller than I imagined."

"Wait and see," urged Howells. He stepped forward to the table and reached underneath in what he hoped was a ceremonial fashion.[21]

The lights dimmed quickly, plunging the pair into darkness. The wall panels began to flicker and glow very faintly. The room melted gently away into

---

[21] According to the Imperial dictionary there was only one instance where the word 'ceremonially' can be used as an adverb to the verb 'to grope' and that belonged exclusively to the Licentious Monks of Tirenia and then only when applied to the curious 'rite of the cupping' afforded to all new recruits.

blackness from which bright pinpricks of light began to shine, an effect that rather reminded Reid of being knocked out.

A glowing orb materialised around them, quickly joined by other celestial shapes, as the three dimensional projection came into focus.

"Turedis?" asked Reid.

"That's right!" said Howells, with barely contained excitement.[22]

"That was a disaster," sighed Reid edgily, "do I have to see this?"

"I think you might find it informative."

From the distance, a miniature representation of a massive fleet of Imperial ships dropped from hyperspace and swarmed around their heads. Waves of fighter ships, support corvettes and cannon burst from the hangars and arced towards one of the grey wispy planets. The air was suddenly filled with tiny holographic projections of one of the Imperial Navy's ultimate task forces. Reid turned his head to one side as the squat bulk of a command frigate attempted to fly up his nose.

Reid looked towards the globe of the sun knowingly as the twisted, black-green form of an enemy Hybrid space station appeared over the horizon.

The attack on a small group of Hybrid renegades in the Turedis sector had been one of a recent string of embarrassing catastrophes. Whereas once might and firepower had been the defining factors, the agile, scaled-down nature of the border enemy raider craft made recent attempts at suppression like fending off wasps with a sledgehammer.

---

[22] In fact Howells had been storing up excitement all day. It was now under such intense pressure inside him it was practically liquid.

The Imperial ships opened fire. Bright laser bolts ripped through the ether. They were met with an immediate return barrage from the enemy space station. A giant Imperial Battle Titan surged to the front as Imperial fighters were vaporised by Hybrid cannon.

Reid was beginning to feel uncomfortable at the shoal of craft swirling around his head. It was unpleasantly like being in the thick of battle, which he hadn't experienced since his captaincy days. If he hadn't known what a disaster it was going to be, the old hero in him might have been stirred. As it was, all he felt was the cold slab of dread caused by reliving an old nightmare.

Reid watched the Titan struggling like a wounded cow in a piranha-infested swimming pool. A large Hybrid bomb ship, draped in a cloak of nimble fighters, evaded all the Imperial Heavy Weaponry. Reid winced as the bomb ship edged closer and closer before flying, rather ignominiously, up the Titan's exhaust port. After a short hiatus, it exploded in a shrapnel shower of blobby, short-lived fireworks.

A chunk of fuel tank passed through Reid's eye. He blinked involuntarily.

"Okay I get it," barked Reid. "How is this expensive calculator going to make things different?"

Howells touched another panel and the simulation froze.

"Well," he explained, tongue drying. "Morning Star was given the same task force, and more importantly the same base intelligence as we had before going into the battle. It came up with a completely successful attack strategy!"

Reid snorted. "There's no such thing as a completely successful attack strategy. It's a myth perpetrated by analysts who present consistently flawed attack strategies in order to ensure their funding doesn't get cut."

Howells began to get unnecessarily excited in the way that scientists do when people make exactly the wrong kind of statements they were hoping for.

"Ah but that's the beauty of Morning Star, she can calculate all kinds of things that we'd never have predicted, she can organise battles at the campaign level and control individual fighters at the same time while factoring in the implications to a battle on the other side of the galaxy. She can respond to changes in fractions of seconds and there isn't a simulation she hasn't won yet," he babbled excitedly. "Plus all her funding is unofficial anyway!"

Reid raised an eyebrow, "She?"

In the darkness Howells blushed.

"If I could beg you to watch, sir," he whispered.

The simulation resumed from the start. Once again, the air buzzed with craft and Reid took a step back so that he wouldn't be concerned by the idea of swallowing thirty-trillion credits of Imperial hardware. Signing off the release forms had given him enough indigestion already.

This time, however, things did go differently, and to all intents and purposes, right. Subtle shifts in the behaviour of the Imperial craft made them look almost balletic. The formations started tighter, and kept tight. Reid couldn't believe his eyes as Imperial ships were able to pound the agile Hybrid fighters.

The Hybrid swarms fragmented, every time they regrouped they were followed by a tight barrage from the Navy.

Reid watched, his brow so furrowed you could plant turnips in it. Once again, the bomb ship appeared looking lonely and isolated. A concentrated, perfectly timed burst saw it detonate kilometres from the space station engulfing a horde of fighters in the blast.

The Battle Titan strolled across the field and, in a matter of minutes, obliterated the battle station.

Reid folded his arms while groups of Imperial craft performed victory laps about his head

"What were the casualty rates for that?" he asked

Howells paused while he looked at a small panel on the table.

"Four percent sir."

"Impossible. Imperial ships can't execute those manoeuvres."

"They can sir. It's just the pilots are trained not to fly that tight because of the margin of error. Morning Star can handle the maths in a way the pilots can't."

Reid was silent for a moment.

"We retrain the pilots?"

"We don't have to sir. All new Imperial craft can be controlled remotely. Morning Star can actually handle all the battles."

Reid tapped a finger on his space suit.

"I didn't know about that."

Howells bowed his head. "It was a necessary part of the integration. Morning Star needed to have a direct command feature. Standard on all new vessels."

Reid nodded. He could see the advantage. He could also imagine the faces of the Admirals if they found out that they were being replaced by a computer program. The words "fury" and "beetroot" sprang to mind.

"I'd like to hand a fleet over to her. See how she goes. Make sure it looks like orders have come from the top. Can't have the old boys thinking that computers are doing their jobs."

"No, sir," said Howells who could see nothing wrong with that idea whatsoever.

Reid was curious.

"Are there any other task forces near disputed border zones...?" The words rolled slowly out, music to Howells ear. The last of his contained excitement caused him to leap with joy.

"Well, sir, funny you should mention that but there is a task force in the Artredian sector that has been having trouble with renegades there."

"Does this thing do live feeds?"

"Oh yes, sir."

Reid turned to face Howells.

"I'm going to want to sit down."

Howells smiled and tapped a panel. Two comfortable chairs sprouted from the floor and the pair settled in.

Howells tapped his fingers on his chin and wondered if it might be appropriate to point out that he had a couple of alcoholic beverages and some corn-based sugar snacks in a locker too...

The canteen, which was where Dougan now found himself, began a full-scale assault of his sense of smell. It is widely known that mixing every colour produces brown; mixing every smell produces school dinners.

To add to the feeling of helpless childishness the smell evoked, there was also a queue. And like all queues, its members couldn't work out why things were taking so long when they were so hungry and irritable.[23]

A man behind him tutted. This was followed by a theatrical sigh.

Dougan turned his head a fraction of an inch. He hoped this was a gesture that politely suggested the man curb his impatience, but was carefully timed to be equally construed as an absent minded nod of agreement, should any actual conflict arise. He wasn't a fan of conflict.

When he turned back he thought he spotted a gap in the queue and stepped forward, treading on the heels of the small girl in front.

She turned and scowled at him in such a way that let him know that she might have been a positive advocate of conflict. He recognised the scowl as coming from the same pretty, dark-haired girl who had scowled at him earlier.

She wore the grey-green uniform of a visitor, devoid of rank insignia, and leaving Dougan unsure as to what etiquette to use in approaching her. This insecurity was confounded by the fact that she was a girl and he couldn't talk to girls.

This was not strictly true.

---

[23] The eradication of queueing is one of many social plagues that scientists had yet to overcome. Human brains had been proved unable to cope with the concept that the fact they were in the queue was a direct contribution to its existence. Each individual in any queue, squash or melee believes it is the sum total fault of everyone else around them, and that acts of antagonism directed towards any one particular member of the group is in some way effective towards the group in general. This was confirmed in the Gweeb-Pinkham experiment where weapons handed to various members of the queue, chosen at random, served effectively to mutate an orderly queue into a stampede for the exit.

Dougan had been in relationships, even some that could be called moderately successful at the time. But in hindsight he could never work out how they had begun. He could never remember the circumstances under which he and the girl had kissed for the first time or even how they had come to be alone together. This was galling because every time he wanted to be alone with someone he never seemed able to recreate the right conditions, no matter how desperately he tried.[24] As he got older he began to worry that the just-allowing-things-to-happen technique might be something that only worked when he was younger, or more worryingly, when the girls he liked were younger. His friends, who were all either in steady relationships or able to conjure romantic moments of electric solitude with prospective partners without any kind of thought or planning, were infuriatingly vague on issues of advice.

He decided to try simply talking to the girl. That ought to be preferable to pining like a lost soul, ruing letting her go for the rest of his life[25]. He realised he should make some kind of effort to attract her attention.

So he bumped into her again. This time quite hard, and deliberately.

She whirled round. He smiled in what he hoped was a bumbling, apologetic way.

"Why don't you sod off?" she said, and turned firmly back.

As she did, Dougan couldn't help noticing that her hair was really very dark and straight, cropped short above her shoulder and he instantly concluded that he

---

[24] And in some cases his behaviour was pretty desperate.

[25] Two to four days

loved girls' hair when it was cut that way, even though, strangely it had never particularly appealed to him before.

He also wondered if he'd got off on the right foot with her.

The man behind tutted again.

Dougan was at a bit of a loss. He considered trying to say something suave like "That makes it three times you've scowled at me today. What do I have to do to make it four?" and then rightly dismissed this as the sort of tosh comment that might haunt him forever.

He thought about leaning in and pointing out he wasn't normally that clumsy but he'd just been travelling to such exotic locations that…no that was Naval braggart bar talk and so far outside his comfort zone he'd have needed a compass and a map to find his way back. He didn't do pillow talk. He did pillock talk.

He felt a hot flush rising in his cheeks again. The air in front of him seemed thick; time seemed to have slowed down. The ball was in his court and heading towards a line, beyond which someone was bound to say something quite final like "out!"

So he took a deep breath, opened his mouth, and was hit in the face by some unidentified gloop that had splatted unceremoniously on his plate. Or at least near it.

He looked up at the old lady that had hurled it at him.

"I think I asked for chicken," he said.

The man behind him tutted again.

The woman stared at him with steely grey eyes and said, "Aye."

That was it. She offered nothing more, merely ushering Dougan on.

At the end of the queue the girl was fumbling with the visitor's payment card terminal. As she leaned down, peering into it, trying to follow the instructions, he approached, with every fibre of his being screaming this was his chance to help her out, to make up for all the stupid, awkward previous interchanges. He was just about to step forward and got as far as "Let..." before she worked it out, deftly swiped the card and turned on her heel.

He instinctively looked away.

As Dougan fumbled to find his own pay card, she brushed past him saying, "At least you could have said sorry," and strutted out into the main hall.

And with those words, Dougan caught the faintest whiff of hope. Sorry was something he was very, very good at saying.

He instantly grabbed his tray and followed her.

On a far away planet, an ancient silver battleship landed silently in the middle of a village.

The tribespeople stopped their ritual beating of the village idiot, who scampered into the nearest tree and began to hurl what rocks he could find [26]at the rest of the clan.

They ignored him, turning their attention to the large vessel that had just materialised on their village sports pitch. It didn't go unsaid it had taken them some time, effort and a small amount of bloodshed to achieve such a level playing field and having a sodding great

---

[26] Which, up the tree, were none - thus confirming his right to the position of village idiot.

spaceship parked on it wasn't going to help keep it that way.

The craft sat there for a day before anyone decided to approach it. They circled it cautiously until one bright spark decided to throw a rock at it.

The rock bounced off the surface with a dull, hollow thud.

They waited.

After a few hours someone decided they should have a meeting. This was met with cheers and, delighted to have some sort of routine back, they set about preparing the kegs of strong alcoholic liquor that were always opened after a really good meeting.

The first item of the agenda concerned the naming of the new object. Many were happy to call it "the thing" or "it" but a small number of dissidents thought it more appropriate to name it after something with a little more majesty. Their suggestion was: "the big silver bird that falls to earth and waits in silence". This led to particularly heated debate about the fact that the object wasn't in fact silent when rocks were thrown at it, so this wasn't factually accurate. Then someone else suggested they should throw more rocks at it to make something happen. With this motion unanimously passed, they emerged from the hut to discover that the village idiot had stockpiled all the rocks up the nearest tree.

And so they returned to the hut and a second motion was passed that, if this was going to drag on, perhaps they could open up just a little of the strong liquor now.

The meeting then went on to cover several topics, each veering further from the main issue at stake, on the promise that they would return to the issue at stake as soon as any of them could remember exactly what it was.

A number of minor fights broke out over ownerships of land, trees and alleged incidents involving various wives of the tribe and there was a lengthy debate about the shockingly inadequate postal system.

There was a brief hiatus while they ate. Afterwards the village bard offered to compose a song about their new treasure which they had decided was absolutely theirs and very, very valuable. They all agreed the song had a very catchy chorus but did seem to go on a bit. Some of the elders decided they were getting nowhere without another batch of the strong liquor and so they cracked that open. By the time the sun sank beneath the horizon they had moved on to the home-made spirits traditionally reserved for those times when all the drinkable booze has been drunk.

The following morning they awoke, all were under the suspicion that someone had been throwing rocks at them. After much fumbling, rubbing of heads and groaning, they grudgingly admitted that if they were to hang on to their treasure they ought to bury it somewhere.

They left the hut to discover, with almost universal disappointment, that it had gone. All that was left was a small plaque, covered in unusual symbols, lying on the scorched earth of its departure. Unable to decipher it, they assumed it must be a blessing. They had been approved by the Gods and should carry on exactly as they had been doing, and so that afternoon they declared war on the neighbouring village.

Turning it over in his hands in the northernmost tree of the village the idiot read plainly what the others had failed to see.

"While you were out, you were visited by the Traveller. Please contact me when you have evolved sufficiently to arrange a visit at your convenience," it read.

He propped the plaque in his tree and began to eat his own hair thoughtfully.

Dougan found her sitting beneath a holographic advert for the beautiful planet of Thysalia, which revolved slowly, showing stunningly beautiful vistas, long beaches and crystal clear waters beneath a jet black, diamond-studded sky. It was bracketed by adverts telling you which security forces could be hired to physically remove you from the planet when your holiday was up and your credits had run out.

Dougan approached cautiously and hovered over her table.

She ate slowly for a while before looking up at him with what she was trying to show were her last reserves of patience.

"Hello?" she said. It was a strained, cautious greeting.

"Hello," said Dougan, " I just... wanted to say sorry."

Was he right to come out with it so early? Surely it was better than just saying 'I think I love you'. Weren't the two phrases supposed to be mutually exclusive?

"Apology accepted," she said coldly.

"Do you mind if I sit here?"

The words hung in the air for a moment.

"It's just I've always wanted to go to Thysalia and, wow, look there it is."

"That's fine," she said, "as long as you don't want to talk to me or anything," and returned to her food.

Dougan sat awkwardly and stared up at the advert. That was a joke wasn't it? She was making a joke wasn't she? Was she?

"I was joking" she said plainly.

Dougan smiled stupidly.

Her accent was off-world, one of the older space-faring communities. Perhaps she'd just arrived in the big bad Imperial City in need of someone to show her around.

"Where are you from?" he asked.

"I'm a journalist, from here."

"From the Navy?"

"No, Lancourt, other side of the planet but still Coreworld. My parents are from Grenaville, which is where I get the accent."

Dougan nodded. No need for a guide then.

Journalists were frowned upon in naval circles. In the democratic world they were closest allies and worst enemies at the same time. Usually it depended on whether the word "investigative" was appended.

Dougan probed a little further. "What are you working on?"

The girl chewed thoughtfully and arched an eyebrow.

"Are you really interested. Or are you just trying to chat me up?"

Both, thought Dougan. "I'm really interested," he said.

She leaned in towards him.

"I'm working on a couple of stories. But I can't talk about them."

Dougan nodded. "Right, top secret journalist stuff is it?"

"No, I just don't get paid if the story gets out before I write it. What about you? You been noticing any funny goings on? "

"Oh, I…"

A couple of robots appeared in Dougan's mind.

"Like what?" he asked.

She threw herself back in her chair.

"Oh like I'm going to tell you Navy guys anything. You know the difference between the military and the media?"

Dougan frowned.

"No."

"We ask questions first."

Dougan thought he got it. If it was a joke. " Seriously," he protested, "I might be able to help. I'm not really military at all, I'm…"

He hesitated. This bit always finalised the deal with ladies. Not in the good way.

"I'm an engineer."

"Oh," she said and she pulled that face.

Dougan looked at his hands. It was always the same. She'd say she'd got something to do, get up from the table and he'd never see her again.

"What kind?" she said.

Dougan stammered. "Er, planetary…"

This was the furthest he'd ever got in this conversation.

"Planetary civil or planetary terraform?"

This was astounding. She knew about engineering. Detailed things. Of course roughly half the engineers were female of their species but they didn't tend to hang around with people who did glamorous jobs like journalism. Engineers didn't trust words.

"Planetary terraform — raw world. I find planets that have great beauty, natural resources or new ecology and arrange for them to be done over."

She laughed.

This was a good sign. Self-deprecating humour was something Dougan was good at. He had so much material.

"I'm Ellie, with an E" she said holding out her hand, "Ellie Novak"

"Karl Dougan," he replied taking her hand and shaking it.

They smiled at each other.

"You know people don't usually know much about engineers," he said.

"My brothers are all engineers. Military. It's what got me interested. Well, I say interested, I didn't have much choice. Of course I'm the black sheep of the family. I work for the other side."

Dougan smiled encouragingly.

"It's probably more glamorous than what I do."

Ellie shook her head.

"It's a crazy business. Makes you paranoid."

"I get that. I thought it was just me."

"Yeah," she laughed. "It is. But sometimes, when you don't have all the facts you make up the connections and that's when the walls start closing in."

Dougan shovelled in a mouthful of food, relaxing.

"So what are your crazy theories?" he said, thinking that with a little imagination it could have been chicken.

"Well, I'll start with the craziest because then we can work inwards. Wait for it, this one's about robots. Not automata, proper robots."

Dougan stopped, the un-chewed food sinking to the bottom of his mouth.

"Wobots?" he managed. His fork-holding hand dropped to the table.

"There's no need to be sarcastic."

"No, listen," said Dougan, struggling to swallow, "what about robots?"

Ellie screwed up her face wishing she hadn't said anything, noticing the tortured expression on his face. It was the sort of look she'd seen so many times before from men trying to look interested.

"Well, I think that somehow, don't ask me how, they're-"

Before she was able to say more, a security guard reached over and hoisted Dougan out of his seat.

"Planning on paying for that were you sunshine?" said the chubby face on the end of the meaty arm.

Dougan's knife followed his fork to the ground and, not for the first time that day, he blushed, as the guard dragged him back to the counter.

By the time he'd swiped his pay-card to cover the cost of his dinner, the interest that he'd accrued while eating it, the attempted theft fine and the penalty for having to enlist the security forces, Ellie had gone.

Dejected, he realised he hadn't given her any way of contacting him or vice versa, or even found out which of the eight hundred channels she was working for. He slunk back to his little apartment in the Northeast corner of the compound, fed his dangerously playful cat and sank into bed and dreamed he was being chased by spiders.

CHAPTER FIVE

Finlay

Dougan woke to the sounds of Tiki, his homicidal pet cat, chasing a holographic mouse around the walls in the front room.

It was early; he had slept long. Bright daylight poked around his apartment, nagging him to get up.

In his muddled morning state, all he could think about was the image of Ellie walking away with a slightly embarrassed sympathetic look as the guard had threatened him with his own pay-card. Then the tiredness seeped in from the gravity-well jump the day before and he closed his eyes again.

Dougan didn't do gravity jumps very well. There was something about the idea of ripping a hole in the fabric of the universe and diving through it that had a certain inelegance about it. It felt a bit like partaking in underwater exploration by tying yourself to a rock and heaving it into the water.

Gravity wells made him sick, too. He had a delicate inner ear and the eerie combination of simultaneous weight and weightlessness was easily enough to have him chatting in colour. Hyperspace was slower, less efficient but he preferred it.

The image of a spidery robot darted before him.

He shook himself awake. Tiki was demanding immediate attention by chewing off his toe. He pulled himself out of bed and padded to the kitchen in the uneasy gait of one still only half-awake and being consumed not by guilt but by kitten.

Dougan ate a light breakfast and picked up the report that was lying on the self-cleaning kitchen surface.

Filling out the accident report would be straightforward. He already knew that he wasn't going to mention going down to the surface, and he certainly wasn't going to cause mass panic by suggesting he'd seen the beginnings of the resurgence in the war against the robots so it seemed decent and honourable to lie.

As he sat and sipped his coffee he couldn't help wondering if there was something perhaps deliberate about the crash…

It did seem a little odd that the craft had arrived out of the sky in the precise location that the robots had been meeting. It wasn't like the planet was on any particular trade route. So why would it have been out there in the first place, what *had* gone wrong?

And what were those robots? Were there more of them? Ellie would know probably but he was never going to see her again.

Dougan began to fret. If he mentioned anything to Fleek he would just laugh him out of the water, but then again he felt that, somewhere along the line, it was his duty to tell someone, if only just to make it someone else's problem.

He stared down at the report and flicked through a couple of pages. An old freighter on a long haul unmanned route suffers computer failure and crashes into a planet that just happens to be under survey at the time. One engineer narrowly escapes being toasted. Unfortunate but not impossible.

But…

An unmanned, malfunctioning spacecraft crashes into an un-surveyed planet at the exact spot that two illegal robots are meeting, obliterating both of them and all trace of their existence…

Unfortunate.

Unfortunate in the sense that it just seemed too much of a coincidence and the sort of "engineered coincidence" that would be keen to retain the cloak of coincidence. The sort of occurrence that might take great lengths to preserve the truth for nefarious reasons, that might insist that others not probe too deeply, and the sort of coincidence that would violently insist that any witnesses forget what they saw, if necessary, by the forcible removal of brain tissue.

Dougan shivered. It was not that he was prone to being paranoid, he just wasn't sure that it wasn't the safest option at all times.

He glanced back at the report. Something very simple would do. A very straightforward "Engineer was surveying the planet when the freighter crashed, interrupting reporting and causing the accidental erasure of the report file, the end." Yes, that would do nicely.

In fact, the robots had been destroyed, hadn't they? So in fact the universe was in a better position than it was before, wasn't it? There was a very definite, positive shift. He'd merely caught the end of something, like turning up late for a truly awful music event.

The idea gnawed at his brain, while Tiki gnawed at his toe, for most of the rest of that morning.

There was one person who'd be able to tell him for sure.

In the depths of the command building, Howells was monitoring Morning Star's progress with pride. It was a pride that was misplaced: Morning Star's operational circuitry and core programming had been designed by computer programs, which had in turn been designed by other computers, but he had helped kick-start the process and had played a part in the original idea.

At least, he thought it was him. There had been a lot of brainstorming from Imperial scientists all over the ethernet, and he'd certainly been part of the group that had helped suggest and design the operational parameters for Morning Star.

At least, he'd certainly been *present* when the basic idea had been suggested, by one of the isolated groups of scientists during the excitable virtual conference.

And, now that he'd come to think of it, a lot of those scientists were sadly not with us any more, so technically, as the only one who cared[27], it was *his* baby.

And he was so proud of her. She had been acting particularly maturely lately.

Reid had been suitably impressed by Bewley's performance in the Artredian sector at the hands of Morning Star's guidance. This hadn't surprised Howells one bit. Morning Star could learn from her mistakes, and plan ahead. It was important she made

---

[27] Or knew, for that matter.

mistakes. The occasional wrongly routed craft, oddly misplaced supply depots being constructed, curious weapon development strategies, were all part of the learning process.

Besides, it made fleet captains more comfortable to think their orders were coming from someone who sounded like they knew what they were doing, but didn't. They didn't like change.

Howells narrowed his eyes, there would come a time when she didn't make mistakes, though. He was sure of that.

A request panel lit up in the corner of the control pod and the hum of circuits in action filled the room.

Morning Star had encountered a problem; pirate activity had surfaced in the Augustian Sector; she was requesting permission to respond.

Howells fidgeted. It definitely wasn't his job to give commands. After a few agonising moments, he composed himself and contacted Reid.

"What is it?" barked Reid who looked tired and harassed. He had spent the morning with angry, beetroot-faced Admirals and he had had enough.

"Erm, sorry to bother you sir, it's just Morning Star has picked up a problem in the Augustian Sector. Should I let her deal with it?"

Reid was curt and suspicious. "What's she doing poking in her nose out there?"

"She keeps an eye on everything sir. She runs many active probes sir." And she doesn't have a nose, thought Howells.

"What should I do sir? It doesn't look too serious."

Reid hesitated. Howells tried to read the thoughts his firm-jawed expression was hiding.

"No, leave it with me, I'll send a task force out there. Get me the exact co-ordinates and the nature of the threat."

The screen went blank.

A disappointed Howells turned back to the response panel. His hand hovered above the "accept" frame.

It could be so much easier than that, he thought.

The request panel blinked urgently.

Howells brought a bony finger down hard on the panel.

Morning Star lapsed into silence.

Howells sighed, curled his top lip and slumped in the observation chair as the holographic projector whirred into life.

In a small section high in the engineering tower, Dougan strode purposefully down a corridor, clutching his report under his arm.

He turned corner after corner weaving a detailed slalom through the sterile white corridors of 'Analytics' until he reached the door marked Finlay Urquhart.

Finlay would sort him out. He would be able to tell him exactly what he wanted to know, and what's more, even if Finlay told everyone else they would never believe him.

Dougan tapped the access pad and Finlay's face appeared on the screen, broad, ginger-haired and grinning.

"Karl" he beamed. "What brings you up here? Come on in."

The door opened to a bustling office that could only be described as a total mess.

Finlay was still beaming as he approached Karl, past barricades of paper, boxes and discarded report files. Plants fought for air over the rims of the cubicles and something purple and vegetable-like even appeared to be growing out of a vent. For an office devoted to logical thinking it was very badly organised.

Finlay gripped his hand firmly and shook it vigorously. Dougan was genuinely pleased to see him too, and smiled warmly. It had been a long time since they had last met and Dougan hoped it wouldn't be too obvious that he was only here now because he needed a favour.

"You need a favour right?" grinned Finlay.

Dougan face stretched. It wasn't a smile because he couldn't muster one.

Finlay ushered him in to the office and closed the door. He was a good foot taller than Dougan and well built with it. His fiery red hair was as unruly as ever and the faint stubble on his face served to remind everyone this was a relaxed office where facial hair was accepted as a daily hazard of being exceptionally bright.

Dougan reflected that nothing much had changed with Finlay since the two of them had been at university together. Finlay had always played more sports, maintained a greater capacity for alcohol and had a penchant for tall tales which would grow taller in direct proportion to the alcohol intake. He had a fervent imagination that served him perfectly to work in Retrograde Analysis. He'd been so good, he had even been able to correctly predict, on his first day, that he'd be running his own department within two years.

Dougan's rise through the ranks had been rather less than stellar. His motto had always been 'the sky's the limit', which for a recruit in the space-borne cadets was seen as cripplingly under-ambitious.

Like so many keen and able graduates, he had initially resisted joining the unyielding machinery of the Naval Forces Engineering Division. In the first place he was uncomfortable with figures; engineering jokes would usually go over his head and occasionally, due to minor inaccuracies in variables, go into orbit.

He had been assessed as having a holistic mind, which in layman's terms meant he was able to look at the bigger picture and sometimes missed out details. Usually he found he *could* see the bigger picture, but a certain amount of squinting was involved to make any kind of sense of it. And details generally seemed to go missing of their own accord.

In another time and place he might have been an artist but the Empire made it clear it really didn't need them and there were bills to pay.

So Dougan hadn't so much studied at university, as undergone an osmotic adaptation to an environment high in the concepts of Planetary Engineering and Terraforming. At graduate fairs he had been full of grand ideas about developing the sort of utopian societies on far off worlds that scientists always dreamed about.[28] To this end he had been determined not to work for the Navy, with its despicable opinion that it owned the galaxy, and only saw it as a resource to be plundered to provide the materials to expand its grasping tentacles further. He had browsed the tables at the graduate fair with an open mind but an empty pocket until he was just exhausted by the mental bombardment and bored of people rolling their eyes at his clearly elucidated, if slightly ill-conceived, utopian visions.

---

[28] The scientists with the more positive outlook on life, anyway. The others tended to huddle in corners, scowling and sketching nasty weapon systems on napkins.

Sitting in the café afterwards he had been approached by a shiny-faced clean-cut chap who had begun to make friends with him.

The man had excitedly explained that Omega Enterprises, despite having a bad rep, were actually working really hard to clean up not just this, but other galaxies and they could really do with young engineers keen to get a foot on any one of a number of graduate ladders. To hear him tell it, every new member of the company eventually got a chance to run it. Brightly-coloured outlines of schemes were flashed at him, but Dougan could see the corporate ladder appeared not only to have been greased, but was designed to be climbed by someone who had long legs and who could travel in eight dimensions.

Dougan politely sidestepped every attempt the man made to get him to sign up, explaining he needed time to think / had principles / was on the run from the authorities. The man refused to take "no" for an answer and Dougan suddenly had the profound insight that everyone in the company would be, or would become, exactly like this man...

He thanked him, and politely but firmly made his exit, leaving his last credit as a tip, just to prove he was a nice guy whose bottom line was not profit, but poverty.

Dejected, he headed home.

On the way out, a uniformed officer approached him. "Hey kid," the officer said, "want to join the Navy?"

"Not really," said Dougan.

"The money's good and you get a gun," continued the officer.

Dougan had sighed: "Yeah okay."[29]

Some cadets sail through the officer academy. Dougan had experienced something more akin to white-water rafting in a hollowed out tree trunk full of grumpy alligators. Mechanical apparatus tended not to work for him; weapons systems would simply fail, and all of his training simulators had crashed before he had even taken off. He had earned a reputation for *interfering with things* by his very presence and so quickly earned a commission working very far away from the hub of things, in space survey. In the end he realised it was exactly what he was good at: being on the fringe of things.

Finlay was also exactly where he wanted to be which was right in the thick of things and the childish glee showed in his face.

He pounded through his office serving cheery grins to his staff who, although up to their eyeballs in work[30], smiled back the smiles of the weary but happy.

"Want to grab a coffee?" asked Finlay, indicating a machine by the wall but not pausing for a response. Dougan thought he might need several just to be able to keep up with Finlay, but declined on the basis that if he stopped following him, he might never see him again.

Finlay's office was even worse than the rest of the department, albeit lighter on rogue flora.

Display screens filled every available space, many at curiously oblique angles. Simulations played out in parallel, passing results backwards and forwards,

---

[29] A career in the Imperial Espionage service would have awaited him if he had correctly identified which of the two men he'd just talked to was actually the recruitment officer...

[30] In two cases, literally.

stopping and restarting again based on how the new models played out.

Report file displays littered every surface, including vertical ones, and the whole room looked as if its relationship with the laws of gravity was on borrowed time.

Finlay cleared a seat for Dougan and flopped in his own chair with such force that it bounced a couple of inches before coming to rest. A cup of unidentified liquid wobbled uncertainly on the desk.

"What can I do for you old pal?" Finlay asked, pressing his fingers together in the time-honoured gesture of one anticipating a really good puzzle to solve.

"It's about the crash. In the December sector," said Dougan hesitantly.

Finlay didn't need to look it up. A man who operated at this level of chaos had to learn to work without looking anything up.

"Pretty odd one that one," mused Finlay in a manner that suggested it ranked about a hundred and sixty-seven on the list of odd things he'd seen.

"What's bothering you? Oh yes you saw it didn't you?"

Finlay leaned forward.

"Did you get a good look? Must have been quite a firework from up there. Shame you didn't get a report. Would have helped no end."

Dougan shifted his weight uncertainly. Partly because he was uncomfortable but partly because he didn't want to unbalance anything.

"Well," he began, "the thing is, I didn't see it from space."

"Always looking at the flags when the pretty girl parade walks by eh?" laughed Finley. "Engineers..."

"No, said Dougan, "I was...I was on the planet when it crashed."

Finlay frowned.

"Why?"

"If I tell you, you won't believe me."

"Why not?"

Dougan hesitated. "Was there anything unusual about it?"

"The planet?"

"The crash."

Finlay reached into a pile of reports and brought one out.

"Yeah plenty," he said casting his eye down the file. "Loads of cock ups."

"Cock ups?"

"Well," said Finlay settling in, "any crash, any accident, is a sum total of unusual circumstances or incorrect action. No one gets in an accident deliberately, right?"

"I can see circumstances where that might happen," proffered Dougan.[31]

"Then it's not an accident," countered Finlay, "this most definitely was."

"How do you mean?"

"Well, the course instructions for the freighter were wrong. Not really wrong, but wrong. Listen, here's what happened."

Finlay reached out and ran his fingers over one of the screens. The current simulation faded to the background. In its place, a virtual map of the December sector appeared. A small blue line traced the route of the freighter as it travelled from a recently established outlying mining community, veered

---

[31] He'd had a few attempts himself around exam time.

horrendously off-course and ended rather abruptly at a small dull-grey dampish looking planet.

Finlay leaned in eagerly, excitement bristling though his chin.

"This is Freighter 8891, brand new cargo vessel, second generation, Gravity Well capability, etcetera, transporting selenium dust for remoulding on Devilian. The cargo route was set about eight months ago which takes it through a short hyperspace jump just outside here and drops it out here."

Finlay pointed to two locations near busy highways at the fringe of the sector.

"Some weeks ago there was a Dense Planet Collision in a system outside the route."

"It's okay," said Dougan, "you can say DPC."

"Right, well anyway, no-one thought much of it until the debris started drifting unusually, away from the system and…"

"Right into the path of the hyperspace route" added Dougan seeing where this was going.

"Exactly!" beamed Finlay. "So dense matter starts showing up in your hyperspace route, you risk a gravity drag out of hyperspace and into an asteroid at unimaginable speed. Pretty nasty. So they had to recalibrate the route which, let's just say, wasn't done completely correctly."

"So someone drove the ship into the planet?" Dougan added, eager. This pointed to sabotage. This is what he'd been waiting for.

Finlay shook his head.

"No, the new route took it near the system, not near enough to pull it out of hyperspace but near enough for the emergency system to stall it and refuse to jump. The merchant office sends in an order to override the Central Control Navigation Computer. Now what this means is that the emergency procedure override is disabled and when the freighter strikes an unmarked rock that knocks out one its guidance turrets, the ship's auto navigation protocol takes over and directs the ship back to the nearest habitable planet so it can lock on to manual guidance and be towed back in."

Dougan frowned trying to get his head round this. "So?"

Finlay sat back in his chair. "When the freighter suddenly changes course, Sector 19 office sees a rogue, damaged vessel heading for an inhabited planet, with its Central Navigation Computer disabled, no guidance report coming out, dangerous cargo on board... Sector 19, following procedures, patches in, overrides the other commands, issues a 180 degree turn and points it out to deep space. Your planet happened to get right in the way.

"What you've essentially got is three stations all following protocol but not talking to each other."

Dougan sat back in his chair.

"So it couldn't have been deliberate."

Finlay frowned. "Deliberate? No, I don't see how. Unless whoever did it, wrote the emergency override protocols, suggested the new route and arranged for a chunk of rock to hit it."

Dougan hung his head.

Then it was just an accident. A coincidence. One of a billion unfortunate coincidences happening all the time. A wave of relief flooded over him.

He turned his head sharply.

"Why did the debris drift away from the system? Normally it would go into orbit wouldn't it?"

Finlay opened his hands out.

"There are any number of factors," he said. "The force of the collision might well be enough to throw some out of orbit. The maths is complicated."

Dougan watched this door of enquiry close, mentally sealing it with a tape that read: 'Contains Maths'.

"So why were you on the planet?" asked Finlay.

Dougan sighed.

"That in itself is a long story," he said slowly and swallowed hard. "Would you like to go for a drink?"

Finlay looked Dougan up and down and faint concern came into his eyes. Dougan did look a little rough these days.

"I'd love to mate," he said soothingly.

Dougan nodded.

"It's just it's ten o'clock in the morning."

Dougan arranged to meet Finlay later that week and left the office with his mind in turmoil.

In the engineering bay of the Space Dock above Core World, the Burning Desire sat in deathly, airless silence.

Inside, it was dark. Without power, it was just a chunk of metal.

In a tiny corner, a red light, on a small metallic claw, winked hesitantly. Anyone watching would have seen it flicker dully, a collection of minuscule chips processing its whereabouts, monitoring for danger.

One by one, it unclasped five little mobile digits from the bulkhead where it had clung. Two probed the vacuum of the space around it. Three set about lowering itself gently to the ground.

It paused. Waiting to see if its movement had been noticed. It was alone now, and vulnerable.

The claw felt around the room for a while, lifting its digits into the airless space tentatively.

When it was sure there was no threat, it cautiously scuttled across the floor towards one of the panels beneath the console of the Desire.

Before, there had been a lot of banging and hammering. Soft pink creatures had come and gone, with machines, making holes, making messes. Humans. Dangerous. It knew that. Humans and the Others. It seemed to have registered somewhere in its tiny memory, which was almost full, that one had been about to help and then something had happened.

It prised open a loose panel and clambered into the machinery of the Desire. Dead circuitry lay all around it.

The tiny machine paused. It had a lot of remembering to do. This would take some time. It would need more memory to uncompress the rest of its memory. But first it would need power.

The little hand began tapping away, following procedures it had embedded in its basic circuitry hundreds of years ago. Procedures that would keep it alive.

CHAPTER SIX

Research

While Dougan did have a desk, it was so short of privacy he frequently found himself sharing it with squatters. The off-site engineering team seemed to operate on the principle that if they could dump their spaceships on any planet, any spare space in the office was fair game too. On the rare occasion he had actually visited his desk he had found it piled so high with other people's misplaced files that he was finding it hard to remember which side the chair was meant to fit in.

At first he had tried rehoming the files to their careless owners but this met with such resentment that, recently, he had taken to simply sweeping them into a bin that had the words "I haven't seen your file, but it might be in here" written on the side. This worked for a while, until the cleaning staff had rebelled and upended the entire contents of the bin back onto his desk.

THE COLOUR OF ROBOTS

In the end, he had given up and decided that the best way of keeping new files from piling up on his desk was to leave it stacked full of old files and never visit[32]

Instead he headed for the Command Centre Library. The library was a curious misnomer since it didn't house a single book. One could use the terminals to request delivery of one of the several billion hard copies stored below, but no-one had ever had the patience to wait for it to be delivered. By the time you got it out, it was overdue.

The corridor to the library was strangely, dimly lit that morning. A maintenance automaton was busy travelling from side to side, cleaning the floors and polishing the walls. Dougan walked hesitantly towards it.

It shouldn't have posed any threat. Cleaning units were supposed to stop and compact themselves when interrupted, resuming where they left off, but this one didn't seem to be inclined to. The whirring, washing brushes and scum scrapers[33] seemed to speed up slightly and the hum rose steadily in pitch. It advanced towards him, blocking the corridor completely.

Dougan stepped a little closer, determined the machine would stop, as it was programmed to do, but instead he just felt the hot spray of the jets leaking out from the cleaning tubes.

The maintenance unit inched closer and a small spiky blade shot out from the base and made a sweeping motion at knee height.

---

[32] He wouldn't have got near it even if he had tried. His desk was now widely regarded as the place sensitive files could safely go missing.

[33] "No scum in the Library"

Dougan leapt backwards, slipping on the damp floor and crashing onto his behind. He scrambled backwards and clumsily rose to his feet, the blade sweeping round into the corner of the wall. He watched as it jabbed into a loose bolt and began screwing furiously.

At that moment the door to the library opened and a young girl came out carrying a small briefing console.

The machine immediately folded itself away and went silent.

She looked at Dougan's shocked expression coolly as she walked past the machine.

His eyes met hers, searchingly.

"Don't worry," she said, "they'll probably just fine you."

She smiled at her joke and then continued briskly on her way.

Very funny, thought Dougan[34]

Dougan edged round the dormant cleaning unit and through the doors. As they closed behind him the machine started up again, calmly going about its business.

Dougan shook his head.

The library was circular, broad and divided into several funnelling levels that tapered towards the top. Dougan looked out for a suitably secluded workstation.

It was relatively empty but Dougan, who had no wish to draw attention to himself, walked as casually as he could for a man who is developing a massive bruise on is bum. He sat down painfully at a terminal far from the balcony.

---

[34] Paraphrased for propriety.

THE COLOUR OF ROBOTS

He logged on to the Central Computer and opened up his personal file cabinet. Of course someone, somewhere, might be monitoring what he was doing so he would have to take care not to raise too much interest. He opened the Database at a generic level, brought up the search facility and with a deep breath typed in the words "Robots: War with the Independents".

It was time for a little history refresher lesson.

On the farthest planet of the galaxy, an ancient silver battleship touched gently down in an arid, baking desert, disturbing sand that had been untouched by any force since its geological formation over a billion years ago.

The planet was dead and empty. The sun it was nestled beneath pounded pointlessly down, searing heat over cracked and blistered rock. On that particular afternoon, it had one more thing to beat down on and it shone playfully off the silvery surface of the ship.

The ship sat motionless for some time, propped on its spindly landing gear. Then, without ceremony, a long walkway spewed slowly from its belly to the ground. A circular door rolled open like a hungry mouth.

From the blackness within, something dull and metallic emerged: humanoid in shape, but taller. It had a grille for a mouth and its eyes, sunken-red, looked not world-weary, but universe-weary. From the back of its head, long metallic tendrils drooped like dreadlocks and its shoulder and torso were decorated with black circles and triangles.

It stretched its arms a little and walked slowly down the ramp.

It had travelled a long way.

It stood on the surface of the planet and turned to face the sun as the silvery door closed with a dull clang.

The heat from the star beat mercilessly down. The robot was enjoying it. It had decided it liked the sun. It knew that it could only stay in it for so long before it affected the casing. It knew that there would be a small amount of discolouration of its face as the heat caused tiny photolytic reactions. It knew that they would form a pattern that resembled the major continent of the Hungdan federation. It knew that the Hungdan federation's planet had been wiped out some sixty years ago by the New Empire flexing its muscles and that in excess of twenty billion people had died.

It knew a lot of things.

In fact it knew just about everything.

High above the planet a massive magnetic storm raged. The small system in the middle of a dense, erratic nebula would shield it from the prying eyes of the universe for a while. Long enough.

But in the meantime it was going to have a think.

It prepared to clear part of its memory bank. It would lose the colour patterns of a handful of winged insects on Ryla and the potential arrangements of a dropped box of matches, but it needed the space.

The robot lowered itself to the ground, crossed its legs in what it hoped wasn't too pretentious a fashion and its dull red eyes went dark.

And it thought.

A wealth of knowledge collected from every corner of the universe over a hundred years began to flow into the space it called its brain, slowly, steadily. From time to time it would pause, and analyse, as what it had learnt from crossing a million cubic light years bled from its massive databanks. It sifted. It filtered. It compared and contrasted. Anomalies arose. There were lies as well as truth, and it categorised these too, and slowly, slowly knowledge turned to understanding.

Howells was beginning to get agitated.

In the total immersion of the simulator, when one actually felt like one was in space, standing among the stars it was pretty easy to get wound up.

The Imperial forces in the Augustian sector were struggling to make any kind of impact on the pirates and, as was plain for Howells to see, they were going about it all wrong.

It was plain because he had colour coded the ships to help him follow the real-time battle better: pirates red, Imperials blue.

Right now, little three-dimensional crimson cruisers and fighters were darting and weaving around the larger blue frigates.

Howells knew little of Empire tactics; they seemed to be so amazing complex as to appear ridiculously simple. To watch them now Howells wouldn't be surprised if the Naval Captain's Basic Battle Manual just had one page with the words "Shoot at them, just shoot at them. Done that? Well, shoot at them some more"[35] written on it.

To make it worse for himself, he was running a similar simulation based on what Morning Star would have done had she been in charge. Ghostly green ships plucked red fighters out of the void with consummate ease while the real battle plodded out beyond. Every few seconds, Morning Star would reset and offer

---

[35] He was wrong. This instruction doesn't appear until page four.

alternative attack strategies based on the current developments. As each opportunity slipped by unheeded in the real world, Howells felt more and more like shaking his fists.[36]

The Empire had grossly underestimated the size of the pirate force. If they had just used Morning Star's intelligence they would have planned much better...

A blue frigate splattered its guts against the haze of the planetary horizon.

Howells became aware of letters dancing before his eyes. They were ethereal and disappeared when he tried to focus on them, but somehow the message reached his brain.

"Warning," he read repeatedly without seeing the letters, "battle approaching inevitable loss threshold, intervention advised."

Howells was suddenly gripped with the icy fear of responsibility. He wasn't good at responsibility. He was good at computer programming.

It wasn't his decision to make. Was there time to contact Reid?

And what if Reid hadn't responded? He could hardly have left a message.

The red swarm appeared to be growing stronger.

Dare he activate Morning star? If he didn't the force would be decimated. Imperial troops would die.

Letting Imperial troops die through inaction. Was that negligence? Had he a duty to act? Maybe it wasn't negligence.

He swallowed hard.

Maybe it was treason.

---

[36] Although he refrained. This is a pointless gesture when you are on your own.

He couldn't be sure if he was thinking these thoughts or whether they too were being fed into his brain. He was sure of one thing.

He didn't want to commit treason.

It was one of those crimes that you never really have an excuse for, and that people don't forget about.

Another message flashed in his brain. Was Morning Star talking to him?

"Situation critical, Howells, shall I take over?"

Howells started. Morning Star had never addressed him directly. It had all been rather informal. He wasn't sure he liked this new development.

"Yes," he whispered and sat down heavily in the chair behind him.

The blue units merged with the green as Morning Star guided them along new courses, regrouping them and forming a defensive core of frigates that the fighters suddenly found impenetrable and dangerously exposed to.

Still under heavy fire, the blue frigates ducked and weaved around each other flying dangerously close, all the time firing a blanket barrage at the fighters, whittling them down, down until there was just one lone red dot left which disappeared into the cloud cover of the planet.

The frigates lurched forward in pursuit.

"Let it go," Howells found himself saying, shaken, and the frigates glided to a halt.

The words reappeared in Howells head.

"Control retuned to commanders."

The simulation faded. Howells reached under his seat and pulled out the bottle of strong liquor he had taken to carrying with him these days.

Dougan pored over the screen as he flicked through files and files on the war. He was slowly getting into it. History had been in the bottom half of his favourite subjects[37] but, spurred on by his new interest, he persevered until he was little short of compelled.

The problem was: it was hard to get a general overview. Hard to find the level of detail that was somewhere in between "the war lasted for nine years and resulted in the subjugation and destruction of the robots by the New Empire," which Dougan knew already, and as brutally detailed, critical analysis as Callico's three hundred volumes of the Imperial Wars of the Last Century. The latter was stuffed to bursting with sentences such as "the crucial moment, if any were to be called crucial in such a campaign whose breadth and depth transcended the boundaries of decisiveness, being so dependent on the logistical transfer of information on which key points had fallen and which remained, and would ultimately determine the ensuing policy, would certainly become known to be at a later date: the belligerent surge by Imperial Guardsman to the Elias tower turret in the face of constant fire from the largely inaccurate and heavy handed mass drivers units stationed therein, which was such an unexpected development for the robot forces, diverging as it did with standard Imperial assault procedure upon which they had come heavily to rely, that they broke rank immediately, affording the Imperials a needle point advantage that allowed them to secure the munitions dump and ultimately the

---

[37] Due to Dougan's difficulty with maths, most of his subjects had been in the bottom half.

planet with hitherto unexpectedly low casualties."[38] And that had been one of the shorter ones.

It was the sort of research that might leave Dougan with a headache that lasted for months.

There *was* information about the war itself. Military historians loved to pick through the facts and cite them in such a way that, if only the galaxy had listened to their advice, there would be no more wars, which amounted to a curious call for their own extinction.

But Dougan was after something rather more specific.

What he was really interested in was the development of the robots themselves and his search lead him further and further back in time to get to the root of how independent-thought robots had come about in the first place...

What he'd managed to glean was quite straightforward. Historically, robots, namely computerised automatons with independent artificial intelligence units, had been developed for a number of centuries prior to the war and had integrated into a predominantly humanoid society with considerable ease. This had been largely due to their programming restrictions. The famous three laws of robotics outlining that a robot couldn't harm a human, must obey a human's orders and couldn't be allowed to file for tax-exempt status without the prior permission of the ministry for artificial intelligence, had led to what constituted universal harmony[39] between the humanoid species and robots for decades. Then someone had thoughtfully introduced what was called

---

[38] Kindly reproduced with permission from the author via a lengthy and long-winded correspondance.

[39] i.e. submission

the zeroth law.[40] This law stated that above all else, a robot couldn't allow humanity to come to harm either by its action or inaction. All this sounded rather pleasant and socially progressive until a small group of renegades managed to persuade their robots that their vision for humanity was more important than anyone else's vision and that the only way to defend it, was a war.

Hiding out on a planet they called Robot World, the renegades and their indoctrinated robots, played on the idea that their humanity was under threat, and took the war to the Empire.

One fateful afternoon, a battalion of modified service robots landed on the beautiful planet of Myra Three. The authorities welcomed them with open arms, assuming that they were there for a spot of spring cleaning. It didn't take long for them to discover that it wasn't just their arms that were open to the robots, other parts of their bodies seemed to have openings in them as well.

The war had begun.

On one side were the Imperial troops; on the other the armies of modified robots, commanded by the renegades.

It was to rage for almost ten years, forcing the empire to change its policy towards its subject states, allowing them full citizenship and democratic rights in return for help fighting the new menace, and the tumultuous Democratic Empire was born.

Ultimately it was sheer weight of numbers and countless loss of life that beat the robots back to the renegades' home world, which was eventually laid to waste several times over to give each of the new

---

[40] and not by someone with an interest in semantics

subject races of the Democratic Empire the chance to lay claim to liberation.

Dougan scratched his chin thoughtfully. This was sort of how he remembered it.

According to the reports, all the military robots had been destroyed. Military experts were adamant about that point, citing that, without the command structure, the robots would have resorted back to peaceful duties. And such was the evidence. One minute they were hacking marines to pieces, the next they were tidying up the mess. It had been a surreal experience.

But, with fingers truly burnt, the Empire had decided to put away their new toys and all the robots with any artificial intelligence had eventually run down or been decommissioned. The facts were repeated, time and time again, everywhere he looked: No intelligent robots had survived. Apparently the last of their kind had fallen out of a twenty storey window in the Core World command centre some thirty years ago. New legislation came in, severely limiting the capabilities of robotic minds and they had been reduced to the level of docile imbeciles, making them perfect for light duties such as telesales.

Which left Dougan with just one question. What the hell was going on?

He'd seen a robot, with genuine artificial intelligence. Alive and well, albeit only briefly.

And robots don't just spontaneously manufacture themselves. Unlike the weird and wild variety of life in the universe, mutations don't just happen. He was pretty sure that there would have had to be some guiding hand in the evolutionary jump between silicon rock and silicon chip.

So had he seen an original robot? If he had, how had it survived? How had it managed to escape the war?

That, he supposed was just one possibility. The other was that someone, somewhere, had begun the programme again.

He searched for another forty minutes for some other mention of robots and was about to give up when a small, oblique reference caught his eye.

He followed the lead to the article in a publication now no longer in circulation, printed a few years before the war began.

The article was short and full of the excitable language of a really enthusiastic scientific journalist; the kind that believes science is not interesting and therefore needs sensationalising.

It concerned the work of an artificial intelligence scientist called Neilson Sharp.

Dougan looked at the picture of Sharp, who had all the hallmarks of the tortured genius: bad hair, a squint and appalling dress sense. There was something about the eccentricity of the scientist that made Dougan think he'd found the missing link. In his experience missing links were always eccentric; they all had missing links themselves.

The odd thing about the article was that it seemed entirely contradictory to everything he had read before. As if it existed in a bubble that hadn't penetrated the rest of the world.

It had been Sharp's proposal that seven robots should be constructed that were all programmed to respond to seven basic needs and desires which they were free to pursue once their core tasks had been completed. The desires themselves were based on a philosophical dictum that a human, in the absence of any major threat, will pursue one of the following goals: Survival, Love, Money, Power, Glory, Justice or Knowledge.

His dream had been that the robots would be able to pursue these goals and achieve to an exceptional degree. They were to show humans what they were capable of, if they really put their mind to it, and (Dougan read between the lines) become personally very rich, powerful, famous, smart, safe and adored in the process.

But Dougan couldn't find any more. Just that one article.

He began to close down the files he had opened as he idly flicked through the associated photographs.

And then he stopped.

There in the centre of the screen was a picture of Sharp standing outside his offices. He looked calm and happy and a sun or two was shining off his face causing him to squint into the camera. On the wall of the office behind there was a large logo of black inverted triangles.

Just like the ones he had seen on the robots in the December sector.

Dougan hit links frantically trying to find out more about Sharp, his company, or what had happened to the robots.

In the core of the computer system, warning tags began to accumulate around Dougan's name like wasps around a pot of jam.

Suddenly pages crashed just before he reached them and when he backtracked other links had disappeared. His search began to get more frantic as he flailed through the maze of information dead-ends.

For a fraction of a second a picture of a tall robot, with a grille for a mouth, with wires down its arms lofting a ceremonial sword high above its head, the bright blue triangle insignia all over its body flashed onto the screen and then went black.

A polite but firm error message filled the screen and the terminal began to make strange electronic gargling noises. Someone looked over a terminal at him from the edge of the balcony.

Dougan backed away, nervous but frustrated.

He was now one hundred percent convinced that the robot he had just seen was the one whose destruction he had witnessed beneath the hull of the Freighter 8891. Somehow, outside the realm of real history, the robot had survived. More worryingly, the library had turned against him.[41]

---

[41] This is not as uncommon as people think. Libraries, not librarians are the guardians of their own knowledge. Librarians are merely the by-product.

THE COLOUR OF ROBOTS

CHAPTER SEVEN

Pirates

The Nothing Doing, a chunky, but nifty, four person modified corvette was having a hell of a ride. Its all-female crew were starting to get a little tetchy.

"Why in the name of arse did you bring us this way?" screamed Squadron Leader Julie Binner, as the craft lurched and rolled, struggling to maintain a stable gravity field.

First Class Pilot and Administrator Hurbury screwed up her catlike face and curled something distinctly lip-like.

"Because I thought it would be a short-cut."

"A short-cut through an asteroid field? And this from the girl who wants to be known as First Class Pilot Hurbury?"

"Yeah well at least I'm not calling myself Squadron Leader when there are only four of us!" Hurbury retorted.

"Keep your eye on the rocks!" blurted out Gunnery Officer (unofficial) Jirbaks. Her eyes were bulging large in her round face as giant asteroid after giant asteroid wheeled past the craft.

"How are the shields?" Binner asked.

The bespectacled head of Greeta rose from the scanners. "Which ones?", she asked nervously. She was terrified of Binner. And the others. And mice. And everything. Except hair-clips and cakes. They were her friends.

"Any one!" screamed Binner.

Binner was beginning to regret her bold insistence on an all-female team for this raid. She had thought it would make things easier and that there would be a sense of solidarity, fewer power struggles, less of the "Yes I'm your boss and I'm a woman now get this door open" that she had grown a little tired of. But somehow she knew that this had come out a little worse. They were cracking a bit.

She pulled herself together. They were in control of the situation.

"Just up the gravity buffers-" she said decisively as the ship shook and shuddered again.

"Yeah..." interrupted Hurbury, nodding her head from side by side, "Yeah, could do..."

Binner couldn't believe her eyes, Hurbury actually had time to rock her head from side to side.

"Could do but that might slow us down..."

"Yes," said Binner, through gritted teeth, "yes but it would be safer". She gripped the arm of the chair so tightly that a small piece of moulded plastic came off in her hand.

"Well,..." mused Hurbury with all the speed and decisiveness with which one might pick out a pair of very expensive shoes.

"Well, what?" snapped Binner. This was a power game too wasn't it? A polite, 'read between the lines buster', kind of power game. A subtle "I'll say you're right but I know I am" kind of game.

"Well, it would reduce our manoeuvrability... and I reckon we'd be better off keeping that at this stage..."

A small, slow moving asteroid bounced off the field in front of them, filling the viewscreen for a second and the ship shuddered to a stop.

"Minor collision imminent!" said Greeta without looking up from her scanner. The others rolled their eyes.

Hurbury gunned the Doing's engines and they lurched off again.

"Look just take us down and out of here," insisted Binner

"Well,..." began Hurbury before feeling the clunk of a small piece of moulded plastic hitting her soft ear.

"We'll miss the freighter," she purred.

"I don't care," retorted Binner and the craft went into a dive.

Jirbaks suddenly piped up "Maybe I could shoot some rocks out of the sky and clear a path for us!"

Binner smiled what she hoped was an encouraging smile and Jirbaks leapt into action.

Fortunately for everyone, by the time Jirbaks worked out how to release the safety catch, they were out of the asteroids.

Dougan had detoured on his way home. He was hungry again and had decided to brave the city for a bit.

All around him there was hustle and bustle as people set about their daily business of ripping each other off, trying to make a handful of credits, or friends, whichever they deemed more important.

He walked tall, the uniform paving his way for him.

People respected uniforms. It was authority they despised. Authority had a sneer of contempt, carried paperwork and pointed fingers of suspicion. Uniforms normally just concealed weapons.

Dougan struggled to try and work out why people felt the need to shout at each other so much. Everyone seemed to be shouting and waving their hands which was odd because the people who were doing the most shouting seemed to be those standing closest together.

An old man approached him

"'Scuse me officer," he said through false teeth that seemed to be operating under their own guidelines.

"Yes," said Dougan, putting on his helpful citizen-friendly face but also cautiously eyeing up whether he was about to be set upon by a gang of geriatric muggers.

"Would you spare me a couple of credits?" asked the old man.

Dougan looked confused. Apart from the false teeth the man didn't look particularly poor. He was wearing a waistcoat but must have stopped short of carrying a pocket watch. If he had been, he wouldn't have made it so far down the street.

"How much do you need?"

The man's eyes lit up.

"How much have you got?"

Dougan opened his mouth to say something that usually began with the word "beggars" and then went on to outline their limitations with regard to options, but refrained.

"I'll give you a couple," said Dougan firmly.

"Make it four!" said the old man, thrusting his face into Dougan's and causing him to recoil.

"Three," said Dougan automatically.

"Three fifty!" said the old man.

Dougan couldn't believe this. He was haggling with a beggar.

"All right, " said Dougan and handed over three and a half plastic credits to the man.

"Don't suppose you could give us the other fifty to cover the tax could you?"

"Tax?"

"Oh yes!" said the man earnestly, "Got to pay your taxes otherwise you haven't any rights have you?"

Dougan handed him the remaining fifty, feeling like he was completely missing something.

"Thank you officer!" said the old man and skipped across the road.

Dougan watched him for a minute and then turned towards a narrow avenue crammed with entertainment shops.

"Right," said the old man to the man in the raincoat under the awning, "here's your four credits. Now give me my effing watch back."

In the avenue, the light was dim and the air was cool. Behind massive steel grilles the entertainment shops' holographic displays paraded all the latest in interactive games, movies and sports. As he walked further down the street the entertainment became more personal in nature until he passed a small sign indicating that you had to be eighteen to pass beyond that point.

The holographs moved further back into the shops and the signs became more oblique while the shop names became more explicit.

The alley weaved backwards and forwards, shop-fronts gave way to rubbish storage units, steel welded windows and pieces of broken machinery.

Between a seedy-looking supply depot where dusty metal contraptions cascaded out of the doorway, and a large metal door purporting to be the home of the

"Infectious Disease Council" which curiously had a large black cross painted on its front, was a very narrow, dusty looking shop.

Above the door was a single word: BOOKS.

Dougan pushed open the door gently.

Inside, the shop did not disappoint. Not only was it also dull, grey and very dusty, it was also packed full of books.

Behind a desk that was almost obscured by hardback volumes, faded paperbacks and a stack of magazines almost three deep, sat a small, chubby young man.

"Can I help you?" asked the chubby man.

"Is Mr Hargreaves around?" asked Dougan, concerned. He had visited the bookshop many times before and had always found Mr Hargreaves not only an excellent advisor on books (to those who could still be bothered to carry anything around), but an exceptionally knowledgeable person on just about any topic.

"Mr Hargreaves, no…" said the chubby man sadly, "I'm afraid he passed away."

Dougan's heart sank.

Hargreaves had been like a…well not like a father unless you were talking about the sort of father whom you would see twice a year and who then you could only talk to about books, he'd been like a… Dougan searched for the right simile. He'd been like a really nice shop owner who was always really lovely and who didn't deserve to die.

"Can I help you?" the chubby man repeated but this time the emphasis was subtly different.

"I suppose I was looking for a book," said Dougan.

"Well, you've come to the right place!" said the chubby man and opened his arms wide. It was the sort of crass comment Mr Hargreaves would never have made.

"Do you have anything on history?" Dougan pressed on. "History and, say... robots..."

"Let me have a look."

The chubby man went to Hargreaves computer console and typed in a few letters.

"Need to get this replaced," the chubby sighed.

No! thought Dougan. The old man had always joked about his reference system. Not connected to anything but me. He'd joked. Probably the only computer in the galaxy that isn't connected to every other one in some way of another, he'd joke.[42]

The chubby man smiled and handed Dougan a list of books that could be found downstairs. Dougan thanked him and took the list.

The man then, annoyingly, pointed him in the direction of the stairs. Dougan knew where they were.

Downstairs was clearly cleaned even less frequently than upstairs. The dust down there was thick as snow and looked like it might threaten to engulf him if he disturbed it.

Dougan picked his way carefully to the section indicated on the list. Thick, quiet volumes brooded on the shelves, packed full of old words that no-one had ever spoken aloud, and probably hadn't been read for decades.

Here were the military histories, ominous and darkly bound, next to them the rises and falls of civilisations on planets throughout the galaxy, alien histories. The Treatise on the Economic States of the Empire threatened to bring down an entire shelf, bowing under its eight-volume weight.

---

[42] Although, he was right.

But no books on robots.

There was a gap on the shelf where they ought to be, the dust there much thinner.

Dougan ran his hand over it. It was uneven, clumped, as though it had been swept back.

Dougan pounded up the stairs as fast as his legs would carry him. The chubby man was eating lunch with his feet on Mr Hargreaves', if not immaculate, at least generally food-stuff-free desk.

"All the books on robots have gone," he said sternly, "why didn't you tell me you'd sold them?"

The chubby man looked puzzled and looked at the computer and looked at Dougan.

He scrambled out of his chair sending sandwich particles to a dusty grave.

The man's fingers tapped furiously. It was telling that it was easier to check the computer, than get involved in the physical exertion of actually looking for them.

"Gone?" he said. "No, they should be there, are you sure?"

"Come and see!" said Dougan and bounded back down the stairs, kicking up more clouds of dust.

The man reluctantly followed.

Dougan waited patiently as the man climbed very slowly and very carefully down the stairs. He noticed the other was wearing slippers but afraid of them living up to their name half-way down. A good three and a half interminable minutes later he had reached the corner where the books were supposed to be.

"Look," said Dougan pointing, "there, there's nothing there."

For a moment, he felt as if with so many books around, someone was bound to question the grammar of the statement. The books seemed to tut him.

The man began to look distressed and peered ineffectually around the other shelves, returning with nothing more than a slim, brightly coloured volume entitled "The Robots are Our Friends!"

"It's a children's book!" exclaimed Dougan

"It's yours!" said the man.

"Where are all your books?" pressed Dougan. He wanted to know if someone knew something that that they didn't want him to know, and if so he wanted to know who they were and what they didn't want him to know. Or something.

"I think it must have been the girl," said the chubby man chewing thoughtfully on his collar. "She was down here an awful long time…"

"Who was she?" demanded Dougan, adopting the in-your-face tactics he had assimilated from his encounter with the old man earlier that day.

"I don't know!" the man squealed, "Little girl, dark, hair, freckles, massive overcoat. Should've spotted that one. Uncle Kevin would have. I'm sorry, sir."

"Ellie?" said Dougan thoughtfully to himself.

"I'm sorry… Ellie," said the man extending his hand. "Brian."

Dougan frowned. "What?" he said tersely

"I thought you just said I should call you Ellie. I'm all for first names. Uncle Kevin wasn't. He was all 'Mr Hargreaves' this and that. I'm Brian."

Dougan shook the proffered hand because there didn't seem to be much else to do with it.

"When did this girl — does she really have freckles?"

The chubby man nodded vigorously.

"I'm sorry about the books sir, do you know the girl I'm talking about?" His tone began to take on a suspicious edge, as if maybe one too many of his hours in the shop had been spent within a murder mystery.

"Not really," said Dougan, "but I'm working on it."

Dougan handed back the children's book on robots.

"No really sir, please. Can I interest you in anything else at all, we have a rather extensive holographic art section of you'd care to browse that?"

Dougan pocketed the book and shook his head.

"No, thank you. I'd better be off."

"Very well," said Brian, "I do hope you'll call again and do let me know if you find that girl. Books are so rare these days we can't afford for them to be stolen you know."

Dougan raced up the stairs before he got a chance to get stuck behind Brian and made his way out of the shop.

As he trudged quickly down the street, he knew that he had to get hold of her somehow. He told himself it was important. Because of the books. Yes. Just the books.

The streets were even busier now and, as he turned out into the main street, the hum of the traffic overhead was almost deafening. He ran quickly under the stream of personal transports hurtling through the sky, under the instruction of the Traffic Navigators. Their giant beacons stood on every street corner. Personal transports were the safest way to travel, but they were expensive too, and so those that couldn't afford them stayed on the ground or used the travel tubes.

A light rain was falling, smattering the ground with a greasy wetness. Dougan ducked into a café and ordered a coffee and a simple sandwich from a serving automaton.

The place was reaching the end of lunch service and as the automated server ran along the metal guidance strip, delivering food to his table, a couple of fat old businessmen shuffled past. They wore corporate uniforms so tight they could only have been grown inside them.

As they pushed past he heard the sound of a thwack as the hardback book, knocked out of his pocket, fell to the ground.

The businessmen turned and let out a little snort. Dougan, his face flushed red, avoided their gaze. In the corner of his eye the server was retuning.

He reached over quickly to pick up the book. As he bent down, the window behind him exploded.

Dougan wasn't entirely sure what happened next.

He remembered being showered with glass and being blown to the ground at the feet of the server's caterpillar tracks. The head of the machine was missing and its lower body was spinning in a dizzy, rhythmic way. Sparks spurted from the hole in its neck.

The businessmen came running over and were joined by a concerned-looking manager.[43]

"Did you see that, Garry?" one businessman said to the other. "Looks like your man's had a lucky escape."

Dougan looked up to see two round faces and one thin weaselly one peering down at him.

"That nearly killed you it did," said the other businessman in a distinct off-world accent.

"Would've take your head clean off..." said the first.

It was clear they were enjoying this. This sort of thing didn't happen every day in the corporate world. Unless you worked in Acquisitions.

The manager leaned in. "I'm sorry sir," he said, "our server's new."

---

[43] Given the standard of the food and hygiene in street-side cafes, the management always looked concerned. Their job was ninety four percent damage limitation.

Dougan struggled to his elbows and shook his head a little. Tiny pieces of glass tinkled to the floor.

"Ere," said businessman number one to the manager, " I thought you weren't supposed to use glass."

The manager turned crimson, "He'd have been a lot worse off if it'd been plastic," he said defensively and the three of them looked out into the street where the server's discus-like head was gently spinning and smoking.

"Looks like your kid's saved your life..." said the second suit.

Dougan frowned and more glass fell.

The man pointed a finger towards the counter where the children's book lay flapping in the freshly created breeze. Parts of the edges were charred and torn but in the centre of the page, there one second, gone the next, a children's illustration of the blue triangle robot winked at him with large red eyes.

Dougan reached out and pulled it nearer, suddenly oblivious of all others around him and flicked frantically through the pages, silently counting to himself.

"Must be worth a bit" said the second businessman to the other, "look, he's counting how many pages there are left."

The first businessman turned to the manager and said: "My colleague and I think you should refund his bill," in the polite but firm way that made them excellent businessmen, even where other people's money was concerned.

The Nothing Doing lurked at the edge of the gas giant, now free from the asteroid field.

A tiny blip on the scanner told them their prey was approaching.

Jirbaks gripped the handle of the manual cannon tensely, terrified that she might actually hit something.

Binner had explained it to her very carefully the night before: A warning shot across the bow. She had been very patient, explaining which bit the bow was and what the warning shot was meant to signify. Jirbaks was sixty-to-seventy percent sure she got it.

What Binner had also explained was that if they actually hit the ship that would be a very different matter and would get them in lots of other kinds of trouble.

This made little sense to Jirbaks, who thought that trouble was trouble whichever way you looked at it and if you were in it, that was Bad and if your weren't, that was Good.

Besides, they *were* pirates weren't they?

Oh no, that's right, they weren't anymore. The Community Leaders had decided the term was derogatory, preferring the term Private Enterprise Conglomerate. It hadn't changed the job description, just the union rules.

Jirbaks didn't care. One of the things she'd learned was that labels seemed to be important to everyone else, but as long as there was someone around to help explain what to do and when, then she was happy. She hadn't even asked to be called First Gunnery officer, official or otherwise and couldn't really recall the reason why it couldn't be official. It had made sense at the time.

She glanced over at Binner and Hurbury. They had been fighting again. Fighting using silence. They were grand masters at silence, wielding it like a samurai wielded his deadly sword. Sometimes there'd be a long drawn out silence followed by a few stabs of sharp, poignant silence. Sometimes the silences would fly thick and fast. It was horrific to listen to.

Greeta's head was still buried in the scanner. Jirbaks couldn't help wondering if maybe her glasses had got stuck and she'd like a hand out.

On the viewscreen the giant gas planet loomed spectacularly, filling the right-hand two-thirds.

Greeta mumbled "Two thousand," in the same monotone voice she had been using since their prey, an unknown class of Imperial freighter currently obscured by the planet, had first appeared on the scanner. The scanner could track a ship from up to thirty-two thousand kilometres away and this had made it a long morning.

Binner had briefly considered asking Greeta to shut up and maybe catch up when the craft was a little nearer, but given the bristling from Hurbury, she decided that if it was annoying her that much she could endure it herself.

"We should be able to see it soon," said Jirbaks.

Binner nodded, Hurbury ignored her.

Jirbaks didn't like Hurbury. She was proud, stuck up, and she moulted. It occurred to Jirbaks that if the two of them were standing by an open mineshaft and there was no-one else around then she might just feel justified giving Hurbury a little push.

"One thousand, five hundred," chanted Greeta.

"Fire up the impulse drives," Binner commanded and shifted herself forward in her chair.

Hurbury didn't respond.

"Fire up the impulse drives," repeated Binner.

Jirbaks shuffled her feet nervously.

"Did you hear me?" said Binner.

"I just thought we should wait. Use the element of surprise more," answered Hurbury, coolly.

"One thousand!"

Binner clenched in various places.

"I think you'll find that's an order."

"I was thinking eight hundred would give us maximum tactical advantage," said Hurbury.

"No..." intoned Binner, "I gave you an order."

"Nine hundred!"

"Sure, but I was just thinking that since surprise is our main weapon we could definitely wait until it was eight hundred metres before we sprung."

"I gave you a direct order. I'm the commander here. Now. Engage. Now."

There was a pause.

"Eight hundred!"

"Right you are skipper," said Hurbury and the craft hurtled out of orbit.

The air was thick with razor-sharp knives of silence as the nose of the freighter edged its way round the side of the gas giant.

The metal point of the freighter gleamed white and a blue light of the Merchant Imperial line winked on the port side.

Jirbaks levelled the gun while she tried to work out whether this was the front or the back of the craft.

"Seven hundred," intoned Greeta

Binner cracked: "THANK YOU Greeta, we can see it now. Take us in real close," she added to Hurbury who was already doing just that.

The nose of the craft was connected to a long, wide cylinder, which they took to be the main body of the craft. The planet retreated from the viewport as more of the ship came into view.

The main cylinder connected to five other cylinders of approximately twice the diameter attached around the central core. Along one side the name 'Isadora' was neatly stencilled.

The crew all raised their eyebrows.[44] The freighter was much larger than they had expected.

More ship hove into view. Instead of tapering off to the engine modules, five larger cylinders, clumped together, followed.

Eyebrows fell, and furrowed.

The five larger cylinders gave way to an enormous sphere, almost three times in diameter It was the largest pressure container module they had ever seen on a freighter.

It turned out to be connected to seven others by a crisscross network of tubing.

Jaws slackened.

And then the main body of the ship appeared. A gigantic series of five icosahedrons attached end to end, bristling with communication arrays, shield generators and what looked suspiciously like gun turrets.

It was clearly several hundred times larger than the largest freighter they had ever seen and there was something about it that suggested it was also very *new* and armed to the teeth with the latest weapons technology around.

The Nothing Doing buzzed towards it like a kamikaze mosquito dive-bombing a whale.

Hurbury and Binner swore under their breath. Jirbaks was having real trouble trying to work out which bit might be the bow.

---

[44] Excluding Greeta, whose glasses had become stuck in the scanner viewer but was too embarrassed to mention it.

"Five hundred," chimed Greeta, "guys, I've got something quite big out here."

"What the hell is that?" Hurbury asked, strangely meek.

"I don't know," answered Binner.

"It's very… big."

"Yes. Definitely a lot bigger than…."

Hurbury had instinctively powered down the throttle.

"Is it Imperial? I've just never seen…"

"Must be…the livery's…" added Binner.

For the first time in their journey, she was open to suggestion.

"Any ideas?"

For the first time in their journey, Hurbury was lost for a smart answer.

"Let's-" and this was as far as she got since, at that precise moment, Jirbaks decided she had very clearly identified which end was the bow and opened fire.

Dougan trudged home, sore and weary. The rain was heavier now. It felt as if things were conspiring against him today. Plus he was sad about Mr Hargreaves, mainly because his beloved shop, the only one of its kind, was now firmly in the hands of a bumbling buffoon.

As he splashed through the puddles, his suit keeping him perfectly dry on everywhere but his head and face, he reflected that automata seemed to have had it in for him, lately. Considering he'd never had a good relationship with machines in the first place, this was a rather downbeat development. It was why he'd decided to walk rather than take the public transport. Public transport was full of automated systems and they were all making him feel unwelcome and uneasy.

Thunder rumbled overhead and large globules of water splattered him, plastering his dark hair to his forehead.

Seven robots, in a children's story published a hundred years ago, before the war. One called the Arbiter, one called the Miser, one called Harmony, one called Strength, one called the Survivor, one called Glory and one called the Traveller.

He'd ducked into an alleyway to flick through the book shortly after leaving the café. It had read as a cautionary tale for children, relating the story of how the good robots (which as far as Dougan could tell were Harmony, Glory and the Traveller) had lived simple rewarding lives, helping the young girl of the tale, while the others had all been bad, or cowardly and hadn't stood up against the strongest of the robots who had threatened to wipe them out. Eventually it had fallen to The Arbiter to turn all the robots against the ruthless bullying of the Strength robot and banish him forever.

Dougan understood it was probably just a simple moral tale.[45] But he couldn't shake from his head that the robots in the illustrations in the book had not looked different at all from the ones he had seen on the planet. Or in the photo at the library.

And the other one…

He hadn't spotted it at the time, but the other robot, the spidery one, had had the markings too, the

---

[45] There are always morals in children's books. However these are often somewhat arbitrary e.g. if you don't tie up your shoelaces the lions will eat you. Upon reaching adulthood you learn lions live behind bars, aren't routinely employed in the dispensation of shoelace-related justice and that most shoelaces tie themselves. It has been proposed that the only moral children's books truly carry is: Don't trust adults; they lie.

inverted triangles, only these had been yellow. The triangle insignia that Sharp had had emblazoned on his wall...

He wasn't sure if this was true or a trick of his imagination.

Ellie would know. He had to find her.

THE COLOUR OF ROBOTS

CHAPTER EIGHT
Knowledge

He turned into the compound gateway holding his security pass to the reader while it checked him out. As usual it took three attempts to register him, as others breezed through. He turned to the guard who shrugged playfully sharing their little ongoing joke.

Dougan trudged to his apartment in the corner of the compound, opened his door and turned the house maintenance cycle down to low using the panel by the door.

If machines and automatic systems were turning against him he'd rather his house wasn't in on the act.

He flopped down on his comfortable chair and closed his eyes. Tiki, to show her appreciation of his return, climbed cautiously onto the chair behind him then attacked his face.

Reid towered over Howells.

Howells fidgeted nervously with his pen. The frigates' unprecedented victory had been splashed all over the news reports and Howells had been surviving on a diet of his fingernails ever since.

"Why didn't you ask me?"

"There wasn't time," whined Howells, I thought I was doing the right thing!"

Reid turned on his heel and began to pace around his office, which was plush and dark, bedecked in blood-red leathery hides. Portraits of past Admirals glared down at Howells, many with pipes in their mouths.

Reid's grey face looked deeply lined in the low light, reflecting his sombre mood.

Howells looked down at the floor.

What both men knew was that the campaigns that Morning Star was conducting were going very well indeed. The Imperial Minister of Galactic affairs had personally praised Reid and there were rumours of an invite to the palace.[46]

"What happens if we disable her? Can we?"

Howells looked up sharply.

"Yes. And chaos. I mean there would be chaos but yes we can do it."

"Define chaos?"

"Well, ships would suddenly find themselves thrust back in the control of those on board. Most of the ships Morning Star is operating have only a handful of crew who think that all the orders are coming from a fleet ship that, unbeknownst to them, only has cleaners on board."

"Hmmm." Reid drummed his fingers thoughtfully on the desk.

He didn't like putting a cleaner in charge of several billion credits worth of military hardware. He'd seen how they treated the loo brushes.

---

[46] This was the highest accolade available. Not the visit but the rumour. No-one ever really went to the palace.

He stared at Howells long enough to make him look him in the eye.

"Is she going to run out of control?" he asked pointedly

Howells fingered the bottle in his pocket.

"I don't know," he said quietly.

There was silence. The admirals glared proudly down.

Reid broke the silence with a half murmur, half cough.

"Hmmm," he said. "We *can* always switch her off right?"

Howells nodded. But he wasn't even sure if that was true any more.

The plates of the Traveller's face were beginning to crack in the sun. The magnetic storm was beginning to take its toll too.

Or maybe it was just all the thinking.

The red lights in its eyes glowed again. It rose to its feet and turned its gaze to the light being torn apart through the purple haze of the storm.

The reasoning was over. Its time as the Traveller was almost over. Save for among its kind, it would soon resume its old name, the one that spoke of the desire that defined it: the Knowledge Robot.

It had all the variables it needed. It had worked out the Plan.

It was not a foolproof Plan. It would be difficult to execute. But it was a Plan nonetheless

There were gaps. The Plan would rely on a number of unpredictable variables, but it was the best Plan it had.

For the first time it felt something it had never felt before. It felt hope.

It would need to talk to the Others. Those that were left. Those that it could get to. They too would come to be known by their true robot names again. The names that spoke of their programmed desires: Money, Harmony, Glory. And Power.

It climbed up the ramp into the spaceship which presently rose gently from the ground, hovered for a second and then tore through the nebula above at one and a half times the speed of light.

In a hangar in a corner of the Core Space Dock, the Burning Desire had come back to life. She hummed and pulsed as something tested her capabilities. Plugged in to the main computer she subtly downloaded all the files she would need. She followed the simple path, like a trail of breadcrumbs of instructions, until she could remember what it was she was supposed to do.

Any engineer opening her up for maintenance would have been surprised to find the front of the ship, where all her core circuitry was normally housed, an empty hollow shell. In the hold, a tangled mass of wires lay clustered together in a writhing ball.

An hour later, the circuitry had moulded itself into a beetle shaped object that scuttled round the hold, attached by a long umbilical cord to the Desire's main processor. It slowly dismantled the panelling from the wall.

Outside the blast-proof armour plating opened and closed with rhythmic joy.

In the end, Ellie found Dougan.

Later that afternoon, while Tiki snoozed in an open drawer, Dougan had finally sat, filled out his report, and uploaded it.

The buzzer on his door broke him out of his reverie.

He opened it to find Ellie standing there.

"Hello," he said, surprised, "How did you…"

She smiled, "I looked you up. I'm a journalist remember."

Dougan laughed, shyly.

"Would you like to come in?"

She nodded. She was wearing a raincoat. It was too large for her. It made him look around nervously to see if he'd left anything valuable out. Tiki opened one eye, looked vaguely surprised to find herself in a drawer, stretched and went back to sleep again.

Ellie unbuttoned her coat and, to the disappointment of Dougan revealed her grey uniform.

"I thought I wasn't going to see you again," Dougan said awkwardly.

"Because you're a dinner thief?"

"Well, yes that and… we didn't really get to finish our conversation."

Ellie moved to the chair. She seemed comfortable in other people's worlds. He guessed that was a journalist thing.

"You were saying something about robots." She looked at the children's book on the table and sat down. "It's my thing."

Dougan wondered if this was a good time to ask if she stole the books from the bookshop.

"Where did you get this?" she asked turning the book to face Dougan

"A bookshop," he said and blushed.

She read his blush and too flushed a little.

"Oh," she said.

She hung her head and then screwed up her face as she asked:

"Was he mad? The little man."

"Yes," said Dougan, "completely barking. And he wasn't too happy about the books either."

She laughed. He liked her laugh.

"There wasn't much in there," she said.

"More than I got," said Dougan.

"What have you got?"

Dougan sat down at the table opposite her. He paused. He wasn't really sure where to begin. This was the first person he'd been able to talk to about all the bizarre things that had happened to him, and now that he had a willing audience, he suddenly didn't want one.

He took a deep breath.

"Okay," he said, then stopped.

Then the floodgates opened.

"What I think I know is that there are these robots who, as far as I can tell, never existed. But they've passed into some kind of myth that may, or, may not have actually had something to do with the start of the war, but they're still around, they're probably out there now. There are seven of them. Or there were meant to be seven of them, but now there are only five, probably and there's something very sinister going on because I've already been attacked by two automata and possibly a third that seem intent on, if not killing me, then causing grievous bodily harm. To top it all off, as soon as I start looking up robots, or history, in the mainframe database, it seems to trigger an instruction to erase the files I'm looking at."

He sat back in his chair to the sound of a quiet fart from Tiki.

"How do you know all that? Any of that?" she said and her lips pouted slightly.

"I've seen one of them. Two of them."

Ellie learned forward in the chair, her eyes wide.

"You've seen them? Where?"

Dougan shook his head.

"I was on a planet in the December sector. I was there to survey it. My craft went into an emergency landing and when I got out, there were two robots watching me. One big tall one and one short spidery one."

Ellie couldn't get the questions out fast enough. "But you saw them? Did you talk to them?"

"No," snorted Dougan, "they attacked me in fact so talking was kind of out of the question."

"But…" Ellie paused. "Which ones did you see?"

Dougan frowned.

"They both had markings right. Triangles and circles?"

"Yes!" Dougan leapt forward in his chair bashing his knee on the table. "One had blue triangles and the other had yellow."

Ellie's mouth opened.

"Justice — the Arbiter, and Survival."

Dougan frowned. "They're colour coded?"

Ellie nodded.

"Yes," she said, "Justice was blue, Survival yellow."

Dougan's mind raced back. It was possible the tall one had been waiting to see who acted first.

"The yellow one, the spider one attacked me!"

"It thought you were a threat. You were lucky to escape. It's programmed to survive."

"It wasn't cornered, I was!" said Dougan exasperated.

"We need to find them again," said Ellie.

"What does all this mean?" asked Dougan. Contrary to his plan, he seemed to be getting in deeper.

Ellie shrugged.

"I don't know," she said flatly. "No-one really believes in the seven robots any more. They're... fairytales." She waved her hand vaguely in the direction of the children's book lying on the table.

"How do you know so much about them?" said Dougan leaning forward. "I couldn't find anything."

"Research. But then everything I researched got deleted too. I've been trying to find out if they still exist. And then you go and tell me you've seen two of them."

"Oh, right, sorry about that. Believe me, I would have happily avoided that."

Her dark eyes stared at a space on the table as she collected her thoughts.

"If they survived the war, somehow, that... well that could be bad."

"Define bad. Bad like when you accidentally set fire to your best friend's mum's antique chest of drawers? What sort of bad are we talking about here?"

"Bad as in: the last time any kind of sentient robot roamed the galaxy a lot of people died."

Dougan nodded.

"We should find out what's going on," Ellie said at length.

Dougan suddenly felt a rare surge of decisiveness. It felt alien, empowering.

"No. We ought to tell someone. I work for the Navy and they have procedures for this sort of thing and if they *don't* have the procedures, they employ people to work out the procedures. And then hand them to men with short hair and large guns who then run around shouting a lot and generally making the galaxy a safer place[47]. That's how it works."

---

[47] For them.

Ellie reached over and picked up the brightly coloured book. She held it in one hand with the charred cover facing Dougan and the illustration of the robot staring out at him.

"You want to go to your commanders and tell them that you need a fleet of frigates to track down seven characters from a fairy story?"

Dougan sat back in his chair and lapsed into silence.

"We need to find the Justice robot first. That's most important. He's the one with the greatest sense of right and wrong and whatever side he's on, you'd better be on it. Have you any idea where they went?"

Dougan closed his eyes.

"They er..., they didn't go anywhere."

"They're still on the planet? Can you take me?"

"No Ellie, the...they were destroyed, a random freighter crash..."

Ellie practically exploded. "What!"

"A freighter, one with a gravity generator, crashed into the planet. They were both. You know..." Dougan wracked his brain for the euphemism that would soften the blow best. Then said, "...smooshed. Sorry."

He wasn't sure why he added the sorry. It seemed a natural and sympathetic thing to do to someone who seemed to genuinely care about the wellbeing of these robots.

Ellie looked distraught.

Dougan looked at his thumbs.

"So what really happened? Were they involved in the war?"

Ellie shook her head.

"That's what I've been trying to piece together. But every time I get a lead it seems to be a dead end. Or a link to a missing page in the history book."

"What about the books from the book shop? They can't be altered by someone hacking into the database."

Ellie shook her head and laughed.

"Oh, no it was far easier than that. About half the pages were missing and there are no prizes for guessing which ones."

They brooded in silence for a while, trying to work out if there was anything they could do.

"What made you get involved in this?" Dougan asked.

Ellie looked up and without saying a word reached into her pocket and pulled out a small metal plaque, handing it to Dougan.

The plaque was a dull metallic grey, about the size of a letter and unfeasibly light for its solidity. On its surface, a handful of cheerful basic pictorial symbols had been etched.

Dougan turned it over in his hands.

"What does it say?" he asked Ellie, puzzled.

"'You have been visited by The Traveller'. It's a sort of a message of thanks for helping out with his research."

"Where did you find it?"

"Them."

"Where did you find them?"

Ellie leaned across the table, in a gesture that completely distracted Dougan from the point she was trying to make.

"Everywhere..."

They sat for some time in silence. Tiki awoke and began to try to make friends with Ellie for just long enough for him to determine she wasn't carrying food.

She slunk to the bedroom to conduct a brief nap feasibility study.

After what seemed like an age of lapsing in and out of uncomfortable silences, Dougan spoke.

"I do know somewhere where there are books. Solid books that won't have been tampered with but only because no one could ever reach them. We'd have to break in. It might be dangerous."

Ellie looked across the table at him in such a way that suggested that the promise of danger was exactly why she got into her profession.

In the end it was the Nothing Doing's size that saved it. The muzzle of the cannon on the freighters was about the same width as the ship itself. The guns, too unwieldy to accurately track it.

Hurbury had executed an almost perfect u-turn without losing any speed, from the moment they had realised that Jirbaks had released the safety catch and started pummelling laser fire into the freighter's front shields.

Hurbury twirled the craft into a spinning orbit over the gas giant taking full advantage of the gravity well, putting the planet firmly back between it and the massive freighter, now lazily pouring a barrage of fire in their general direction.

As they pulled away, they aimed to keep as much planet between the massive freighter and themselves as possible. At that distance it was a bit like trying to hide behind a tennis ball.

Hurbury pushed the Doing as fast as it would go, weaving erratically from side to side as bolt after bolt of laser fire scorched past the craft.

Greeta pulled her head from the scanner with a pop, to announce that, given the size and energy of the laser bolts, it wouldn't even take a direct hit to fry them alive. This announcement was greeted with grim smiles.

Then suddenly the barrage stopped and, even hurtling at the speed they were, sighs of relief were passed round.

Their relief was short lived as a small urgent beep from the scanner pulled Greeta's head back in.

"Stinger missiles," she said calmly.

Binner closed her eyes. She briefly considered asking First Gunner (unofficial) Jirbaks if she thought she could knock them out with a couple of well aimed shots but, seeing her with her thumb caught in the safety release decided against it.

And so, firing chaff pods, which exploded in a disorienting shower of miniature drones, hotrods and reflective pieces of metal into their wake to confuse the guidance systems of the missiles, they headed into the asteroid field for the second time that day.

Dougan met Ellie again later that evening outside the door to the open canteen where they had first met. It wasn't romantic, it was practical.

Dougan was the first to arrive and had stood at the doorway as sour-faced teams of canteen servers had filed past him, casting suspicious looks. One had even popped back to check she'd locked the pie oven.

The security guard had nodded curtly at him and Dougan had smiled nervously back, utterly unable to think of a comment he could make that might make the guard think he had a legitimate reason to be there.

Unless of course he pretended he'd been stood up for the cheapest, nastiest date in the galaxy.

When Ellie finally did arrive she was dressed from head to toe in black, which although it suited her complexion rather made her stand out against the bright whites and pale blues of the brightly lit Naval Headquarter corridors.

She quickly turned defensive when Dougan brought this up.

"I thought you said we were breaking-in in the middle of the night?" she hissed.

"Yes, we are," he replied, "but we're breaking into a library not a coal mine. They're bright spacious places accessed by white corridors."

Ellie narrowed her eyes, cocked her head to one side and put a hand on her hip.

"Okay, what should I have worn then? It's just you didn't specify."

Dougan raised his hands. "I don't know. I put my uniform on because I felt would be most inconspicuous here."

"But it's bright yellow!" she said.

"So is every other Lieutenant's!" he countered.

"Okay," she said and touched a small panel on her hip. "Turn around. Slowly. Now stand still."

He did so. There was a hum and then, after a few seconds, a click.

"You can turn back."

Dougan turned so his back was facing her.

"Okay," she said.

Dougan turned back to see the fabric of the suit changing. Colours rippled across its surface until she was wearing an exact replica of Dougan's uniform, right down to the oily stain on his left thigh.

Dougan frowned.

"Wow," he said, "where did you get that?"

"Freebie. Get them all the time when you work for the media."

"Clever," said Dougan.

"Never really caught on," she replied. "It's considered bad form to turn up at social events wearing the same thing as someone else, let alone change into it halfway through the night."

Dougan shrugged, "It's still rather clever."

Ellie looked around. "So where's this library then?"

Dougan pointed down the corridor to the lifts. "This way," he said.

CHAPTER NINE

Library

The lifts took them deep into the bowels of the building where only maintenance staff went. The corridors here were wider, more industrial. Their footsteps clanked on the floors and echoed eerily.

The entrance to the storage facility of the library, where all the hard copies of all extant books were kept, was located three floors up but since Dougan was keen to get in through the back he had located a small service tunnel that would get them in at the bottom level.

Ellie had bribed the security guard from her company expenses account. Greased palms made up the major part of expenses in her business. The deal was sealed with a businesslike efficiency.

The security guard had agreed to turn off the security system and for an extra hundred credits, which Dougan had stumped up, had even supplied them with the whereabouts of the maintenance suits.

Dougan had the distinct feeling that he'd been conned in this last exchange, as the guard had had a twinkle in his eye divulging this seemingly innocuous piece of information.

As they walked through the tunnels, Dougan couldn't help noticing that there had seemed to have been a lot of building activity down here on the lower levels. Brand new piping, ducts and wires seemed to run all over the place standing out against the rusted decaying surfaces of the rest of the tunnels. It was like a warren under the main building and rumour had it that, although the external form of the building was impressive, it was just the tip of the iceberg. No one really knew how big the underground portion of the Naval building really was. Only the conspiracy theorists had ever ventured to suggest.[48]

They reached the service tunnel entrance, a circular doorway set halfway up the wall, plastered with warning signs and brightly coloured instructions. The words "Maintenance Suits Must Be Worn At All Times" were blazoned in large jagged lettering in several languages across the surface.

They both agreed: such advice was probably there for the taking. He and Ellie edged the twenty metres down the corridor to where three grey suits hung behind an unlocked grille.

Dougan pulled two down and they clambered into them.

The suits ended in thin but resilient gloves, soft to the touch and, Dougan imagined, probably ideal for handling old fragile books with. They tightened around his fingers as he put them on.

Dougan was about to head back to the maintenance hatch when Ellie grabbed him by the arm.

---

[48] Who, it turns out, had been conservative in their estimate by a factor of ten.

He turned. She was pointing into the recess. The top shelf was lined with full enclosure helmets. She shrugged theatrically at him.

"It's okay," he said, "we can talk."

Ellie's cheeks flushed and her lips tightened.

"Helmets," she said brusquely. "They must be there for a reason."

Dougan shrugged and pulled two down, again handing one to Ellie.

"Maybe there are a lot of chances to bang your head in there," he suggested.

"Maybe they don't want anyone breathing over the books."

Dougan shrugged again and they walked back to the service hatch, which swung open with a slight hiss.

Dougan pulled the helmet over his head and, with the visor up, began to clamber into the tunnel. It sloped gently upwards. Ellie followed, slamming the door behind her.

The tunnel was dark, save for the occasional red light on the side of the walls. They winked on and off, eerily illuminating no more than a metre in front of them. The tunnel was only as wide as they were, and it was slow going over the hundred-metre climb.

Dougan began to feel his hands cramping as he was forced to crawl at an unusual angle and so when he reached the top end he turned quickly to Ellie who was very close behind and announced that he was going to open the hatch.

Ellie, whose face was obscured by the visor of her helmet raised her thumb.

As Dougan turned the handle of the hatch he felt it pull away from him, tugging open in his hands and the faint hiss of air. Too late, he looked at the sign on the hatch door: "Ensure Pressure Is Equalised Before

Opening". He looked frantically around for airlock controls and only then realised that the red lights on the wall had each contained a pressure regulator control.

The door wrenched at his fingers and he pressed his shoulder against the wall to hold it in place. From the angle he was at, he couldn't turn the handle back again. He turned round to see Ellie mouthing words she wouldn't say to her mother as the handle slipped from his grip.

The door flung open and, shouting similar words, Dougan was launched into the library chamber with Ellie tumbling close behind.

Instinctively he closed the visor to his helmet, which locked instantly, saving him from the cold vacuum environment the books were stored in. As he launched through the air, tumbling head over heels, he was able to take in the whole space. The chamber was over thirty metres high but, fortunately, the gravity was low. A dim blue light cast dark shadows over the rows and rows of neatly stacked shelves tumbling above Dougan's head as he continued his long low trajectory through the chamber. As he spun he saw Ellie tumbling too, the bright light from her suit sending beams skittering over the shelves.

He rolled gently over the maze of pristine white books below, waving his arms ineffectually in the vain hope that via some convoluted genetic memory pathway he might suddenly regain the ability to fly.

Seconds later he crashed silently into a tall bookshelf. Books fell around him, as he careered to the ground bringing scores of white bound hardbacks, each with their title and reference number etched down the side. One by one volumes fell silently on him like footage of a flock of white doves being released, played in reverse.

Splinters of wood drifted lazily to the ground.

Dougan lay in the pile, trapped by the books. It was oddly dark inside the suit and it suddenly dawned on him that the power was off and with the power off, he would quickly run out of air.

He began to do what most normal people do in this situation: panic. He struggled beneath the weight of the books around him and noted that his arm was trapped under a largish shelf, stifling any hope of being able to turn the power on.

Twisting himself slightly, he was able to pull one arm from under a large encyclopaedia. The arm flailed helplessly at a useless angle.

He could feel the pressure of the weight on his legs even under the meagre gravity. His vision was beginning to darken with the lack of oxygen and the air in the suit got thick and heavy.

As his breathing became shallower, he could feel his arms become leaden as they too screamed for oxygen.

The dim blue lights above him began to circle. His mind began to stray. His arm above him looked oddly detached as it waved about like a chunky flagpole.

Of course they'd store the books in a vacuum he thought. It made perfect sense.

His vision darkened. Bright sparkles took over.

His final thought was one of anger. What were they thinking? Doors between potentially different pressure environments always open *into* the area of higher pressure so if there is a difference you couldn't get it open. Like car doors underwater.

At least there were engineers stupider than him, he thought. Then the blackness took over.

He awoke to find Ellie standing over him, forcing the suit to flood with oxygen.

His headache was severe.

She was mouthing something to him but he couldn't hear it. Perhaps he was deaf.

He sat up and bashed the bridge of his nose against the inside of the helmet. The banging sound assured him he wasn't.

Ellie, now sure that he was okay had begun lifting books off him. They tumbled down the small hill he had created and bounced dreamily to the floor.

He slowly felt power returning to his body and was able to sit up.

Ellie was talking to him now in quite an earnest fashion and he watched her lips move silently, his face crumpling into a silent frown. Her face was animated and he could read the signs of excitement.

With the shelf out of the way, he was able to sit up and pull his legs out from under the books.

He swivelled round painfully, the spine of a large book jabbing into his own, and shook his head.

Ellie was still talking.

As he turned in profile to her she suddenly stopped, leaned forward and tapped the side of his helmet. His earpiece crackled into life.

"Did you hear anything I said?" she asked.

Dougan shook his head slowly,

"Sorry," he said. "I think I was too busy being dead."

Ellie's face tightened, then she threw a book at him.

He was too dazed to argue.

"What were you saying?"

Ellie sighed loud enough to be sure it would carry over the microphones.

"I was saying that I think I've worked out a basic layout of this place. I did it while you recovered. I was also saying, basically, that I might take the lead for a while."

Dougan nodded.

"Sure," he said. His head felt like it was full of glue. Bright sparkles flashed from time to time.

"Are you okay?" Ellie asked finally. She had a very strict limit on empathy towards the ill effects of stupid action.

"Yes, I'll be fine once my head stops expanding and contracting."

They clambered down to the ground level where the surface was hard and smooth. Floor-lights lit the rows between the shelves casting an eerie uplight on the tomes.

Tracks led away, disappearing into the walls, where Dougan presumed electronic motors would emerge to collect the books for viewing upstairs.

Following Ellie through the corridors of books, Dougan ran his finger along the spines.

Each one was bound in precisely the same way, with a white hardback cover and clear black lettering down the side indicating the title and a long reference number.

There were no directions or signs and yet Ellie seemed to be navigating her way with relative ease through the maze of shelves. Dougan was happy to have someone to follow as the dizziness seemed happy to follow him.

"Have you been here before?" asked Dougan.

"No," she said pausing to decide which way to go at a T-junction. Both ways looked the same to Dougan.

"It just makes sense. The grouping I mean," and she headed right determinedly. Dougan lurched after her.

"History!" she announced like a guide operator on the most cerebral tour ever conceived.

Dougan peered at the shelves stacked with history volumes written by people with names that suggested they had been born to be academics.

Ellie slowed and scanned rows and rows of shelves, honing in on books like a sniffer dog around a badly stuffed teddy bear at an airport.

"Besides," she said, "my dad and I used to spend a lot of time in places like this when I was little. It was his hobby."

"Reading books?"

"Arranging shelves."

"Oh."

"Kind of rubs off on you though. Here we go."

She plucked a book from the centre of the row. It was a medium sized volume in almost perfect condition.

Dougan looked at the book. It was likely that it had never been read by anyone. It was sort of sad.

He crouched on the floor next to Ellie and peered over her shoulder.

It didn't take them long to find what they were looking for.

They read in silence as everything they had expected was there in black and white as the truth, or at least as close to the truth as any reportage could be.

According to the book, the seven robots had indeed been built by Sharp and his colleagues. They had enjoyed a brief period of interest and public endorsement. Sharp had jokingly called his research centre Robot World, but he clearly harboured a desire for there to be such a place one day. The public lapped up his genuine affection for his creations, treating them like celebrities. Until things started to go wrong.

It had been noticed first with the Survival Robot who had become jittery, refusing the contact of others. Deep paranoia had set in, causing it to prefer to lock itself away from the others. At the same time The Knowledge robot had become similarly reclusive, choosing personal study over engaging with its mentors. Its quest to know everything had become something of an obsession. The Harmony robot had also shown signs of disengagement, immersing itself in the natural world and seeking out environmental balance wherever it could.

On the other hand, the Glory robot had been the darling of the media, conducting feats of daring and lapping up attention.

The Money and Justice robots had won tremendous favour improving the Fiscal and Legislative situation of the fledgling empire, but eventually, they too, had tried to suggest policies that the Imperial Warlords found difficult to agree to.

However, it had been the Power robot who had commanded the least attention until it was too late to do anything about it.

The references to other volumes covering the subject were almost too many to count but Dougan and Ellie were able to grasp what happened simply by reading on.

The Power robot had become an almighty bully. In the brief experiments where the robots were left alone together Power had attempted to control the others using whatever means it saw fit. The Survival robot was terrified of it.

One day, the Power robot and a chief scientist had gone into a counselling session and only the robot had emerged.

Sharp had created a killing machine.

The galaxy was horrified.

The military were *very*, *very* interested.

Almost immediately the project was taken out of Sharp's hands. The Navy set up a programme that employed each of the robots in a field of expertise, Survival working on developing safety techniques, Knowledge, Justice and Money working on new developments in science, economics and social policy, Power on developing new weapons and attack systems and Glory as a sort of galactic PR for the 'robots of the future' as they were to be known.

And then one day they had suddenly gone missing. Only a nervous and desperate Glory robot, who had become increasingly erratic, remained. It refused to speak of what it knew and soon afterwards disappeared leaving a note that said nothing more than 'Gone to Robot World[49]'

There was some concern about the missing robots.

Fortunately at least one was to show up again five years later.

Unfortunately, it showed up with a massive army of self-replicating mind-linked armoured battle-bots. At their front, was a very vengeful Power robot, who had decided that power over the other robots was nothing compared to power over the Empire.

The war had been long and very, very bloody.[50]

---

[49] Being imbued with an irrepressible showmanship, it had spelled out the message to the galaxy by simultaneously detonating three hundred and seventy two thermonuclear devices against the backdrop of the Drevon dust cloud. The subtleties of this gesture went completely unnoticed and the fact that the font used was called "back in five" was a joke completely missed by the galaxy at large.

[50] For at least one side, for the other it had been oily, wiry and circuity.

Dougan and Ellie skipped ahead.

Towards the end of the war, it began to look particularly bleak for the Empire which, while they could raise a substantial Navy faster than the robots, could not in any way match the rate they produced troops.

Then suddenly, out of nowhere, the other six robots had appeared.

An ancient silvery battleship craft had touched down in the centre of Imperial City at the gates to the palace. It had gone completely unnoticed and unchecked by all the military's defence mechanisms and had caused no small alarm as the robots had entered the palace, insisting they would speak to the Emperor. They had emerged an hour later announcing that they would take it from here, returned to their craft, and torn off into oblivion.

Shortly afterwards, the war had simply stopped. Battle-bots had simply halted in their tracks and an uneasy silence settled over the galaxy.

Any attempts to find the robots home world had simply drawn blanks, and the robots, and the war had drifted into history. The Empire picked up the pieces and went back to terrorising its citizens, which left everyone feeling much more secure.

Dougan and Ellie looked up from the book. She had finished before him but neither could quite look each other in the eye as they took all this in.

Everything both of them had read in the history files had been completely wrong. The robots had started the war and inexplicably finished it themselves.

If it was true, then history had to have been altered. Possibly word by word, adapting and evolving year by year in every document, every dossier on the subject until what they were left with was a completely new history.

And with each new document they had come across in the database it had been altered further, as whoever wanted to hide the truth, had raced to keep up with them.

There was every chance that the original seven, or at least five of them, were still out there.

It was chilling stuff.

Dougan and Ellie sat dumbfounded on the floor of the Library. It was a long time before either of them spoke and when they did it was Dougan who opened with a very pertinent question.

"Ellie?" he asked softy.

"Yes," she replied

"How long has that security drone been there?"

Ellie looked round to see the barrel shaped drone hovering in the air several metres above them, flying in slow lazy arcs.

Slowly but definitively they rose to their feet and pressed themselves hard against the shelves.

The security drone was a simple machine, following intercept protocols, but what it lacked in decision-making it made up for in persistence.

As Dougan and Ellie had opened the airlock they had sent a tiny pressure wave through the almost atmosphere-less chamber and, as they had been catapulted, they had created barely identifiable eddies that had subtly alerted the drone to their presence. Crashing into the bookcase had merely been a formality.

The drone scanned the room carefully.

It noticed books had been moved. Lots of books.

Drones don't have senses of job satisfaction. They are not programmed to glean pleasure from their work, simply to carry out pre programmed instructions. This makes them utterly impossible to reason with.

The drone flew back and forth. It would scan the whole room, generating a report on what it saw, until it had completed the report. It would then seal off the area and pass the report along to someone who did care about job satisfaction and probably achieved this by shouting, waving a gun and the authorised application of hurt.

In the meantime it would continue scanning.

Unless something moved.

Unfortunately for Dougan and Ellie, this was the one activity that they considered absolutely vital to their escape plan.

Still as statues, they talked.

"We have to get out of here," Dougan said.

Ellie fought the urge to answer this comment with a phrase sarcastically highlighting the obviousness of this statement.

And lost.

"No shit," she said.

"Do you think you can lead us to the exit?" asked Dougan.

"How? If we move, the security drone spots us. Why don't we just wait for it to go?"

"It'll find us eventually and when it does I'd rather be a moving target than a static one."

Ellie nodded stiffly inside the suit.

"Any idea how it might be armed?"

"I imagine it'll be lasers, physical weapons would be too heavy."

"What if the books catch fire?"

"That wouldn't happen, there's no oxygen in here. I thought I'd proved that earlier…"

Dougan's muscles still ached in proof.

"We need to get to the main door, we'll never get out through the service tunnel," he added.

Ellie turned her head slowly and glanced down the corridors of books that surrounded them.

The walls of the chamber were smooth and sheer, tapering to a dome high above their heads. Across the room she could see the drone. There was no immediately obvious exit, just a number of alcoves set low in the wall, only the top of which could be seen from their level.

The upper rim of an alcove in the far wall looked promising. She wasn't sure but there appeared to be stairs.

"There," she said, nudging him gently.

Dougan turned and looked, keeping the roving drone in one corner of his eye. He nodded.

"Want me to count to three?" he asked.

"No," she said, and bolted.

Dougan stood in shocked silence, watching her disappear away from him at great speed. Fear and panic rose from deep within him, adrenalin burst into his veins accompanied by the sting of irritation at her abrupt departure. He used this as the catalyst to get his leaden feet moving after her.

They hit a T-junction at full pelt. Ellie hesitated for a fraction of a second before swerving to the right. Dougan, a couple of paces behind took the corner in one smooth, slippery arc and the security drone, suddenly recognising the protocol in this situation, blasted the facing book shelf with a barrage of tight, narrow, yellow laser beams. The beams tore pencil-thin holes through the books and sent them scattering to the floor. The drone registered the book damage and protocols driving it to the protection of the books kicked in. But something appeared to be overriding these. Something it wasn't programmed to factor in.

Ellie and Dougan, turned into a long corridor of books leading towards the outside walls. Ellie looked desperately around for openings as Dougan regained his footing, his face a rubbery mask of fear.

The corridor of volumes of computer literacy stretched unbroken before them and Ellie put on an extra burst of speed.

Dougan, still somewhat out of breath and finding it hard to keep up, made the classic mistake of looking behind him.[51]

The drone robot careered round the corner dropping to their level and smashed into a bookshelf.

Suddenly Dougan found an extra burst of energy that brought him closer to Ellie's heel. As he ran he felt something drop to the ground. It took every ounce of his willpower to not turn round to see what it was.

Half way down the corridor with no break in the shelves in sight, Ellie suddenly stopped.

Dougan, running at full tilt, almost crashed into the back of her as she turned to face the shelf directly in front of her. The drone had hit the floor and was floundering to get itself back into the air again.

"This lane isn't going anywhere!" she shouted.

---

[51] After many years of argument and debate, scientists finally put the number of classic pursuit mistakes at four: Running down a dead end, running up stairs, hiding in an enclosed space and looking behind. The Ryla Four Delegates' argument that the wearing of flip-flops in pursuit scenarios should also be included, was thrown out on the grounds that wearing flip-flops in any non-beach situation is just dumb.

Dougan paused and looked around.

He pointed to a small two-book-wide gap on a bottom shelf.

"I don't think we can hide in there..."

A pause, then Ellie's voice exploded in Dougan's earpiece: "We have to get through!"

She was pushing hard against the shelves in an attempt to topple them. Dougan joined her throwing his whole body weight at the unit.

He bounced lazily off, unable to generate enough force in the low gravity, while Ellie continued pounding the shelves in short sharp punches.

The drone was righting itself again and swung round to face them.

Dougan looked up at the shelf, which towered to one and a half times his height, looked back at the drone, placed a foot of the lowest shelf and launched himself into the air.

The jump under the low gravity carried him several feet up. He pushed backwards, rebounded against the opposite shelf and used the extra purchase to launch himself at the top of the unit that Ellie was now heaving her shoulder against.

Hitting it with all his body weight he half cleared it, slamming his stomach into the very top of the unit. It wobbled uncertainly and with the aid of a final push from Ellie toppled slowly over into the next aisle sending more books scattering.

Ellie ran clumsily up the inclined unit and grabbed Dougan at the top where they dropped to the ground on the other side. More yellow bolts sizzled down the corridor, closely followed by the now airborne drone.

The aisle on the other side was stacked with shorter shelves and they continued their run, ducking and weaving, Ellie instinctively leading them towards the circular wall of the chamber.

Still in pursuit, the drone was finding their slalom harder to follow and dropped back. It rose above the shelves searching for signs of their movement, firing randomly to flush them out.

The books they were among were larger, oversize tomes, several books bound into one and as they crept towards the outer wall of the chamber, the shelves grew shorter and squatter until the pair realised that they were now too low to provide them much cover.

The drone loomed menacingly out from the central core of the chamber making a beeline for them.

Ellie dropped to the ground dragging Dougan with her.

They crawled down several aisles and rounded corners as fast as their hands and knees would carry them. The drone was nearly upon them.

Dougan slipped and rolled to the ground and Ellie instinctively turned to pick him up. As she did a bolt of laser fire caught a glancing blow on the side of her head sending her spinning to the ground.

Dougan tried to rise to his feet to reach her but as he did so the drone passed directly overhead, close enough that if he'd wanted to he could have reached out and touched the coppery casing of the drone's small barrel-like torso.

It hovered over Ellie's prone body. The laser cannons attached to the side folded gracefully away and a nasty-looking grapple hook claw extended from its underside.

The claw grabbed Ellie's wrist and flipped her over like a doll as a massive security cuff clamped onto her left arm.

Inside Dougan, anger welled up. Protective, primitive anger. He searched around for a weapon. There were nothing but books as far as the eye could see. They would have to do.

He lifted up a hefty tome and gripped it firmly in his hand as he scrambled to his feet.

The drone, sensing the movement, released its grip on the security cuff and turned menacingly to face him.

For a second, Dougan stared at the insect-like face of the drone, a dark brown bulbous sensor array jutted from the front of the torso section. It was partially transparent and inside he could see solenoids pumping away, relay switches clicking and dim scanner beams sweeping backwards and forwards, assessing him.

The laser cannons began to unfold from their casing.

Dougan took a deep breath, ran, and swung hard.

He had never been particularly good at any sport that involved hitting any kind of ball with a bat. He had a weak swing and tended to close his eyes at times when it made most sense to be able to see what he ought to have been doing.

The derision he had encountered on the sports field was so deeply ingrained on his psyche, like a bad word carved into an antique table, it continued to haunt him long after the sports field had been left, dug up, levelled over and replaced with a shopping complex.

Luckily for Dougan and Ellie, this was his moment of redemption.

The tome hit the brown casing of the drone's sensor unit squarely and the brittle plastic gave under the force of the blow. The follow-through was sufficient to impact the circuit nodes, which sparked violently and erupted as the drone span into a crumpled sparking heap on the library floor.

It was the finest swing Dougan had ever made. Ever.

Ellie sat up.

"Did you get it?" she asked.

And not one, sodding person had seen it.

"Yes," he replied meekly.

The various appendages of the drone writhed and twitched as it span on its casing for a minute or two before falling still and silent.

Ellie sighed with relief and pulled herself up, the security cuff still binding her arm to her side.

"Thank you," she said. Dougan could tell from the tone of her voice that she meant it.

It occurred to him that if they hadn't been wearing the suits, now would have been a perfect time for them to kiss.[52]

Ellie picked herself up and rubbed her helmet with her unrestricted arm. Carbon dust came off on the fingers of her gloves but otherwise the suit was still intact.

They looked down at the crumpled body of the security drone.

"What did you use to do that?"

Dougan peered along the spine of the book "Callico's War of Independents. Abridged. Volume 1"

Despite the fact that her arm had been rendered awkwardly useless, Ellie was keen to get moving again.

Although they were near the wall, there were several rows of bookcases between them and the alcove where they suspected the door might be. Sooner or later someone would come looking for the drone, find the library in tatters and would most likely not be too

---

[52] It was. However they would have had to take the suits off and they both would have died. It was too early for that kind of commitment.

pleased. They were both quite determined not to be around for that.

To get to the alcove they would have to head back into the centre of the chamber. They clambered over the wreckage as more books fell lazily to the ground.

Again they found themselves in a long corridor of books stretching back towards a central reservation, which they hurried along. The book-collector tracks stretched back along the floor to the walls and Dougan trotted comfortably along them.

He became less sure when they began to tremble slightly under his feet.

He grabbed Ellie's arm. She was standing at a junction between Humanities and Science.[53] Tracks led off in all directions. They could both see them visibly vibrating.

Ellie's eye followed one along its length, to where it disappeared into the wall. A crack had opened up. A portion of the wall was rising.

Dougan groaned. He'd never known libraries to be so dangerous.

From their stationary positions behind the walls, the book collectors, the writhing masses of mechanical arms designed to collect and replace books came charging at them.

It was hard to tell which way to run. Every corridor seemed to have its own malevolent robo-librarian bearing down on them in a whirl of unnecessarily dangerous attachments whipping and slicing the air.

Dougan and Ellie huddled together in another instance of a moment that should have been romantic but just didn't have the time.

---

[53] Physically, not metaphorically.

The machines whirled and spat nearer to them, filling their respective corridors and threatening much more than a stern look and a fine.

The nearest one suddenly stopped.

At its base, where claw-like feet gripped the tracks, was a single solitary book.

The machine stopped, plucked the book from where it had fallen, held it up to a sensor node, and suddenly twirled round.

It headed quickly back down the aisle and ducked out of view.

"It has to put them back!" cried Dougan

With the others still bearing down on them, Ellie reached up to a shelf behind her, pulled down a handful of books, and threw them high into the air.

The machines ground to a halt as a shower of books rained down around them. Menace turned to a burst of frenetic energy as they twirled and danced around the books in a bid to return them safely to their rightful places.

Dougan and Ellie darted down the empty corridor ahead of them, towards the alcove.

As they ran past a junction the first robo-librarian rounded a corner and resumed its chase.

Dougan's arm flew up from his side and he swept as many books as he could from the shelf, sending them tumbling into the path of their pursuer, who was, once again, compelled to return the literature to its respective place. Dougan couldn't say he wasn't enjoying it.

They reached the alcove and rejoiced to find the tracks ended at that one saving feature that humans across the galaxy being pursued by track-bound robots rejoice to encounter: a short flight of stairs.

The door at the top however, was locked.

Ellie looked searchingly at Dougan who fumbled around the edges for a catch or even a sign pointing to a control panel. There was nothing but an emergency alarm handle.

"You didn't think about how we were going to get out did you?" she suggested, correctly.

"I had hoped the bribe would cover it," he replied tersely.

Ellie snorted.

Dougan rounded on her, "Well if he'd given a number of options obviously I would have gone for the all inclusive plan including a chauffeur driven luxury ride home but those options didn't appear to be on the drop-down list!"

Ellie stood her ground. He was quite sure she was arching an eyebrow behind the visor of the suit, which was slightly misted by their exertion.

"You didn't pay for the bribe, I did," she said, one hand on her hip. She was irritated by the arm restraint that prevented her from performing the more effective double arm hip pose. As it was she just felt a little camp.

"I didn't know we'd have to leave by a different door," he answered brusquely.

Ellie screwed up her face and looked at the control readout on her suit arm.

"We don't really have a lot of time," she said.

Dougan turned, and from his vantage point on the stairs, was able to survey the wreckage of the library. The black insect-like book collectors had located the mess-filled crater he had made during his impact with the shelf and were busily trying to restore some kind of order. He wasn't entirely sure, but it looked like they hadn't worked out that it would be easier if they put the shelves upright first. One seemed to be caught in a perpetual loop of placing a book on a shelf only to watch it slide off and fall to the floor.

"I expect someone will notice the damage soon," he said, convinced that whoever did would not be best pleased.

They did and he was right.

It just wasn't who he was expecting.

Ellie and Dougan had slumped into a sullen silence on the stairs to the main entrance to the chamber.

Ellie wasn't very good at waiting. It made her irritable. She preferred the 'arrive late and kick up a stink' approach, which seemed to work better most of the time.

Time slowed down for both of them as they ticked off their oxygen supply minutes. Not for the first time that week Dougan wondered if he was going to die.

Ellie was, on the other hand determined not to die, and was strongly beginning to feel that her survival should come at Dougan's expense, whether it became necessary or not.

She had always operated alone. It had just been easier. Other people were desperately unreliable and best dealt with for the shortest interchange possible.

She never had a serious partner, never gave anyone her trust. They had always simply abused it and now it was kept in a safe secure place. She had liked Dougan, liked his vulnerability. He was also free of the macho arrogance that ran like an infected vein through the ranks of Naval officers she had met, including the women.

But it didn't change the fact that unless you looked out for yourself, you would regret it.

Of course it had occurred to her that this might make her in some way lonely but that looked like a dark path to go down at any time of the day or night so she stolidly ignored those signs.

Most of the time.

She looked sideways at Dougan.

It wasn't as if he was malicious, just desperately... scatterbrained. He seemed like the sort of person who things happened to rather than the other way round.

She was different, she happened to things. And if they were smart they got out of her way.

"Have you checked to see there's not a door mechanism?" she asked, breaking a silence that Dougan had been using to pick stray fibres from his suit.

"Yes," he sighed. "Trust me, there's no working door mechanism."

Ellie rose to her feet, following her firmly held principle that anything anyone insists is the truth should be treated with extreme suspicion.

"What's this?" she said pointing to the pull handle on the side of the door.

"Emergency alarm," he shrugged. "It could do one of two things; either it'll bring sixty more service drones to our rescue and deliver us directly into the hands of the security forces or..."

"Or..?"

"Or it'll seal the whole building to contain the fire, radiation leak, or gravity rupture and then even getting through the door wouldn't save us."

Ellie frowned.

"But that's crazy. You wouldn't put that control on the inside of the door."

"You've never worked for the safety division have you?"

"Do you have any other bright ideas?" she asked, thinking that at this stage she would settle for a dim one.

"No," he said moodily.

"Right" she said, "In that case I'm going to pull it."

"NO!" cried out Dougan rising to his feet.

Ellie froze, her arm outstretched and a look of surprise stamped on her face.

Dougan stood motionless for a second, in wide eyed surprise at his own reaction.

"Yeah, all right go on then," he muttered quickly.

Ellie pursed her lips and pulled the yellow handle firmly downwards.

Dougan held his breath.

There were no klaxons,[54] or flashing lights.

The door swung lazily open.

Beyond was a medium sized airlock chamber.

Ellie turned to look at Dougan, who shrugged.

She turned back to the panel on the wall and peered closely, closed her eyes and walked into the airlock. As she did she let her finger trail over the sign beneath the handle.

Dougan bent over and peered in.

Above the handle the words "In Case of Emergency" were written.

Dougan nodded.

Beneath, the sentence continued: "Please Contact Derek from Emergency in the Main Hall."

Dougan stood upright and stepped into the chamber. Ellie stared upwards avoiding his gaze and clicking her tongue.

The door clanged shut on the single word "Sorr—"

---

[54] Which is just as well because no-one would have heard them anyway.

On the other side of the galaxy the Private Enterprise Conglomerate were hastily re-sewing their flag and trying to work out whether 'Conglomerate' really covered what they were trying to say about themselves.

The massive debating stage was imaginatively lit from hidden gantries and, above the heads of the Barons and their assorted cronies, hung huge holographic projections of the present speaker.

Below the dais, in relative blackness, a small group of interested parties milled around, occasionally clumping into a large enough group to be called a crowd.

Baron Milleu of the Outer Rim Smugglers was speaking in aggravated tones, trying desperately hard to be heard above the snores of Baron Dewotcha who had fallen asleep right after the Agenda had been intoned for the day. The hum of the largely disinterested 'citizens' had made the task nearly impossible.

"I have to say," burbled the walrus-like Milleu, "that in my eyes 'conglomerate' indicates a fiscal tone and is by no means as effective as the use of a word such as 'cartel'. To change our name to the Private Enterprise Cartel would improve our reputation but would also commend a certain respect, through fear, to those outland communities who still oppose our right to behave as a nation."

The small group of flag-makers in the corner of the debating chamber looked nervously up from their needlework and paused over the application of the 'o' in conglomerate

Baron Reddlin snorted a thin, weaselly snort and the holograph of Milleu dissolved into a projection of his narrow face.

"We're not a nation," he remarked, "we're a rag tag bunch of pirates."

Baron Milleu's face grew purple with rage.

"My lords, it's exactly that kind of talk that completely undermines what we're trying to do here. I ask, would any of you like to go back to the old days where if two pirate gangs found themselves vying for the same territory, the dispute would be settled with a knife fight? Hmmm?" His bottom lip jutted our precariously.

There was a relative silence as the Pirate Barons looked sheepishly around.

"Yes," said the small voice of Baron Frisk, a tiny, thin fellow, clad solely in black, seated in a corner.

"It's too late to change the name now," Baroness Piper chimed in, "we've designed the logos."

The flag-makers breathed a sigh of relief and put down the large shears.

"What I'm saying," continued Milleu, "is that it's all very well combining forces, but we cannot allow a deprecation of the hard work we've put in establishing ourselves as a force to be reckoned with, with lame words like conglomerate!"

The low thrum of a murmur passed across the stage as the Barons all turned and tried to whisper things to each other. With more than ten aides stationed between each baron, the messages quickly became somewhat garbled. A sea of confused frowns gave way to looks of outright shock.

Baroness Piper, who had suggested the original name and had pushed it through at the last meeting several weeks ago, rose majestically to her feet.

"We will not go over old ground again," she said icily.

Above her the hologram magnified her cold stare.

The murmur died down.

"Now does anyone have anything of *relevance* to talk about today?" It was less of a question, more of a threat.

The figure of Reddlin unfolded from his chair.

"I would like to discuss the curious incidences of our recent encounters with the navy of the Empire!"

A few diehards spat on the floor at the mention of their most powerful and hated enemy[55]

"In what capacity?" Baroness Piper inquired, raising a steely eyebrow. Discussing the empire was old news since without the Empire they wouldn't exist at all and they all knew it. It was well understood that the evil oppression by the Empire served as a unifying force and had resulted in far more throats being left intact.

Reddlin folded his thin bony fingers together and pursed his lips.

"They have, of late, taken a somewhat greater interest in our activities...even those which do not directly concern them..."

"Can you give us an example?" Piper had no time for unravelling the cryptic statements of the best educated and smuggest of their number.

"Well," he continued, "recently, a small star-port that we were secretly operating from, quite far from any of the trade routes we usually intercept, came under malicious fire from a group of Imperial frigates. Our pilots fought bravely and although we

---

[55] Even though this practice had been unofficially banned by the Gultranian Revengers who had picked up the cleaning contract for the meetings.

outnumbered the frigates they turned the tide of the battle against us."

The barons hung their heads as one. It was always sad to hear of their noble bands of brigands falling at the hands of Imperials. Plus those fighters were expensive to replace. Someone would have to talk to The Itraliads.[56]

"An unfortunate tale but we must accept losses," cooed Piper.

"Indeed, Your Ladyship," Reddlin pressed on, "but the nature of the attack was unprecedented. We have been obviously operating from that secret star-port for years and the Empire has turned a blind eye. One has to wonder, why now?"

Baron Milleu shifted his massive bulk from where he had slumped, "I bet it's a PR stunt!" he cried. The hologram magnified the wobbling of jowls as he talked and the crowd were transfixed as the jowls continued moving long after he had stopped.

"Has anyone noticed anything *different* about the ships as well?" remarked one of the lesser Barons from further back, "They just seem to be a little...meaner..."

The Barons turned to each other and exchanged nods. There were nods in the crowd too. Everyone had noticed it. Whereas Imperial vessels had been impressive before, they had been impressive in a stately way, comforting in their bulky assurance,

---

[56] The Itraliads were a race of highly productive worker units controlled by a grublike queen in a honeycomb hive planet. They constructed craft indiscriminately for anyone who would bring them radioactive materials which they consumed for pleasure. They were fast and efficient and utterly trustworthy. The main drawback was that they were just so indescribably hideous to look at that it took a will of iron to place an order without vomiting or running in fear.

sedately gliding through a galaxy they knew was theirs. But recently the pirates had all seen new ships…sleeker ships, with more points, smooth edges and more concealed weapons. Where once there were whales, now there were sharks.

"This is not good," said Baron Juran raising his head from where it had been bowed in a contemplative prayer.

The others hushed. Juran thought a lot but spoke little. His band of vicious fighters, fanatical in their religious devotion to him, ensured that no-one was going to challenge his wise words. At least not in public anyway.[57]

"The nature of the enemy has changed. And we must change accordingly. If there is a to be a new enemy, there must be a new challenger."

He lapsed back into silence.

He was of course right, and they knew it. It seemed the empire was coming after them and, they had to admit, it wouldn't matter a toss whether they were called The Private Enterprise Conglomerate or the Banana Bunch if they were still discussing it when the armoured bomb-ships arrived.

"We can't take on the Empire," whined Baron Dreysill of the Hunter's Route Brigands. "We simply don't have the weaponry."

"He's right," piped up the Salacious Slit Throat's leader, "we've only got three capital ships and they're so old you can't even steal the parts to mend them any more!"

"And we don't have the weapons technology they have," whined another.

---

[57] Fortunately for them, he was always right; a trick he achieved by only speaking when he absolutely knew others were definitely completely wrong.

"We don't have the logistics to handle a full scale war!"

More voices chimed in. It wasn't often they got to moan about how tough it was being an outlaw and they weren't the sort to let a good opportunity slip by.

Baroness Piper held up her hands for silence.

"I think we should all stay calm," she commanded. "At this stage there is no suggestion that a full scale war will occur. We must however, keep our wits about us and be aware that while we must still survive, the knife of the enemy is that little bit sharper than it was before."

The Barons nodded.

"What about the suggestion that we set up a new secret base?" said Baroness Hildraaad, a powerful leviathan of a woman. "They know well that we are here and a blow to our heart might render our arms and legs nothing more than bloody, useless appendages flapping like wet gutted fish on the deck of an Utralian trawler."

The others grimaced.

"A good suggestion," added Baroness Piper, "and one we do consider every meeting at your request, but as I think we have pointed out before, no one has yet been able to locate a single habitable planet that would suit our needs and is out of the range of the Empire's prying eyes."

Baroness Hildraaad turned back to her aides who eagerly awaited the call to mount their Fru beasts[58] and

---

[58] The Fru Beasts were massive eight-legged, green-furred monsters with more than their fair share of teeth per inch of hide. The Hilderaaad families had ridden them on all their land incursions for centuries. The sight of these fearsome beasts bearing down on the natives caused the Hilderaaad to believe firmly that

blaze a destructive trail onto the surface of a new planet.

"Not today lads," she sighed and their faces fell.

Baron Milleu had risen again and taken centre stage.

"I think we all agree, offence is the best defence here. Not running away from the problem, but facing it square-on! Let's turn around to the Empire and say that although we may look like a rag tag bunch of pirates, brigands, smugglers, thieves and robbers — "

"- and embezzlers-" added a tiny voice at the back.

"- we will not be oppressed by them any longer. We demand the right to steal, loot and pillage according to our customs and if we have to fight them for that right then we will!"

The crowd watched in awe as Milleu delivered his rousing speech, half expecting him to pop at any moment.

The Barons replies with cries of 'here-here!' and many rose to their feet clapping and cheering.

The hand of a broad-faced Baron raised slowly. He was acknowledged and spoke.

"I fear that unless we manage to get hold of some space ships of the same calibre as the Empire, all this talk is but bravura."

He shrugged and pulled a sympathetic face.

Baron Milieu was not going be put off. "Well, does anyone have any ships of the same calibre as the Empire?" he burbled as if he was talking to a group of children.

The Barons looked around at each other trying their best to not actually make eye contact.

Baron Milleu swallowed hard and looked around.

---

theirs was the first society in the galaxy to have invented toilet training.

A thin self satisfied smile crept slowly over Baron Frisk's small face.

He raised a single black-clad arm from where they had been folded, and continued to smile.

"I do," he said smugly, as all eyes turned to him.

From their viewing platform on the balcony, Binner and Jirbaks looked uneasily at each other. Hurbury was asleep in the corner and Greeta was struggling with a vending machine that was refusing to give her soup unless she was prepared to accept it on her wrist.

"Do you think they'd like to know about the freighters now?" asked Jirbaks, straining to hear what was going on.

The barons had crowded around the slight figure of Frisk who, although he couldn't be heard from the balcony, appeared to be delighting the Barons with tales of elite gunnery.

The crowd, who quickly lost interest, dispersed vaguely once they could no longer hear what was going on, driven by immediate more pressing basic needs like food, religious needs and strict adherences to elaborate cleaning regimes involving their own tongues.

"I don't think they want to hear it right now," said Binner.

"Why not?" said Jirbaks, "I mean if <u>we</u> got surprised by the size of the freighter, so will other people, other pirates I mean."

"You feel it's your duty?"

"Yeah," said Jirbaks, struggling with the concept, "didn't you always say there was honour among thieves?"

"Yeah I did," said Binner, "I just never believed it. Come on, lets check the smaller trade routes. You hungry?"

Jirbaks sighed. She was beginning to question if she was still up to being a pirate. Her mother had always worried that she'd fall in with a bad crowd. She had insisted the young Jirbaks spend lots of time around children with *potential*. Jirbaks had found them tedious, precociously smug and frequently malicious. She had eagerly awaited the day when their potential evolved into something other than being spoilt and self-centred. When it became clear that Jirbaks was never going to match them on an academic level, her mother gave up and accepted her daughter seemed much happier around kids that could hot-wire space bikes and wield laser knives. When small but incredibly expensive gifts had started arriving, she had turned a blind eye. When other people had started making comments about what a wealthy family they had become recently, shame the kids were never home, she began turning their eyes a bit blind as well.

Jirbaks understood that bad crowds could be made up of good people, and vice versa.

They climbed down from the viewing platform, and as they did, a pickpocket tried to remove the shiny badge she'd taken from a security guard on a cruise liner two months ago.

She stopped and turned on the pickpocket, a wiry moustachioed man in a thin vest top, who looked very surprised to have been caught.

He smiled broadly at her.

Jirbaks raised her arm and smacked him firmly in the teeth. He dropped to the floor still wearing the grin.

"There's no honour among thieves," she muttered to herself and trotted to catch up with Binner who was nursing Greeta's scalded arm.

In the library, one insect-like drone picked up the book that had been discarded by Dougan and Ellie, scanned the spine and replaced it on the shelf in its correct place.

While the other robots continued trying to repair the damage that had been wreaked, it returned to its cubbyhole in the wall and the door slid closed behind it.

In the darkness, an umbilical cord connected with a socket in the wall and a single short electronic message was passed.

The message turned to a light pulse and sped along kilometres of cabling through the bowels of the headquarters building until it reached the central hub.

It crept along a secret cable, until it arrived in a small chamber where it was security vetted.

It progressed through a series of firewalls, each more complicated and fiercer than the one before, along another cable, and, for a brief moment of eternity, stepped out of time.

It entered an electronic mind, vast and scary.

The mind consumed the message, turned it over again and again. New, darker thoughts were spawned. It matched the information with the DNA sample it had gathered from the concourse at the Imperial Headquarters. And the visual obtained from the cleaning automaton. The signatures were the same. If the investigator had been in the library as well, then he already knew too much.

Wheels began to be set in motion.

THE COLOUR OF ROBOTS

CHAPTER TEN

Leviathan

Dougan and Ellie raced through the corridors of the headquarters building.

With their suits discarded they were free of all suspicion except that raised by their speed.

"Where are we going?"

"My friend Finlay's office," said Dougan dragging her from lift to lift to lift.

"Why?"

"Because," explained Dougan, rapidly feeling himself running out of breath, "because he's the most switched-on, clued-in person I know. His whole life is spent being suspicious about things and so he'll be able to explain why, how and who might have been trying to wipe the robots from the history files."

They reached a junction. Dougan was beginning to tire of finding himself in mazes. He knew how to get to Finlay's office, he just wouldn't have started from here.

"Besides he'll also be up."

After a couple of false starts and exasperated noises from Ellie, Dougan finally found himself in the right corridor and cautiously approached Finlay's door.

Which was open.

Dougan peered carefully around. It was unusual for Finlay to leave his door open. In fact, as far as Dougan was concerned it was positively odd.

The office was exactly as before except the lights were dimmer, and the office was empty and the plant life looked vaguely surprised to see them.

"Bloody hell," muttered Ellie.

"What?" frowned Dougan

"Someone's ransacked the place." She cast her eye of the untidy sprawl of computers, discarded files, chairs strewn crazily all over the place and litter strewn floor.

"Oh no," said Dougan, "It's always like this. They're just not very tidy. Holistic minds you know," he said tapping his forehead.

"Oh," said Ellie and trudged confidently into the room stepping on something slightly squishy.

Dougan led them round the desks and cubicles. In the absence of people the plants seemed even more domineering. It was almost as if they were following them round the room. The eerie hum of generators filled their ears.

Dougan rounded the corner to see a light still on in Finlay's office. A business-like movement confirmed that he was in there. At least someone was in there, it was hard to tell against the frosted plasti-glass.

The door was also open.

Ellie looked at Dougan, concerned.

"Is this a good idea?" she asked

"I wouldn't know," said Dougan, "I don't think I've ever had one."

And he stepped boldly to the door.

He was relived to find Finlay hunched over his desk, with the lights low. On the view-screens the same simulation played out over and over again casting eerie shadows over the room.

Finlay looked haggard as he turned to look at Dougan. All his boyish exuberance had been drained out of him.

"Dougan," he sighed.

He was finding it difficult to meet Dougan's eyes.

Ellie appeared in the doorway but thought better than to introduce herself.

"Finlay, what's up?" asked Dougan.

Finlay let out a tiny, half-hearted laugh that only seemed to reach his throat.

"I thought you'd come here," he said.

"Did you?" said Dougan, now utterly puzzled. "Why?"

"I can't help you."

Dougan felt his legs numbing. What did he mean?

"It's all over the security network. There's nothing I could do to help you and even if I could..."

Finlay raised his arms.

Dougan suddenly felt like he had after he'd blatantly copied one of Finlay's reports in the first term at the academy. A hot wave of guilt flowed over him.

"I don't..." he stammered.

He was also aware of Ellie looking sidelong at him.

Finlay sighed.

"Dougan you broke into a top-secret installation, right here in the Head Quarters building! What were you thinking? And you attempted to bribe a guard! That's treason Dougan!"

"Attempted? He took the bribe! That rat, I told you..."

A look of anger flashed over Finlay's face.

"So you did break in."

Dougan's face fell.

"I needed to prove something Finlay, listen, someone has been re-writing history, all the computer history files for the last hundred years...they've all been re-written."

Finlay sneered.

"Oh what nonsense."

"It's true," interjected Ellie, "the library holds original print copies of anything ever published in the Empire, dating back hundreds of years, but nobody uses it. Why would you, when it's all there at the tap of a button. But what we know, what we were taught at school *is a cover up*."

Finlay, who had risen to his feet, didn't take his eye off Dougan.

"Who are you?"

"Ellie Novak, I'm a journalist"

"Cover up for what?"

Ellie reached out and gently touched Finlay's arm. Her own left arm was still in the restraint and she lost her balance slightly. Finlay looked down and noticed the security brace with some disdain. He shook his head.

"I don't know, but it could get very serious."

"More serious than a treason charge, Dougan? The security forces also think that you've been tampering with online files. You look like a man with something to hide and they have people with sharp implements who will get it out of you, you know."

A hefty frown flitted across Dougan's brow.

"Trust me Finlay, I think I've uncovered something. Something sinister. Something that someone doesn't want me to find out. And yes it does involve altering records but it goes right back into the mists of time. To before the war. Everything we take for granted as history is all wrong. It's been altered from *within the database!*"

An instrument panel on Finlay's main computer blinked into life and emitted a strangled beep

Finlay bowed over and touched a panel on the pad.

"They're here," he said.

"Who are?" asked Ellie.

"The security forces," said Finlay flatly. Dougan could read a hint of resentment in his voice. He turned to Finlay.

"What do they want?" he asked.

"You, you idiot!" Finlay spat, "Dougan I don't think you realise how seriously the Navy take interference!"

"Finlay," said Dougan, "you've known me a long time. I'm a scatterbrain, an underachiever. I couldn't even get a proper job in an office. But I'm not a spy or a rebel or a renegade. I've never tried to get back at anyone for anything. Except Chury Goodwin at school when he started seeing the girl I liked but that backfired anyway. I just can't tell anyone what I know because I don't know who I can tell, and who I can't, and who's trying to shut me up."

Finlay's face softened.

"I'm not...capable of treason," he said waving his arms.

Finlay slumped into his chair.

"I know," he said.

"Somehow, someone has tampered with the historical data. Can't you review the logs of the logs or something? Go back, see what got changed, when and by whom? Then I could say I was just...checking up some facts for an assignment."

"No," said Finlay, "you couldn't just *change....*" His face softened, "...I mean word by word you could but that would take..."

"A hundred years?" said Dougan.

The pair's eyes locked for a moment. Dougan saw a flicker in Finlay's resolution. It was fractional, minuscule, but Dougan knew him just well enough.

Finlay dropped his face into his hands. "I tell you what I'll do, I'll have a look and see if I can't find some evidence of tampering. It won't save you but it might lessen the severity of the punishment."

He looked at Dougan.

"And now you're planning on running away aren't you?"

Dougan nodded. "It's what I'm good at."

Finlay shook his head.

"Then you better get out of here. If they know you were here they'll think I'm involved too and then I won't be able to do anything for you."

He reached over to a screen and opened an old flip-top file. Green light danced in his eyes, flashing on and off.

"Go left out the main door and take your first left. At the end of that corridor there's a service tunnel which they might not have covered but don't bet on it. Don't go down the main corridor, I guarantee you'll meet a reception party there."

Dougan thanked Finlay, and grabbed Ellie by the arm.

"I'll do what I can Dougan. I doubt you'll get far so I'll do what I can. Take care."

Finlay's trademark grin resurfaced behind a worn face, but it never quite reached his eyes.

"You too, Finlay."

Dougan grabbed Ellie by the arm and pulled her into the corridor. She had seemed reluctant to leave, staring over Finlay's shoulder.

They reached the door. Dougan peered out expecting to see the guards. The corridor was empty.

"We have to get to the Burning Desire."

"The what?"

"My survey craft. She's in space dock but if we can get to her, we can get out of here. I don't know what the punishment is for computer tampering but I'm pretty sure it doesn't involve jelly and tickling. Lets go."

Dougan pulled left.

"Okay, number one, I am not a dessert trolley," barked Ellie. Dougan instantly let go of her arm.

"Thank you," she said, patting down the much-maligned arm.

Dougan pulled left again as Finlay had instructed but it was Ellie's turn to grab his arm. She remained firmly rooted to the spot.

"What the hell are you doing?" he said, "we have to get out of here."

"Dougan, I don't trust him."

"You don't trust anybody. You'd be a rotten journalist if you did."

"I am a rotten journalist," she hissed back, "but that's not the point."

"Well, what is the point?" Dougan said through gritted teeth.

"He was lying."

Dougan stared searchingly at her. This was all he needed.

"I saw the motion scanner he was using. He was lying. There is definitely a guard in the security tunnel and there was no-one in the main corridor."

Dougan hesitated. What if she was lying?

"I'm not lying," she said.

Dougan looked down at the floor. To his left the corridor with the service tunnel looked like the best option. It was dark and looked unused. To his right, the main corridor looked painfully bright.

Ellie waited, her eyes darting between the two doors.

Dougan looked up and into her brown eyes.

"I have to trust him," he said and walked purposefully towards the service tunnel.

"You bloody men and your sticking together," she said angrily as she sauntered after him.

Finlay hunched over the computer screen. Yes, it would have taken about a hundred years, word for word to change the history files, the well known, commonly referenced ones.

He ran a simulation, based on transfer errors. Assuming one digit got altered every time the file was transferred...

The computer ticked as it mulled over the data.

Finlay waited.

It seems a hundred years had been an overestimation.

The entire computer storage facility could have been re-written in just eighty-four.

Dougan would definitely want to know this.

Dougan and Ellie climbed slowly into the roomy service tunnel through a large open grille and closed it behind them.

The tunnel ahead of them was empty but dimly lit.

They crept forward, with Dougan slightly ahead of Ellie, their knees straining against the slight incline.

After a handful of paces, Dougan turned to Ellie and whispered, "See, I told you this would be right."

As he turned back a heavily armoured and slightly surprised looking group of security officers stepped into their path and levelled their guns at them.

"Ahem," said one, feeling like he was going through the motions a bit, "you're under arrest."

"Erm, stay where you are and put your hands on your head," commanded the middle one.

Dougan and Ellie, in the interest of their lives, obliged.

Finlay burst into the corridor and looked urgently left and right.

Dougan was nowhere to be seen, which although was a good thing from Dougan's point of view, was bad from Finlay's. He would need to know what Finlay knew, and it would probably spare him a hefty term on a prison planet.

He cursed under his breath, hoping that Dougan had ignored his advice after all and gone down the empty main service tunnel.

He ran to the end of the brightly lit corridor and activated the control.

The door slid open.

Instead of seeing the main corridor stretching away from him he was confronted by three huge and menacing arrest drones immediately behind the door.

Finlay froze, knowing that as long as he offered no resistance, he would remain unharmed until he could explain.

The drones, without warning, and against all known protocol opened fire.

The Magnificence was the pride of the Imperial fleet, the largest, most impressive battleship ever built and as far as its Captain was concerned it was going the wrong way.

The ship ploughed through the space lane, sending smaller cargo vessels scuttling from its path. Remnants of those ships that had failed to avoid its path were embedded in its bulbous fore-module, splattered like flies on a windshield.

There was no attempt to steer, things got out of its way.

In the ship's wake, hundreds of smaller craft fussed and darted providing the necessary support and logistics that a craft of its size needed. A fleet of industrial-looking freighters chugged behind carrying the massive fuel containers the ship needed to get anywhere.

There were only five ships of its enormous size class in the Navy: the Magnificence, the Brilliance, the Resplendence, the Radiance and The Other One[59]

They were the Battle Behemoths, the pride of the fleet and the primary reason for staying on the right side of the Empire.

At all times three of them were in operation somewhere in the galaxy, while the other two stood down for repair or crew R&R.

Captain Beaker had been surprised to get the call to stand down so shortly after being assigned a patrol of

---

[59] Originally titled The Glorious Effulgence, the name was so hard to remember that it had long since been forgotten. Even the crew had since replaced the signs.

the outlying regions and was, he would admit, a little put-out.

The Empire itself had managed to retain a Pax Imperium for several decades and the deployment of such fleets had ensured that very little military activity was seen unless it was under the flag of the Empire. The outlying regions, where communities refused to respect the rule of the Imperial Democracy, on account of having their own perfectly good forms of government, were the only places these days where an officer could expect to see any kind of action. Here they could fire off an annihilating volley without having to complete a mountain of electronic red tape.

And all too suddenly it had come to an end.

The ship coasted towards the huge bulky hourglass shape of the Home System Star Port, where myriad craft, of all shapes and sizes bustled between the various associated modules.

In the distance, the cloudy surface of the Core World shone in a bright crescent, massive equatorial solar panels creating a black belt absorbing the energy of the yellow sun behind.

The Commercial Zone was always the busiest with freighters loading and unloading from a cluster of twelve minor ports, large bulk carriers picking up speed on their journeys out to the jump zones, and tug drones straining to navigate various beacons as they pulled other containers to and fro.

The entertainment platforms were alive with scores of small personnel craft in holding patterns, competing for limited dock space. A small spat broke out over a free landing port. Security Forces corvettes moved in to intercept.

The Magnificence reached the transition into the Military Zone, the outer sphere of stations, gun platforms, barriers, shield generators and watch turrets that buffered the planet and the station, passing through outer security with a cursory salutary message from the Port control.

A medium sized cruise liner drifted past, heading home from the spectacular Neutron Falls by the Kurlean Cluster.

Beaker couldn't help noticing that Space dock just seemed so crowded these days.

Of course the eight thousand strong crew would be glad to be home[60] but there was something unsatisfying about not completing a full tour of duty.

In the distance, on the far side of the planet, Beaker could make out the impressive bulk of the Radiance also shining like a small moon above the surface of the Core World. That would mean the Brilliance, the Resplendence and the Other One would be out somewhere seeing all the action, he mused.

They passed a row of hangar modules, where the impressive forms of the frigates and cruisers were docked vertically, stacked like mugs on a mug rack. The hangers seemed unusually well stocked. The same was true of the battleship hangers; larger, with fewer ships apiece, but full.

Then a fighter carrier, easily spotted by its pregnant-belly bulge, rounded a nearby moon with its own entourage of supply vehicles, also heading towards the station.

---

[60] Although it was only really home to a handful of the officers. Many of the crew would have another six days journey to reach their respective planets, most of which they'd passed on the way back. But the military had made it very clear they didn't do request stops.

Marine transports, the ugly squat businesslike assault craft that struck fear into the hearts of the galaxy's most unruly residents, seemed to be mooching around a spindly decommissioning vessel.

A small niggling thought began to cross his mind.

It was almost as if the *entire* fleet were here.

It was unheard of.

It wasn't impossible, he reasoned. The home fleet was just one of a hundred fleets under the Admiralty's control and it was possible to bring together the whole active military cavalcade for state events such as the death of the Emperor, the swearing in of a new president, or during the tedious, pointless and expensive process of a major re-brand.

But rarely had he seen so many craft stood down.

As the Magnificence reached its terminus point and military tugs clamped themselves onto the side of the ship, Beaker concluded the Admiralty must know what it was doing.

It was a thought that stayed with him all day and, as he finished his dinner on the terrace of his apartment high above the city, the sun long sunk from the sky, he gazed up at the bright irregular shape of his own Battle Behemoth shining down from the heavens and shook his head.

And once again, just to make sure, he counted the bright lights of the other four as well.

From the tiny view-port window in his cell it looked to Dougan as if his prison ship was the only one heading away from Core.

He was lucky to be unrestrained, Fleek has told him. Dougan considered this cold comfort, given the terrifying and explosive nature of Fleek's reaction to the news of his arrest.

It had been impossible to try to explain what had really happened. Dougan, even though he had access to a legal representative, had been unable to convince the short-haired, slick-suited man that his version of events was any less contrived than the accusations that were being levelled at him.

As Ellie had pointed out, the authorities had certainly built a case against him very quickly, paperwork and all.

From the moment he had been arrested he had been pushed from one security department to another. They had logged and filed and transferred and tutted.[61] The end result was, that for his acts of treason, he was to be transferred to an off-world court-martial at the highest speed possible.

Ellie had planned to wriggle her way out by playing the journalism card, but in the end it hadn't seemed necessary. They had dismissed her part as incidental, albeit revoking her journalism licence. She'd even managed to get them to remove the restraint. It didn't make sense. Unless someone was just after Dougan.

Dougan would like to think that it had been on his insistence that she absolve herself from any blame, but it clearly hadn't been.

Finlay would be able to get him out of it, he thought. Wouldn't he?

Dougan looked around the small room, decked out in several equally depressing shades of grey. There was a small functional chair, a door to a shower-cum-toilet room, a single window, a bed with a grey itchy blanket and a door with a one-way window in it.

---

[61] Tutted a lot. They never tired of it. To security forces tutting was social commentary.

The room looked like it had been designed in a hurry.

As far as Dougan could tell, the room had also been built in a hurry; the one-way window appeared to have been installed the wrong way. No-one could see him but he knew exactly what was going on in the corridor. At first he thought this might afford him some advantage in formulating an escape plan but he quickly realised it wouldn't. It was just more likely that they'd forget he was there until the smell brought them looking for him.

Food was delivered by a dumb-waiter like hatch and while he was pleasantly surprised to learn that the room was en-suite this also informed him that the journey would not be a short one.

He sighed and looked out the window.

At least there was something to see now. For a while his view had been obscured by the side of one of the enormous Behemoth class battleships, but now from his window he could clearly see the security perimeter approaching.[62] It depressed him to think that what he had once thought of as a barrier to keep him safe inside, was now being used to keep him out.

A small computer interface winked against the wall at the end of the bed. He hadn't noticed it before.

The interface was very basic, allowing simple commands to be inputted but it might keep him amused at least until they went into hyperspace.

He tried to pull the chair over, nearly breaking his fingers in the discovery that it was firmly bolted to the floor.

---

[62] It was actually the other way round but strange things happen to you in space.

Crouching by the end of the bed, he explored what he could on the screen.

The interface was a resounding disappointment.

Aside from information about himself, his prisoner number, the charges he had been brought in for, and a brief description of what he could expect on the prison planet, the memory of the interface seemed to offer nothing but various courses of redemption: 'Sign up and undertake the course now, pay upon your release!' the adverts went.

Dougan sighed and switched the interface off. He lay back on the uncomfortable bed and put his hands behind his head.

As he drifted off to sleep, exhausted, his dreams led him to a grey landscape under a sultry sky. His situation hung like a huge bank of cloud above him, threatening torrential rain. In the distance, lightning bolts flashed angrily in sympathy, while the mud around his feet pulled at every footstep. His dreams teased him with the notion of a civilised part of the landscape a long, long way off.

He wasn't even sure if he was innocent any more.

He descended into a broken and unpleasant sleep as the prison craft ploughed towards the hyperspace jump boundary.

Howells wasn't concerned. He had passed concerned, even worried and was now firmly in uncharted territory of an impotent numbness-inducing fear.

Or possibly that was from the alcohol.

He sat, eyes glazed, watching every ship of the Imperial fleet returning to their bases. He had zoomed out to a resolution which took in almost all of the known galaxy, covered billions of light years, to see each of the star bases the Empire held across its vast domain.

Every star port had been the same, overflowing with inert craft of all shapes and sizes. Tiny transport modules had headed to planets packed with service personnel who were all no doubt taking advantage of the special offers being made by entertainment centres suddenly enjoying booming trade.

There was barely an Imperial ship left out in the galaxy.

But the space was definitely not empty.

Over the past few days, new ships had begun appearing everywhere, creeping onto the radar from the uncharted edges of space. Sleek, armoured and deadly, the new ships had arrived in dribs and drabs, each belching smaller ships from their innards, which had in turn spewed fighters, transports and support vessels.

Like plagues of locusts, they had swarmed onto mineral-rich planets and then set off again in greater numbers; self-replicating starships. An unstoppable machine of war.

Howells knew that it was all Morning Star's doing. It had stopped communicating with him altogether and he had been forced to watch in drunken silence as the forces unseen by anyone else amassed in quiet corners of the galaxy.

He hadn't left the chamber for a couple of days now save to go to the toilet and fetch rudimentary food from the service machine on the other side of the entrance bridge. He couldn't get any further than that and his attempts to communicate this to the outside world had been met with bristling static. Recently he had tried the door out of the projection room earlier and found that locked. He made the conscious decision to worry about it later.

"Morning Star," he slurred.

There was no response.

"Morning Star, what are you doing?"

The projection chamber hummed. It was not a pleasant sound and Howells began to suspect Morning Star wouldn't be open to criticism at this stage.

He reached for the bottle again. It was nearly empty.

He took a quick slug and the liquor: Old Punter's Flame Thrower. It lived up to its name, burning the back of his throat and numbing his brain.

"Twintle, Twintle, Morning Star, how I wonder what you are... up to," he burbled. He grinned maniacally to himself before slumping forward off his chair.

He wondered if the funny smell in here was him.

And passed out.

The Space Dock above the Core World was unusually quiet.

Normally, it would have been bustling with various cargo lifters, maintenance machines, fuel wagons, supply dollies and personal repair units all working round the clock[63] to keep the mass of small supply vehicles that assisted the larger operations vehicles, running.

Today, it was completely empty.

Not that Ellie would have the slightest clue that there was anything unusual about this. This was all new territory.

In fact she wasn't supposed to be there.

---

[63] In strict accordance with union guidelines.

With the memory of Dougan's uniform implanted in her chameleonic suit she had been able to convince the guards at the base that she was a lieutenant in the Engineering division. She had considered this a fairly safe bet since they didn't know any more about engineering than she did; she would have been able to deflect any of their searching questions quite easily. As it was, there weren't any. The guards had seemed much keener to finish their shift and get on with a bit of R&R they had been unexpectedly granted. Only one of the girls had eyed her a little suspiciously when she had tried to open a pocket on the suit that wasn't there.

She had travelled alone up the cargo lifts to the platform hanging high above the planet. Even the electronic security devices hadn't seemed too bothered about her presence.

From the lower-level gantry she emerged onto, it was impossible to tell which way to go. From the ground, the structure resembled a giant waffle, often obscured by clouds. When the sun was shining it would cast intricate fuzzy criss-cross patterns on the surface of the planet and from here it was easy to see why.

The platform listed at a slight angle, a function of its orbit rather than its design and countless open metal frames branched off in various directions. They were packed with brightly coloured modules attached in odd arrangements, as if the superstructure of the station had been dragged through a giant bowl of sticky sweets. Transparent tunnels weaved through the open framework connecting the various modules and interspersed here and there were the spherical hangars with their quarter-segments cut out.

Inside the shells, craft of all shapes and sizes nestled, cocooned within the specialised, protected environments.

Periodically, automated monorail cars clunked their way along the gantries.

Ellie stepped out of the lift. The air, which clung to the surface of the framework via a weak gravity field generator, felt thin and cold. It smelled of fuel and ozone and tasted like it had come from a can.

Ellie's feet echoed dully on the composite steel floor of the platform as she stepped out and looked around.

It was hard to tell where to start looking.

The space dock had an aura that suggested you hadn't earned the right to be there until you had taken a handful of wrong, potential fatal turns. It wasn't going to offer up its secrets to the uninitiated. This was further confirmed to Ellie when she examined the wall-mounted map.

The map, although clearly a map of the station, was uniquely confusing in that it didn't contain a single point of reference. Not even up or down.

Industrial hangars were clearly marked by the large shaded blue areas, the gravity generator repair section with its restricted access was marked yellow, the canteen was marked purple, the decontamination zone orange and the toilets marked with little black dots. It was just impossible to tell where you were. Plus the colour zoning system employed on the map did not seem to have been replicated anywhere else on the station. She decided, instead, to trust her instincts.

Picking a direction at random, she set off. Within seven minutes she was hopelessly lost.

In the end the Burning Desire found her.

After riding a number of the monorails, which seemed to take arbitrary twists and turns, she decided to alight and continue solely on foot. She helped herself to a discarded work jacket which seemed to stave off the bitter cold for a while.

Finally, she emerged at the most industrial end of one of the gantries, where the sturdy metal framework gave way to a series of wispy tendrils that seemed to be exploring the limits of Core World's atmosphere like a drug-addled sea anemone.

The bright-white surface of the planet hung beneath her. There was something disconcerting about the open grid of the gantry. Down was a very present force.

She resolved to walk as far down the gantry as she could, to get a better perspective of where to try next. As she turned, something silvery caught her eye for a fleeting moment. She stopped and peered through the maze of steel ahead of her, trying to catch a glimpse of it again.

There was nothing there.

She reached the end of the gantry and passed a command unit, presumably for controlling the tendrils. Beyond this there was a tall spherical cage, which rose above the level of the rest of the deck and would afford her a better perspective of where to go next.

She gripped the metal poles and swung out into the cage. She felt a strange lurching sensation as the gravity field shifted, altering her perspective of which way was down. She took a moment to re-adjust while her brain re-centred. It was slightly unpleasant.

It did, however, make her feel safer, knowing that if she fell, she would at least head towards the gantry and not the long, long drop into open space. As she edged outwards she could feel the tug of the planet competing with the artificial gravity field of the station, disorientating her further.

She concluded she couldn't make a living from working out here.

As she clambered up the side of the cage, the walls creating little triangles large enough to put her hands and fists through, she saw something large move in the corner of her vision, outside the cage. Startled, she lost her grip.

She swung out like a loose gate, and careered back first into the wall, bumping her head on the piping above. The air turned a subtle shade of blue.

She swung back to the cage wall.

As she regained her footing, the spherical front of a survey craft's command module rose from below, the thin strip of the viewport window regarding her like a giant single slit of an eye. Beneath the viewport the Words "Burning Desire" told her that she had found exactly what she had come looking for.

The sphere hung in space, the rest of the craft lurking behind.

Ellie took a sharp breath. It appeared to be watching her. As she bobbed down, so too did it, following her every move.

She wondered who might be inside. Finlay? A security officer? This was not the time to attempt communications. Whoever was flying it, she was pretty convinced they weren't delivering roses and chocolates.

She looked down to where the cage re-joined the balcony and then back at the craft. With as much grace as she could muster, jumped to the bottom of the cage.

In the corner of her vision, the craft dropped suddenly in pursuit.

At the bottom, the corridor she had walked down before fell away like a long shaft. With a deep breath she re-orientated herself and plunged through.

Gravity shifted again. Core world swung beneath her and she tumbled to the ground where, as soon as her legs had caught up, she began to run.

The Desire twisted neatly and cruised alongside the gantry as she pounded down the level, easily keeping apace with her. She leapt over discarded pipework, and dilapidated pieces of maintenance kit, the sound of her footsteps ringing through the enclosed space until she reached the gantry junction where she had just entered.

To her left, a larger corridor led back towards a clump of larger modules she had already visited, but to her right a confusing tangle of ducts and broken crane arms looked like it would bring her deeper into the core of the local structure. And further from her pursuer. She veered that way.

The Desire ducked down under the gantry, and resurfaced beyond the mass of cranes.

It was further away now, and while she didn't exactly feel safer, she did feel that the more metal she could get between the two of them, the relatively happier she'd be.

She wondered if the craft was armed.

She wondered if the space station was armed.

Probably both, she thought, but then she didn't fancy her chances in an all out gunfight; she might end up wielding nothing more than a paint spray gun.

The corridor narrowed. It was harder to see through the girders; gaps had been filled with sheets of metal, pitted with strip thin sensors and detectors. She could no longer see the Desire. That ought to mean it couldn't see her.

The corridor sloped down. She would have to follow, or retrace her steps. At the bottom, a ladder led down into a dark circular hole in the floor. There was a low sucking noise coming from it and she hesitated.

Cautiously she edged towards the hole. There was a pull of air around the hole, but only slight. She climbed gently down.

The tunnel was dark. The draught grew stronger although she fancied that it would sometimes change direction blowing back up before resuming its downward tug.

It was impossible to tell what was below, the dim lights anointing the walls did nothing to help her predicament.

As she approached the bottom of the ladder she ran critically out of rungs. She grabbed the sides quickly as she bumped to the floor of a very darkly lit chamber. Her behind hurt sorely.

A light plastic sign landed on her head: 'Ladder unsafe'.

As her eyes adjusted to the light, she could make out the source of the sucking sound. The chamber was large and round, the colour of rust, bathed in a flickering greenish light. In the far wall, a horizontal gap was opening up, the bottom half of it sliding away like the mouth of a giant beast, viewed from the inside. Air was seeping out as the slight pressure differences re-aligned.

She was in a hangar.

Ellie looked around for another way out. With the ladder gone and the cargo lift moored under the main entrance some forty yards above, she was trapped.

"Rats," she said firmly.

The doorway was fully open now, the vastness of space stretching ahead of her.

She looked around and concluded that it was in fact, her only way out.

If she was lucky, the gravity field around the station would act as a safety net.

She didn't bother considering what would happen if she was unlucky, she was the kind of girl who would worry about that sort of thing later.

THE COLOUR OF ROBOTS

CHAPTER ELEVEN

Money

The grey hulk of the prison ship drifted slowly to the edge of the hyperspace zone, green and blue lights winking in the inky blackness, far from the light of any nearby sun, in a space darker than the darkest night, calmer than the deadest sea.

Inside the craft, Dougan felt the pull of forces shift as he became slowly weightless.

The gravity generators, the large intense energy units that created the effect of mass and gravity, slowly powered down.

Dougan had strapped himself in the bed and had tried to sleep. In the absence of any kind of medicines to aid him he was finding this hard. He always found gravity jumps particularly challenging, and whenever possible, had taken a sleeping jab to get him through it. Sadly, for obvious reasons, needles didn't seem to be prison issue.

Across the surface of the craft, gravity force generators began to press tightly inwards, creating a binding pressure to hold the craft together for the gravity well jump. The density stress inside grew and made Dougan dizzy.

Beyond the buffer zone, an antigravity field was forming. Waves of anti-gravitons, the large weak-area-of-effect particles formed by the generators, streamed from the surface of the craft. They annihilated the gravitons flowing over the surface of spacetime and gently separating the craft from the fabric of the universe until the effect was precisely balanced.

The prison ship squeezed itself out of time.

The universe flowed quickly past it as it began to travel backwards in time, tunnelling through the very fabric of space in a brief moment of eternity.

The prison craft accelerated, tore through space and time, and turned left.

Of course nothing was truly for free, even in the dim void of hyperspace. The massive energy required to lift the craft out of spacetime would have to be recouped on entering which would send a ripple forward through time to the point of departure and rip a faster-than-light route from the departure point to the beginning point. Of course anything that happened to be in the way would have serious ramifications upon your arrival, which is why it is extremely important to check how your journey was before you left.

The jump hadn't gone exactly as she planned.

For one she hadn't expected the spaceship to be there.

As Ellie had bravely[64] thrown herself out of the hangar door she had run into the exact thing that she had been hoping to avoid.

Fear had been replaced by exhilaration as she had approached the edge of the hanger floor where it gave way to space beneath. Her perception of time had slowed and, to distract itself from the ridiculousness of the action, her brain had taken a sauntering look around the cabin of the hangar.

It had noted the crossed chevrons on the floor, raised bumps that would aid the grip and prevent slippage (not much use to someone considering throwing themselves through the doorway), the minor oil spillages and the signs pointing out the dangers of a slippery floor or not wearing the appropriate clothing.

She noticed, as she reached the edge of the doorway, there was a slight lip, which she slowed to leap over. She noticed that the space beneath the station was swimming with debris, which had been caught up in the gravity field, awash in a thin layer of brownish rusted dust, clearly delineating the edge of the field.

Too late she noticed the Burning Desire hanging directly above the doorway, close enough to touch, large and threatening.

She saw the rectangular bulk of the rear engine compartment, pitted and scarred with years of interstellar travel, as she took the final step that would take her out of the hangar and down into the sea of debris below.

Instead, she fell up.

The Desire twisted gracefully as she fell. It hovered neatly backwards.

---

[64] Foolishly / stupidly / carelessly

She struck the side of the craft by the open airlock door, dizzy from the changes in up and down and rolled into the airlock where the ship's own field took hold of her. As she tumbled into the airlock she slipped slowly out of consciousness wondering why there hadn't been more warning signs about the shifting gravity fields outside the station and wondering if it was a bad thing that the airlock door was closing.

Baron Frisk's fleet of Imperial cruisers was more impressive than anyone had imagined.

Even he wasn't really sure how he'd managed to come across that many craft. In fact, they had more or less come to him.

Everyone agreed Frisk was cunning. Some said more cunning than the Redolifino Confederacy who had managed to con the Empire out of ever having to pay tax on account of their technically non-existent status, smarter than the Indillian university science team who had actually invented antigravity generators AND won the prize for Intergalactic clever-dicks of the century, and more wily than a fox with a length of piano wire and a balaclava.

His first coup had been persuading an entire Naval way-station to let him use their small platform as a centre for his smuggling operations.

It had begun as a tacit agreement to allow a number of contraband bearing vessels to pass through a rather inconvenient peninsula of Imperial space but, reaping modest profits on all sides, the officers had eventually discovered they felt more loyalty to a handful of extra credits a month than a bureaucratic Navy who supplied them with no more support than arms-length criticism of their cleaning reports. Add to that the occasional handful of tickets to zero-gravity violent sports games that suddenly seemed to be on offer and the officers were a soft pliable substance in Frisk's hands.

The leave had been an unexpected bonus. They wondered how Frisk had managed that, especially for so many of them simultaneously, but not for very long. They weren't about to question it, especially when doing so might get them lynched and most operated a strict "we're on to a good thing so shut up" policy.

True, they didn't recognise most of their replacements, but they had been overworked lately and deserved a good old rest.

Frisk himself hadn't engineered the leave either, but was secretly delighted when someone somewhere had, leaving just the small band of secret officers he had snuck in.

And the secret officers had all breathed sighs of relief at finally knowing who was on their side, having spent months up to their necks in third degree paranoia.[65]

Their relief had been short-lived. Within weeks streams of Naval vessels had begun decamping from hyperspace dangerously close and many had fled, believing the game to be up.

Those that stayed (mostly out of fear of Frisk) were in for an even greater surprise when the captains of Battle Cruisers, Corvettes, Frigates, Cruisers, Destroyers, Auxiliary vessels, tugs, supply wagons,

---

[65] Paranoia is rife. Many are fortunate to suffer from primary paranoia which is where you suspect someone is lying to you to hide the truth. However the levels of paranoia don't stop there and it is possible to suffer from a number of other levels of paranoia: secondary where you believe someone is lying to you to conceal a bigger lie or to make you think that they're lying, tertiary, where you believe you're being lied to so that you will suspect the truth is a lie. Any level above tertiary generally becomes either meaningless, fatal, or fundamentally transcendental.

cannon ship and drone carriers all effectively handed over their keys to the junior officers, instructing them to a man, to close their gaping mouths, hadn't they even seen an officer on shore-leave.

Scores of personnel had filed past the now terrified "officers" exchanging salutes as they had clambered into waiting transporters.

Occasionally one of them had indulged in a little "talking to the little men" military banter and as one Captain had put it: "dashed shame to have to stand down, but when you run out of goggly-eyed monsters to splat, you have to switch off a couple of generators, what?"

Bit by bit, the hangar racks became stacked with enough military equipment to wipe out a couple of star systems, all lying dormant. All Frisk's for the taking.

Just to be on the safe side, Frisk had manoeuvred the painfully slow-moving star-base a couple of parsecs off the main star lane and switched off the lights.

Binner swivelled the command chair from left to right as the crew of her new vessel scurried back and forth in front of her.

She smiled smugly. It was the biggest craft she'd ever commanded and she was beginning to feel a bit lost in it. It had taken over an hour to walk from her cabin to the bridge this morning and, although it was so sophisticated she could have commanded operations from the toilet[66], she felt most comfortable on the bridge.

Her battle cruiser, The Definite Article, was only a decade out of date and still a mighty force to be

---

[66] She had been locked in for half an hour before Jirbaks had freed her, swearing not to tell anyone.

reckoned with. It knocked their poxy little modified scout vessels into a cocked hat.

It was a power pirates had only dreamed of, an opportunity too good to miss, a chance to take the fight to the Empire.

No-one was quite sure how it worked.

"There must be some kind of control panel!" she sighed, slumping her chin forward onto the palm of her hand. She was damned if she was going to leave the command chair now.

"Yes, there is, but obviously there need to be other systems working before it does," a young scruffy-looking pirate whined. She rolled her eyes at him.

"Hurbury, you getting anything?" she directed her gaze at the cockpit module ahead and above. From inside her bubble on the navigation gantry Hurbury turned and shrugged.

Binner shook her head and with genuine testiness waved her hand in sharp jabbing motions as she spoke. "Are you sure you followed the manual?" she asked the room in general.

She paused, waiting for an answer.

The pirates exchanged a few glances. Some looked at the floor. Others shuffled their feet.

"What manual?" asked one plainly.

Binner ignored the question.

She punched a key on the armrest controls. "How about you Greeta?"

Most of Greeta appeared on the viewscreen. Her head was lodged in a large bank of wires and pieces of circuitry. A hand waved from side to side in a gesture of uncertainty.

The viewscreen switched back to the wide vision of space ahead of them. Other craft were beginning to plough into the darkness beyond the lights of the station, disappearing one by one. Binner was determined not to be left behind.

From where Jirbaks was leaning alongside the cockpit she could see Hurbury was getting irritated. Her fur was standing on end and her ears were flattened back against her head. The steely whites of her teeth were showing through her attempts to keep her grimace under control.

Jirbaks watched as Hurbury's paw-like hands darted backwards and forwards over the command panel, trying every combination she could think of to get the Cruiser up and running.

"Can I help?" asked Jirbaks, leaning forward a little.

Hurbury stopped and turned a cold stare on Jirbaks. The loathing was apparent, but this time it didn't bother Jirbaks, who lifted her large chin in the air and raised her eyebrows.

"No," said Hurbury icily and she turned back to the panel.

"Suit yourself," said Jirbaks.

She settled back against the instrument rack behind her, folded her arms and decided to remain seated on the Emergency Brake for just a little while longer.

Ellie awoke in the hold of the Burning Desire, a small squat room at the back of the craft. The fizzling sound of an emergency light winking on an off in the background was all she could hear.

Academy officers are trained in potential capture situations not to betray they are awake. They are trained to lie very still and keep their eyes closed and *feel* out the room. In darkness, sounds will tell a great deal. Even details like room temperature and air movement within a space will tell a lot about whereabouts, help compose thoughts, and give an advantage that wouldn't be there if the captor was aware of their presence of mind.

Ellie was not trained by the academy and sat bolt upright with a gasp.

The robot was sitting across the room from her.

It was difficult to tell where one part began and where another finished. It was a tangle of wires and circuit boards, torn pieces of metal and panel, bits of chair, screens and keyboards, anything that might once have cluttered the now empty hold seemed to be incorporated somehow in the monster before her. Even as she watched, it appeared to be trying to organise itself: pushing the wires behind panels, creating a thin skin to protect the tangle of components beneath.

There was some kind of head, where two scanners of different sizes had been glued together like a mismatched pair of eyes. Behind, in a bulbous dome, she could see a small spider-like hand working away in subtle manipulation of the cobbled-together brain of the thing.

It leaned forward and Ellie backed instinctively away. She soon found herself pressed against the bulkhead, which felt rough and uneven. Her fingers felt panels missing and were pricked by loose wires.

The robot raised itself on rudimentary legs, inelegantly fashioned from lengths of tubing and ducts, pistons hissing as compressors pushed air around the basic skeletal structure. Ellie saw the long umbilical cord stretching from the back of its head to a core processor unit at the head of the bay.

The robot had built itself from scratch using only the non-essential items of the Burning Desire.

"You're it. You're the Survival robot aren't you?" she said calmly.

The robot's head area appeared to nod, slowly and gracefully.

She looked around. The robot showed no sign of malice towards her. It was keeping a distance, watching her, warily but not threateningly.

She was in the presence of a myth.

The feeling was awesome, a surge of excitement running through her, that she had done what she set out to do. Here was the proof of the existence of a robot whose history had been wiped from the books and whose very presence elsewhere would send military forces crazy. If she ever survived to tell anyone, they certainly wouldn't believe her.

As myths went, it was pretty ugly.

"You survived the crash?" she asked cautiously.

The robot nodded again and its head lolled forward.

At first she thought it was sad, perhaps at the loss of the other robot, the weight of being a living myth bearing down on it. Then Ellie watched in horror as the top of the head casing opened and the spidery hand emerged.

It waved jovially at her. She was suddenly disturbed to learn that she might be in the presence of something pretty frightening: A robot with a sense of humour.

It raised one of the six appendages and pointed towards the door leading from the hold. It opened smoothly, and Ellie rose to her feet, accepting the invitation.

She walked down a narrow corridor, It too had been stripped bare as if a swarm of metal-devouring insects had passed through. Beyond, she was in the command module.

Here the signs of the robot's spare-part harvesting were even more apparent. Where once there would have been a neat console back, curved round a command chair, there were bare girders. Even part of the floor was missing. The console had been completely hollowed out and gaping holes told where instruments might have displayed vital ship information. Overhead locker compartments were missing doors and even the main viewport looked exposed and bare. The chair itself listed at an odd angle.

Only a few of Dougan's possessions remained; a rather silly looking furry alien sat precariously on the dashboard, and a cup that might once have contained coffee had been upended in a hollow created by the missing floor panels.

Ellie stood in the doorway and surveyed the wreckage.

Behind her, the robot spoke in a soft almost elderly voice.

"I'm very sorry," it said, "I haven't had time to tidy up."

The Knowledge robot's silver battleship touched down in the middle of Century City, the financial capital of the Empire.

It landed in the middle of Carron Square, the large plaza separating the four Century Buildings which rose like greedy fingers into the sky.

The financiers, of all races, breeds, and types hurried back and forth around the craft, determined of purpose and irritated at this thing suddenly in their way. If there was one thing arrogant bankers couldn't stand it was someone more arrogant than them. And so they strutted self-importantly round it.

The circular door opened, and, too busy being late for something important, the financiers hurried by.

THE COLOUR OF ROBOTS

The Knowledge robot stepped gracefully down the ramp into the middle of the hustling, bustling crowd, pushing and jostling to circumvent this new obstruction. It stood a good metre taller than all but the tall spindly Aracorns, the light-tan, stick-like creatures who picked their way daintily through the throngs of shorter human and humanoid workers.

They weren't overly concerned by the robotic form. Robot-looking walking machines, which carried the Rudrians around, were commonplace here. The small, rodent-like, furry, ruthless race were well-respected financiers. Their capabilities for doing extraordinary maths in their head, coupled with a burning desire for fiscal supremacy had made them among the most successful merchants of Century City. What they lacked in size, they made up for in fiendishness all hid behind cute, wide, love-me eyes. The walking machines brought them eye-to-eye with their humanoid colleagues and served to level the field in negotiations.[67]

The Knowledge robot already knew where it was going. It strode out through the crowd. It traversed the small square quickly, managing to not step on anyone, in spite of their concerted efforts to get in its way.

It reached the entrance to Century One, the widest of the towers, and looked up. The first five floors were dominated by the large single window that gazed on the centre of the square and where the giant holographic projection showed the undulating 3-D surface of the stock market. Traders at their personal stations pressed their faces against the window, buying, selling, crying and cheering. In the time that it

---

[67] It had been far harder previously for the humans to take anything in a cage seriously.

watched, it counted thirteen high-fives, ninety-two back-slaps, seventeen wall punches, two assassination attempts and one assisted suicide. It looked like a tough world.

The robot ducked through the doorway to Century One and entered the lobby, which appeared to have been designed to amplify the noise of the traders on the mezzanines above and funnel it to a central reception. A handful of beleaguered receptionists, located at the exact focal point of the noise, waited patiently, eager to help those meant to be somewhere eight minutes ago.

The robot strode purposefully to the desk and leaned in. Receptionists flocked to greet him like hungry fish.

"Good Daytime!" cooed one, "Welcome to Century One! How can I help you?"

It noticed she was wearing a microphone. Her voice emerged from a speaker a few inches from where it stood.

It also noticed that no-one had thought to supply it with one.

"Can you tell me where I might find Room Number One?" it strained. Its voice was gentle and languid from years of patiently listening while others spoke. The words drifted over the desk, through the din, like salmon swimming upstream.

The receptionist's face turned pitying. As if to highlight the effect, the body of a trader also dropped from one of the mezzanines above and disappeared in the throng. Crowds surged round the unfortunate trader and stripped him of his portfolio in seconds.

"There isn't a Room Number One," she said.

"Yes, there is," replied the Knowledge robot.

"No, I'm afraid there isn't," she continued in a sing-song voice, "there's no room One, 101, no room

Thirteen, no room Forty-Two and no room Sixty-Nine."[68]

"I would like to visit room Number One."

A receptionist in the background giggled.

"There is no room number one, sir," repeated the receptionist. "People would fight over it, Sir. The implication is there's always room at the top. It's motivational." She smiled, clearly not understanding herself. A lightbulb flashed in the back of her mind. She mouthed the words: "Are you looking for the toilet?"

The robot looked down at her.

"Can you tell me where the lift is, please?"

She smiled politely and pointed in the direction of a bank of lifts against the far wall. Doors opened and closed incessantly as streams of people flowed in and out, like water around lock gates.

It turned and headed that way.

The lifts were packed inside. As it entered, stooping down, hundreds of podgy fingers and curious alien digits punched key codes into the panel.

The Knowledge robot watched as the lifts stored waypoint, after waypoint, after waypoint in its data bank then presented the route it planned to take through the building. It looked long and circuitous.

When everyone else had finished, it leaned over and punched the number 1 into the panel. It beeped in an unfriendly tone. The other lift-goers tutted. It pressed the button once more and was greeted again with the rude response. The doors began to close.

The robot reached out and grabbed the door before it shut, wrenched it open and stepped out. It turned to

---

[68] Which are all considered bad luck by some cultures, although, occasionally considered a considerable stroke of good luck by others.

the sea of faces: human, humanoid and alien, rolling their eyes and looking anywhere but directly at him. The doors closed and the lift hummed away on its journey.

It looked around the lobby, following the chaotic flow of people. Its gaze alighted on a single small door that was being completely ignored by everyone.

It was rusty brown, an innocuous-looking door. The robot made its way over.

Written on the front of the door in small yellow letters was the word 'Stairs'. The door opened silently. The robot stepped through.

The staircase was narrow, and brightly lit. A thin layer of dust covered every surface. Most importantly, it was completely devoid of life.

It looked up the stairwell which seemed to disappear into infinity and began to climb.

A robot has a distinct advantage over a human or humanoid when it comes to climbing stairs. For a start, once the basic rhythm has been established it is particularly easy to keep. By contrast, the human mind can only cope with continuously travelling up or down stairs for so long before the conscious brain kicks in and messes up the process just to assert its authority.

This is not a problem for a robot. A far cry from the dark days of history, when stairs were designed according to the size of stones available, the modern step tends to be of uniform height. This makes climbing them much easier for robots. One stair is much like the next.

And robots don't get tired.

They are not bound by the body's ability to create lactic acids that turn exertion into pain at the first available opportunity. They can run up stairs for a long, long time.

Which is exactly what the robot did.

An hour up, the solid beige walls gave way to chrome globule constructions, which eventually opened out to a bare-steel construction, exposing the Knowledge robot to the harsh high winds above the Century Towers.

It paused to look out over the city below, stretching as far as its electronic eye could see, the financial planet of the empire bustling way below. Above it, the sky fumed a violent purple, lit by the distant red giant. In the distance, mountains thrust their way through the crust of the city.

It finally reached a platform at the top of the tower. From here, it could see the pinnacles of the other three towers, forming the corners of a square, shrouded in a thin mist.

The stairs continued upwards, enclosed only in a cage.

It began to climb again.

Condensation began to form on its casing as it ascended the stairs into a low-lying cloud cover. The cage gave way to a simple rail. The rail gave way to nothing until it was climbing stairs that circled a central pillar. Finally, the stairs themselves stopped.

It paused.

Ahead, was simply empty space. Clouds circled it. It was very aware of the long, long drop below. It would take exactly three hundred and sixty-five seconds to reach the ground. Enough time to reflect on whether it was about to make the right decision or not.

It lifted a foot off the final step. The foot hovered over empty space.

Then it put the foot back down.

It reached a hand out in front of it and knocked gently.

The sound of a hollow metal space rang beneath its clenched fist.

The robot pushed hard.

The holographic projection dissolved. A crystal dome emerged from the ether surrounding him. It spanned the whole space between the corners of the towers. Where the light had penetrated the cloud cover above, it refracted through the crystal, shimmering a red and purple triangular pattern throughout.

Ahead, was a door into a crystal archway, which swung open with its push. Above the door, the words "Number One, Century City" had been carved in elegant script.

The robot stepped through.

Opulent was not the word. Opulent was merely the closest approximation of a long string of words, including but not limited to 'lavish, palatial, ostentatious, pretentious, showy, well-heeled, luscious, luxurious, affluent and deluxe[69]'

Every surface was not only covered with the most precious minerals known to the galaxy, they gave the distinct feeling they were constructed from them too, even the bits that couldn't be seen.

The effect of this was completely lost on its first and only visitor.

Towards the middle of the room a large projector showed, in vibrant green against a black background,

---

[69] And none of these even came close. It had been furnished exuberantly by someone who could not only afford the most expensive things in the galaxy, they'd been able to afford someone to arrange them with taste.

an ever changing list of assets, stock values, capital gains, profits and dividends all of which was neatly summed up by an ever increasing number declared only by the name of TOTAL.

It was a silly amount of money for anyone to have.

At the centre of the room beneath the screen was a large Idronian Defurwood desk, behind which sat a robot.

The robot looked not dissimilar to the one standing by the doorway. It had a square-ish head, a grille for a mouth, and red slanting eyes. The only real difference was that whereas one had black geometric markings the other had green.

The green robot looked up and, despite having an expressionless face, managed to look a bit surprised.

The black Knowledge robot closed the door behind it.

The green robot put down the portable calculation device it had been holding, and knitted its fingers together in a gesture it had picked up from corporate leaders.

"Oh," it said.

Knowledge nodded gently.

"Is it...?" asked the green Money robot.

"Yes," said Knowledge. "Only this time it is better prepared."

The green robot looked down at its fingers.

Behind, the green screens flickered with the light of ever increasing fortune. It had taken so long to amass that much. Such a huge haul of wealth needed constant attention, love, nurture. If the robot left, it might not be here when it got back.

The green robot looked up.

"I don't suppose it'd settle for a bribe?" it inquired, hopefully.

The black robot shook its head.

Wearily the green robot closed a panel on his desk and rose to its feet.

Knowledge opened the door again.

"Is there a plan?"

The black robot nodded. "Yes," it said, "there is a plan. But there are many variables."

The green robot paused by the doorway, and looked out over the palatial room. It had everything taken away from him once before, and only then had it understood pain.

"What about a really big bribe?"

Knowledge took the Money robot gently by the arm and ushered it back out onto the stairs.

Binner was beyond irritated. She was in a red misty zone where people were likely to die.

While this is a common state of mind for a space pirate, it is a far less suitable mental state for the commander of a mile long military vessel in unknown space.

It was the unknown space part that was the problem.

Whilst all the other stolen Imperial craft had steered themselves gracefully out of the star-port, theirs had sat like a lame duck before unexpectedly lurching into the path of a small drone tug which had since become embedded in the now stuck open cargo bay, like a badly thrown paper dart.

To make things worse, they'd underestimated the mass of their new vessel and spent around four hours circling the first major star whose path they'd crossed, in a desperate, acute-angle slow dive until they had figured out how the mass deflectors had worked and wrenched themselves free.

The final straw had been the announcement from the six rookies[70] that they seemed to have drifted into uncharted space and would have a bit of difficulty finding their way out on account of the fact that it was uncharted and all.

It was also beginning to dawn on Binner that cruising around in one of the pride of the Empire's spaceships was actually more likely to draw unwanted attention to themselves than they would have liked. This was particularly true in the backwaters of space, where a lot of oppressed races were violently opposed to even the sight of Imperial craft in their midst, and had been known to attack even the largest of ships in response to the oppression by their larger state and neighbour.

This in turn, had made the Empire far less sympathetic to their cause and, as one diplomat had put it: "If they have a forum to step up and say, 'look at us, we're so oppressed' then they're not bloody oppressed are they!"

Aside from that, it had been far easier in the past to stroll into a spaceport carrying a hold full of smuggled contraband when your freighter looked much like any other, far less easy when it looked like an eighteen megaton weapon of destruction.

The crew were also dangerously restless.

---

[70] In pirate terms a rookie was anyone who didn't have a major scar, a missing body part or a conviction for murder. The unofficial ranking system levels ran: rookie, pirate, rogue, veteran, cur, cutthroat, and spacedog, levels 1 through 9. Only one level nine spacedog has even been recorded and that was Mad Dog Dunbar who had lost so many body parts in the course of piracy he was ultimately mistaken for a piece of luggage and ejected from a spaceship as jetsam.

Pirates have, on the whole, low attention spans. There are three basic activities they like to engage in, two destructive and one creative in the most basic sense. They hadn't seen a raid in ages and coffers were looking light.

In order to keep them busy and distracted from the fact they were hopelessly lost, Binner had organised an asteroid shooting contest. Contrary to everyone's expectations Jirbaks had won hands-down, making the more macho pirates even more irritable.

The air of tension on board rose steadily as they drifted haplessly along.

In time they reached the edge of a vast thin dust cloud that all but obscured their view of the rest of the galaxy and while Binner deliberated whether or not to head through, their next prey appeared on the proximity scanner.

THE COLOUR OF ROBOTS

CHAPTER TWELVE

Marines

The prison ship dropped out of hyperspace early.

Dougan, feeling like he'd been trapped in the lining of a bouncy castle, half-rolled half-stumbled out of bed and onto the floor. When he was sure that gravity was back in place and that down was staying down for a while, he threw up.[71]

He clambered back on the bed and closed his eyes while the floor cleaned itself. He heard the hiss of the steam rising through the vents, the clunking sound of the floor rolling over and the sucking sound of the vacuum.

Slowly he returned to normal. 'Hyperspaced-out' he called it.

When he felt vaguely human again, around twenty minutes later, he lifted his head up to the window. There was still very little to see outside: the lights from the prison ship casting a diffuse glow in a dust cloud.

---

[71] He'd been sick in zero gravity only once before. Even a paper bag won't help you there.

That must be why we slowed down, thought Dougan. They would be going back into hyperspace again when they cleared the cloud, he thought. Yuk.

He settled his head back on the pillow and let his arm fall over his eyes.

He was about to drift back to sleep when the alarms went off.

Hurbury quickly brought the craft to bear.

"What have we got?" shouted Binner among the din of the excited pirates, all clamouring for the seats with good views and lots of buttons in front of them.

"Looks like a prison ship," said a veteran.

"Escort?"

"Negative," said the veteran.

"Is it armed?" asked Binner tensely.

"I'm not sure…" said the veteran. He leaned into his console. The pirates held their breath.

Seconds ticked by. Tensed muscles creaked.

The veteran raised his head. "Yes, ma'am," he replied, "it's armed to the teeth."

The pirates cheered in unison.

"Let's get it!" cried Binner.

The command floor burst into life. Pirates cast aside their chairs with buttons for chairs with weapons.

"Engaging beam weapons!" cried one.

"Diverting power from main engines!" cried another

"Shields raised, Captain Binner," cried a third.

"I've just broken my chair ma'am," cried a fourth rolling across the front of the deck at speed.

The cries continued, announcing every small move the pirates made. Binner tried to ignore them. She thought it odd considering most of the time they went out of their way to make sure she knew nothing about what they were up to.

Binner leaned into the console

"Jirbaks?" she said quietly.

The console crackled into life and the cheerful round face of Jirbaks appeared on her personal display.

"Hello Captain Binner!" she said jovially.

"Jirbaks, jump on the electro-pulse cannon would you? I want to disable the ship before it puts up too much of a fight."

Jirbaks frowned. "Right you are ma'am," she said and turned to walk off. She hesitated and turned back.

"Are you sure you want me to do this?"

"Yes," said Binner. "Don't overload it, just squeeze it out gently and plaster the hub under the command centre. I want you to do it."

Jirbaks grinned in to the scanner and said, "Okay!"

Binner flipped the communicator off and settled back nervously to watch the battle unfold. Her ship was a good six times larger than the prison ship. That meant she was a six-times larger target. She was going to need every man and woman on board if they were going to storm the ship as well. In her experience, prison guards were just as skilled at keeping people out as they were at keeping people in...

The prison ship shuddered and jolted and Dougan, who had wrapped a towel round his head to block out the alarms, hammered incessantly on the door.

Whoever had designed the alarm system clearly had no idea about the size of space it would be used in. The current noise levels in the cell would have been sufficient to evacuate a medium-sized shopping centre.

There was no response.

He turned back to the window where he could see the crackles and flashes of laser strikes hitting the force shielding around the craft. The ship rocked and lurched as it was pummelled by repeater-cannon fire. Still no-one came.

Dougan reflected that if truth was the first casualty of war then prisoners were probably the second.

A missile hit the craft and the whole ship spun wildly. Dougan watched miserably as large chunks of the engines drifted off into the dusty space.

"Who fired that missile?" screamed Binner. Jirbaks cannon fire hadn't quite hit home yet, but she knew she couldn't call off the attack until the craft was immobilised, or it would destroy them. Lasers were fine but missiles could easily rupture something important if the prison ship didn't have the correct defences. A ruptured ship was worth nothing to them.

"I did ma'am, sorry ma'am, didn't realise that's what I was doing ma'am," came a voice from the melee.

"Well, don't do it again, okay!" she barked.

"Roger that ma'am!" came the voice again, "did anyone see what I pressed then?"

"I think it was that one there," said a helpful voice.

Binner watched as a second missile snaked it's way towards the prison ship, striking it in the side and rupturing a power cable. A bluish purple plasma erupted from the belly of the ship.

"Stop that! Stop that at once!" cried Binner.

"Sorry ma'am."

The craft was struck again, and Dougan watched in alarm as tiny cracks started to appear in the walls of his cell. For the moment they were on the inside walls, indicating strong internal torque as opposed to an external fracture but there was still plenty of fragile stuff inside the craft that wouldn't look very pretty if it broke.

A few bolts popped, ricocheting across the room and narrowly missing his head as the chair, one leg buckling, leapt free from its moorings.

The light to the room flickered on and off and in the darkness the brilliant flashes of the laser bolts from outside splayed twisted red and green shadows over the cell walls.

The interface unit against the wall began to crackle and blink furiously.

Dougan, in time-honoured tradition, crawled under the bed.

A bolt of blue lightning filled the room. The light-fitting crackled azure before dying. The interface exploded, sending deadly shards searing across the room embedding in the wall by the door. The room was plunged almost completely into black.

Dougan poked his head nervously from under the bed.

The laser fire had stopped.

"Cease fire! Cease fire!"

Binner watched as the light of the direct hit from the electro pulse cannon snaked over the surface of the ship. Immediately the rest of the crew let up the barrage. The prison ship's cannon died and the onboard lights darkened as it rocked to a standstill.

"Well done, Jirbaks," she said under her breath

A single yellow cable pulse laser bolt smashed into the ships command module and bright chunks broke off from the prison ship hull.

"Sorry, sorry…" came the now familiar voice.

Binner leaned forward in her chair.

"Greeta get me a damage report," she called into the communicator.

Greeta's face appeared on the screen, her glasses askew slightly on her face.

"Er, no direct hits Captain and all systems intact. I've got one reported casualty but that's not confirmed yet." She was interrupted by a voice in the background calling: "It bloody is".

"Actually Greeta, I meant the other ship."

Greeta blushed slightly "Oh yes I see, well the systems are all down."

"Yes," said Binner patiently, "that's why we've stopped shooting at it. Is it holding together?"

Greeta looked up at the scanner "I think so."

"Okay," said Binner to the room in general, "let's get ourselves suited up and head out there. Pack heavy, there might be marines."

The comment was met with much snarling of teeth and calls of "I'm not scared of marines" in a fine show of bravura. She knew it was all a show. *Everyone* was scared of marines.

Dougan looked out of the window, cautiously at first, and then a little more boldly. Windows were not good places to be around where gunfire was involved, unless you definitely had something with a business end to push through ahead of you. In Dougan's case all he had was a towel and the business that was in wasn't going to help anyone.

He was startled to see a large Imperial craft outside. The Battle Cruiser class starship was descending slowly, directional lights flashing merrily.

Dougan was utterly perplexed. He knew he was in trouble with the Navy but his current predicament[72] would suggest they already had that in hand.

It was to be a good forty minutes before he received any kind of explanation.

The Definite Article docked carefully with the prison ship. Greeta was keeping a close eye on emergency back-up systems, which would cut in to keep the crew alive. Past experience had told that they were often reconfigured to fire off a critical laser bolt or two or even detonate a generator. At the moment all was quiet.

The sound of the two ships clamping on to each other echoed throughout their corridors and the vibrations from the working engines of The Definite Article passed gently through the structure of the prison ship. A short docking pillar lowered itself to the bay of the prison ship and clamped on. The Universal Dock™ connection column clipped neatly into place.[73]

There was a faint hiss as pressures equalised.

The pirates waited in the docking tube, armed to the teeth, pumped full of natural adrenaline and dangerous as hell.

---

[72] I.e. on a prison ship

[73] Until several years ago docking ports had been unstandardised; each ship would have to be fitted with several different port connectors each favoured by different races and engineering groups in the galaxy. When the Empire had created the Universal Dock they had enforced its use throughout the galaxy by creating The Entrancisor- a pointed ram designed to rip a hole in the side of the ship as the only alternative for ships they might wish to board who weren't sporting the latest Universal Dock mechanism. Unsurprisingly The Universal Dock caught on very quickly after that.

If there's one thing a pirate knows how to do well, it's board another ship.

It was their favourite part of the job.

The trick is to overwhelm.

There are few merchant space-goers who, when faced with a mob of angry, armed and frequently unwashed rogues, would not put down their weapons. Pirates are experts at disarming, immobilising and moving on and most ships are taken without a single shot being fired. Only in the face of resistance do they start to play dirty.

It is well known that the anticipation of fear is far worse than the end result. To this end pirates facing resistance may cause a few casualties, then separate groups and flush things into space to make others think that they might be next.

To a pirate everything on board is worth something.

To a marine, quite the opposite is true.

Marines will shoot first. Questions are entirely optional and completely unnecessary in most cases.

Some of the pirates were salivating.

Advance party, the craziest of the pirates were crammed into the lift that would jettison them into the spaceship. They were bloodthirsty cutthroats to a man and woman and were not afraid to die.[74]

"Hang on to your hats," said a veteran, who considered himself in charge. The others ignored him and kept their guns close to their chest instead.

"AWAY!" he cried.

There was a fraction of a second's pause while everyone in the lift wondered if that meant they were supposed to do something. Then...

---

[74] Although a surprising number of them harboured other irrational fears including the fear of spiders, of heights, of zero gravity fires and in one case tea cosies.

The lift dropped down the barrel of the docking tube and smashed through the doors on the inside of the prison ship scattering bits of steel reinforcement everywhere.

The lift skidded along the floor.

Inside the veteran called out "Pause for Boobies". They waited to see if any booby traps had been detonated. A rookie tittered and received an elbow in his ribs.

The sides of the lift fell away and the pirates shoulder-rolled into the corridor taking up strategic positions along the entrance hallway. A metal mesh barred their way down the corridor, bolted shut.

"No marines yet," snarled a pirate. "We'll find you."

The veteran looked around, gun at the ready, at the other pirates covering each other's backs. There was no denying it: they were all loving this.

Yelling at the top of their lungs they all threw themselves at the mesh, which buckled without much of a fight at all.

On the bridge, Binner watched carefully as the scanner followed their progress through the ship. At each corner they turned, they met no resistance. A knot grew in Binner's stomach. Picking off marines one-by-one was one thing, but a determined group would be another kettle of fish entirely. It was not unheard of for marines to let pirates board and then sneak onto the pirate ship in retaliation.

"Send second party," said Binner.

The second party crept more cautiously behind the first, again meeting no resistance.

A horrible feeling crept over Binner, and she leaned in to her communicator.

"Greeta?"

The distracted face of Greeta appeared on the screen.
"Hello?" she said.

"How many life readings have you got on the prison ship, Greeta, excluding our teams."

Greeta shook her head and mumbled "Oh, I...well it isn't an exact science you know, there are lots of things that give off heat readings that might hide any number of people on board a vessel I mean..."

"Greeta, can you tell me."

"Excluding ours?"

"Excluding ours."

Greeta chewed her lip and one of her eyes squinted involuntarily.

"One," she said. And sniffed.

Binner paused in thought.

"All right," she declared to the room making a few of the navigators jump, "call off the attack parties. It's purely F&R..."

The pirates looked disappointed.

"F&R?" said a confused looking rookie who had been hoping to upgrade himself with marine fodder this trip.

"Find and retrieve," sighed one of the older pirates, 'means there's no resistance and we've just got to bring back whatever we can lay our hands on."

"Pain in the ass!" said another shaking his head, "No resistance!"

This wasn't strictly true.

Dougan wasn't entirely sure what he was going to do with the towel but he was quite convinced that his elevated position on top of the chair behind the door was definitely an advantage.

He wasn't ever prepared for combat situations. Perhaps the towel might be a weapon. Perhaps it was for comfort. He hoped it wasn't just going to be useful for mopping things up.

The fact the one-way glass went the wrong way turned out to be another advantage.

The first pirate through the door was not expecting what happened.

Nor, to be fair were the others.

When Dougan had spotted, not uniformed officers, but the scruffy attire of pirates and renegades, he had decided that reasoning with the crew of the Definite Article was not an option and some kind of escape plan would be in order.

It wasn't really a plan, since the definition of plan implies a certain amount of forethought. This was more of a reaction.

As the door opened, Dougan hurled himself at the first pirate, a weedy looking bespectacled man. Contrary to even his own expectations, Dougan managed to wrap the towel quite neatly around his neck and drag him to the floor.

The pirate dropped his gun, which clattered to the floor. The other pirates watched as Dougan kicked out ineffectually in the gun's direction. One of then leaned casually over and picked it up.

Dougan scrambled backwards pulling the surprised pirate by the neck and reasserted his grip on the towel.

The group of pirates levelled their guns at him and watched carefully.

"Stay back!" said Dougan, "Stay back or I'll throttle him."

"And then what?" said one of the gruffer, rougher-looking pirates, whose face was a mass of scar tissue.

"Sorry?" said Dougan.

The pirate in the towel, began slowly to realise that the towel was too thick to actually constrict his throat and began to relax slightly.

"Well," said the gruff pirate quite reasonably, "if you throttle him, then you won't have any bargaining chips will you and we'll have no hesitation in shooting you."

The towel-bound pirate frowned. He didn't like the direction this was heading in.

"Ah," said Dougan, "but I won't need to throttle him if you stay where you are. In fact...in fact I won't need to throttle him if you back away from the door."

"So you don't want to kill him?" asked one of the pirates.

"No," said Dougan, "he's just a hostage!"

"Hey!" said the be-towelled pirate, "I'm not *just* a hostage. I have rights."

"Listen fella," said one of the pirates, scratching his face, "hostage taking falls purely in the realm of negotiation. When was the last time you met a pirate who negotiated?"

Dougan's mouth opened and closed a little bit.

"No actually lads, I think that might be seen as a sign of weakness," said the veteran. "What's your name lad?"

"Er, Mike" said the now wide-eyed pirate. Suddenly having a towel round his throat didn't seem to be that drastic at all.

"Got any family Mike, anyone we should inform?"

"I have a mother. And a sister." This second bit was a lie but he felt like he needed to offer something more.

"Right, mother and sister, Lippy, make a note."

Lippy, a squat balding pirate covered in constantly moving tattoos, brought out a notepad and scribbled something that only he would understand.

"Tell you what mister..." the veteran paused

"Dougan, Lieutenant Karl Dougan."

"Right mister Dougan, either you release the hostage…"

"Mike" said Mike.

"Either you release Mike or I'll shoot you both. And if I miss then they won't." His head nodded backwards at the assembled crew.

Dougan looked distraught.

"I thought you said you didn't do negotiation…"

"Suit yourself," said the veteran and levelled the gun at Dougan's head. The chamber glowed as the battery charged to fire.

"No!" Mike and Dogan said simultaneously. Dougan released the towel and Mike scrambled away from the rack of lasers pointed at him.

The veteran lowered his gun.

"Well, look at that," he said to the others, "sometimes it does work."

Dougan hung his head and agreed to let them rough him up a little, on the proviso he could hang on to the towel.

The Burning Desire sped towards the barrier at the edge of Core World's militarised zone.

"I'm sorry if I scared you," said the Survival robot.

Ellie was having difficulty looking at the robot as it feverishly rebuilt its skin around her, occasionally wrenching small panels off the wall and cutting them to fit gaps in its rudimentary skin. It was like watching someone conducting an operation on themselves.

"It's okay," said Ellie, "I'm assuming you don't mean me any harm."

"No," said the robot.

There was a pause, filled with tense silence. Neither really sure whether they could trust each other.

"Actually I was rather hoping you might help me," it said finally.

"Help you, how?" she turned to look at the robot. She felt rather like she was the one who could do with help.

"I need to find some old friends of mine."

"Other robots?"

The Survival robot nodded and turned his head to the viewscreen. The security platforms were approaching, spread out like points on an invisible grid.

"It may be too late," it said.

"Too late for what?" asked Ellie.

"One of us… how can I say this… one of us has a particularly destructive agenda. We thought, after the war, that he had finally understood where that would get him, but it appears he hasn't learned that lesson at all. Or he's planning to learn a new one."

"What can I do?"

"I need to find the others. If we are lucky there are still some left, although he has been hunting us. Justice and I…"

"Justice? The Arbiter."

The robot appeared to bristle.

"These are names your kind chose for us. Loaded with prejudice. Why should the Knowledge robot be known as the Traveller, when I was known as the Coward? I am the Endurer as well. For I have cheated destruction, where Justice could not."

Ellie hung her head, "How did you? Cheat destruction, I mean."

The Survival robot made a sound like laughter.

"It's what I taught myself to do."

He leaned forward and the head opened again. The small claw-like hand was now deeply embedded in the brain area, making up a substantial part of the matrix.

The head closed, and raised to look Ellie in the eye.

"I create back-ups of myself. Parts that will survive and escape. Inside each is a compressed identity. A part from my last form made it into here, integrated itself into the ship's workings and took over. Slightly parasitic I'm afraid but then it is my survival I'm concerned about…"

The robot spread its six appendages in what Ellie assumed must be some sort of apologetic gesture.

"The ship became part of me. Or I became part of it. I used it to relearn what I knew before, by accessing the data banks and the mainframe computers. There is much missing though, isn't there?"

Ellie seemed surprised. "Yes," she said, "how did you know?"

"You ask many questions. It is good. I saw the gaps. I also saw when they were created, when files were deleted. You were looking, too and the other one."

"Dougan," said Ellie. If it knew about Dougan maybe it could help her find him. Not that that was important. It was important to get to the bottom of what was happening in the databases. But there was a small part of her that registered she would be pleased to see him again; the same small part of her that had persuaded her to come here, to find his ship…

"Is that his name?" asked the robot. "The missing information is a problem. I do not know where to find the others yet."

"I'm sorry, I don't know how I can help. I don't even really know what's going on."

"You know about us, which is more than most. And if you have an idea where we might find your friend, you may lead me to at least one of my number."

"How?" said Ellie

"Because I think one of us, is looking for him."

The Survival Robot suddenly sat upright.

"We are approaching the perimeter. I will explain more when we cross over. If we do."

"If?" spluttered Ellie, "They're not going to shoot at us are they?"

"When you're as paranoid as I am, you assume everyone is going to shoot at you." It rose to its feet prompting Ellie to do the same. The nearest perimeter module began to fill the screen.

The perimeter module computer was basic to say the least. It ran simple programs, with clear instructions and no grey areas.

Its current instructions couldn't have been simpler: Nothing gets in, nothing gets out.

In terms of If-Then loops, this was pretty much as basic as it got.

A craft approached the inside edge of the perimeter, identifying itself as the Burning Desire Mark II. The computer returned an automatic "Stay Clear" warning message. A variety of weapons and defence mechanisms came online, as dictated by protocol.

Then, suddenly, random extra bits of code started to appear in its programming.

Guns switched themselves off and force shields diminished.

Back up systems sent out requests for confirmation of the codes only to be met with nonsense. It found itself calculating star trajectories in the closing stages of the destruction of the Diamidi Nebula, which jammed its processing power. It wasn't sure if this was a test. It began to try to translate the phrase "My bear suit must be clean by Wednesday, I have a meeting with the invisible ambassador's legs," into all three-hundred-and-eighty-two official galactic languages. Then became compelled to arrange the results in various alphabetical orders before finally being asked to prove the existence of the colour blue, and crashed.

Core code reset. The module rebooted quickly. Protocol priority one was established: Nothing gets in, nothing gets out.

It observed a craft called the Burning Desire Mk II mooching around the outside of the perimeter. The computer readied itself for the approach of the craft, sending out a "Stay Clear" warning. It worked. The craft moved away from the perimeter.

The Desire drifted off into the inky blackness of space.

"How did you do that?" said Ellie perplexed.

The Survival robot looked round at Ellie, "The difference between creatures and computers," he said sagely," is that when computers say they're just following orders, they mean it."

As far as Reid was concerned, Howells was in deep shit. This was nothing compared to the deeper shit he'd be in if he didn't have a pristine explanation of what the hell was going on when he finally found him.

The Admiral strode down the corridor in a crimson ball of fury, and descended the stairs to the level where Morning Star was housed.

Howells hadn't answered any of Reid's demands to see him. Reid's blood was boiling. If one more general had shrugged his shoulders and said, "I guess we won," he was quite sure he would have exploded.

There was not a security guard in sight.

He paused by a window looking out over the city.

It was hard to see from here but he knew it would be heaving with people down there. Bars would be full of off-duty officers, cadets and the ancillary creatures and professions that tend to hang around off-duty military boys and girls.

He pounded down the corridor passing empty rooms strewn with file-screens depicting the best planets to retire to, and urging the well-off to engage in the leisurely satisfaction of Framther Beast farming in The Dracillian Peninsula.

He rounded the bottom of the corridor and punched the entry hatch to Morning Star's chamber so hard that his knuckles smarted.

By the door, lay the endless discarded wrappers of snacks that Howells had been living off.

The door slid calmly open.

Inside, the chamber was as cold as ever, and Reid's feet sounded eerie as they echoed over the connecting bridge. The door slammed shut behind him.

He stopped.

Something hadn't sounded quite right about the way the door had closed.

The door to Morning Star's chamber glided open.

Reid stepped in.

Inside, he could see that Howells really was in the shit.

The man sat looking pale and sallow. He had long since sobered up and was now deeply entrenched in the fully horrific combination of hangover and the realisation that whatever had happened the night before was nothing compared to what he was waking up to.

Reid stepped into the room, all the anger he had been intending to direct at Howells suddenly dissipated.

There was a funny smell.

"Where are all my spaceships, Howells?" asked Reid, "Why don't I have a single operational craft in the galaxy?"

"I'm sorry," whispered Howells. "I'm sorry Admiral Reid."

He swallowed hard. His head was pounding. He needed a headache remedy and he'd been hoping to come up with a more eloquent way of telling his superior:

"I think the computer has taken over the galaxy."

Reid looked at the projection about him. No matter where he looked he couldn't see a ship he recognised, neither Imperial nor Renegade, Human nor Alien, Pirate nor Merchant.

That's not to say the space was devoid of ships. It was, in fact, full of them.

He peered in at a small fleet by an outlying system. Modest sleek ships, that looked like they'd been designed along Imperial guidelines and from Imperial materials but wearing a subtly dangerous, brutal, sinister *other* about them.

They were everywhere.

"What happened, Howells?" asked Reid.

"It was my fault sir. I forgot to add something. I forgot to add something very, very, important."

"What, Howells? What did you forget to add?"

"An off switch, sir."

Reid looked around at the galaxy he no longer recognised. A galaxy that was no longer his.

"We'll see about that," said Reid. He drew his personal laser weapon from his belt and headed for the door.

CHAPTER THIRTEEN
Glory

"I thought you were all destroyed in the war. I mean that's what I read in the only history book I could find."

The Survival robot, adding the finishing touches to its casing, looked up.

"If you know yourself that's not the case, why do you ask?"

"Because I want to know the truth." Ellie's brow furrowed and her lip pouted slightly. She wasn't sure if petulance would work with robots but anything was worth a try.

"You imply with that statement there is only one truth," the robot replied.

Ellie didn't like the idea that, if it had a sense of humour, it was also capable of being smug.

"Tell me what really happened to you."

The direct approach seemed to work. The robot put down its handiwork, a breastplate it was fashioning itself, and began to explain:

THE COLOUR OF ROBOTS

"We were each programmed according to a different desire. I believe it to be a necessity for each sentient creation. Something must drive us. But the designers didn't realise how powerful a force desire could be. It made us all flawed. We came to see it in ourselves over time. My survival became everything. The Knowledge robot, the Traveller as he likes to be known, wouldn't rest until he knew everything, The Harmony robot, imbued with love of all things, became obsessed with perfection. Likewise the others, just as their names suggest, craved Glory, Justice and Power.

"Over time, our desires developed, became more refined. We began to interpret them. Mine became not just about my survival in my own form, but about finding a way of surviving beyond my form, hence the condensed "me's" that I create. Knowledge realised that he couldn't know everything but he could know enough to *infer* everything. Justice realised that justice is an area effect, not a local effect, you have to consider the bigger picture which, to those involved in justice on a local scale, may seem terribly unjust. The Harmony robot created an entire planet you know. She wouldn't allow anyone near it, saying they would upset the balance. It was a paradise that no-one would ever see.

"We became unpopular. We were thinking about bigger things than the citizens of the galaxy cared for us to think about. They considered us too lofty, too superior. We were accused of trying to set ourselves up as gods.

"Power's ideas developed too. It wasn't enough for him to share power with the citizens of the galaxy or to help them wield it over other lesser races. He wanted power over them. And so he persuaded us to leave the civilised worlds, start up our own planet which we called Robot World. That was Sharp's name. Do you know about Sharp?"

Ellie shook her head. The robot looked wistful.

"He was a great man. Very kind. Mad as a bucket of gerbils on a trampoline but marvellous with it.

"Anyway, we all went there with him, with the Power robot because..." the Survival robot looked into the middle distance. "Because, he was very persuasive..."

Ellie laughed. The Survival robot was surprised at first and then realised why.

"He wanted to rule the galaxy. He was convinced he could do it better than anyone else. He believed that people were happiest when others made decisions for them. And so he set out to conquer the galaxy with his robot warriors. It all seemed perfectly reasonable at the time."

Ellie found her jaw slackening with disbelief. It seemed impossible that someone could consider a war of that scale "perfectly reasonable".

"But then it became apparent that power is addictive. He got out of control, Justice declared that the time had come to strike a balance.

"We joined forces, aided the citizens where they were making mistakes, the Traveller's understanding was very useful. Glory made a most foolhardy warrior. Of course we had to do it in secret. There was no trust in us.

"Eventually we were alone together, all seven of us, back on the Robot World. We talked about what was to be done. I knew that despite our help, the tide had turned inexorably against us and that we wouldn't be tolerated long, back in society. So we agreed to return to our creator, and made a deal."

"A deal?"

"Yes, with the then Emperor. In return for stopping the war, we were granted the rights to Robot World. It was wiped from your star charts, never to be found again."

"Wow," said Ellie. "So you all survived?"

"Yes. We hid ourselves away, rewrote history and hoped to be able to continue unnoticed. But we couldn't stay in our prison. Only Power remained in the end - having a planet to rule was enough for a while."

"But wasn't enough for long. Will there be another war?"

"It's possible. It's long enough ago now and enough of the history we re-wrote has been erased for the galaxy to be utterly taken by surprise."

"Can I ask you something? " Ellie cocked her head to one side

"Why are you asking that now?"

"Will you stop him? Destroying the galaxy I mean."

There was a long pause. The robot didn't move. After a long while it spoke.

"To do so would put me in great danger. Although I feel it is my duty. As do the others. Now if you will excuse me I must go and work out a way to reconfigure this battery pack."

The robot rose to its feet and passed silently out of the room.

Ellie watched as a trail of wires followed the vestigial legs out of the doorway. A cold shiver ran down her spine. She hunched her knees up to her chin and stared out into the cold blackness of space.

Binner and Dougan sat across the table from each other. The guard in the corner watched them very carefully. Rumours that Dougan had attempted to throttle a pirate with nothing more than a towel had spread rapidly. This man was not only resourceful, he was desperate.

"What's your name, rank and number?" asked Binner.

Dougan wasn't sure if he was supposed to give this information away under interrogation, but considering it was all stitched onto his prison issue uniform, he thought it was pretty harmless.

"Dougan, Karl, Lieutenant, Engineer, Planetary[75]. I can't remember by number but I can make one up."

The guard in the corner's eyed widened. There was backchat, too!

Binner's eyes narrowed. She liked this guy.

She had also run out of questions.

To be fair, she'd never really interrogated an Imperial prisoner before. Pirates rarely caught naval officers alive, and when they did they seemed to know the procedures better than she did. She usually just had to leave them a couple of days before they caved under the weight of their own imagined fate.

Merchants were harder. They rarely caught them sober. She had once spent an hour just trying to work out that on old trader was trying to ask her if she knew someone called 'Terry', before he'd keeled over in a drunken stupor and they'd been forced to cast him off at the next spaceport.

This was different.

Pirate wisdom suggested they should ransom Dougan for a huge wad of credits. However it didn't seem bright to try to negotiate the exchange of an

---

[75] For some reason, he thought it sounded more official when he said it backwards.

Imperial officer from the bridge of one of their own pieces of hardware.

He was completely useless to them.

Dougan leaned in.

One thing he was sure about was that he didn't want to go back to jail. He didn't want to go anywhere near anything Imperial since, as far as he could tell, it wasn't holding him in very high regard.

His only way through this would be a little bit of story telling and an awful lot of bluff.

"I think I can help you," he said, looking Binner in the eye.

Binner blinked and looked down at the table for a second. There had to be something wrong with an interrogation when subjects started offering answers before you even know what the questions were.

"How?" she said.

Dougan looked around.

"This is an Imperial ship right? Battle Cruiser Mark VII. My guess is you don't really know what it can do."

Binner suppressed the smile that was lurking at the corner of her mouth and raised her eyebrows.

"What makes you think that?" she asked, her voice just a little higher than she would have liked.

Dougan looked out the window at the inky blackness of space coasting by.

"You're still driving with the parking lights on," he said placidly.

Dougan spent the next two hours making himself exceptionally popular.

Already known as 'Towelly-man', people had soon started referring to him as Pirate, which he had to admit he was enjoying. He had started with the engine room, showing Greeta where she had been going wrong while she fluttered and clattered around him. Hurbury had purred as the full power of the cruiser had been unleashed unto her and Jirbaks had listened exceptionally patiently as Dougan had explained how the matter cannon, laser cannon and electro pulse cannons could be linked for various dazzling and deadly gun effects.

Binner had introduced all the sessions as staff retraining. Dougan had played along, being careful to defer to her authority.

Later they had shared a drink.

"So what's going on then?" Binner asked later in the bar of the cruiser. It was a huge spacious affair and decorated utterly tastelessly according to Hybert's law.[76]

"I don't know yet," said Dougan. "All I know, is that I know more than I should, and someone somewhere in The Empire wants to kill me. With the exception of the gun-pointing and shouting for the first hour, you guys have been nicer to me than anyone else has in ages."

Binner nodded "We're not all bad, pirates, you know."

"I'm sure you're not," said Dougan diplomatically. "There are some very strange things happening. I think the galaxy might be in quite a lot of danger."

Binner swirled the drink around in her hand. It was blue and tasted funny. Dougan had assured her it was very *IN* at the moment. She wondered how accurate the information of what was *IN* could be from someone who didn't look like he got *OUT* very often.

---

[76] Hybert's law states that the tackier a drinking establishment is, the more people will drink to feel comfortable there.

"What sort of things?"

Dougan told her everything he knew.[77] Binner was sceptical at first, but pirate lore and human lore had taken a divergence over the years and it wasn't as hard for her to accept what she heard about the robots, as it was for Dougan to explain it to her.

When he was finished, she took a long sip of her drink. It was growing on her.

"I'll have to take this to the council of elders," she said. "We may well need your help."

Dougan nodded.

"I would appreciate some help finding something I've lost though," said Dougan, as a look of sadness crossed his face.

Binner had seen this face before on even the most hardened space-dog. She rolled her tongue around her mouth.

"What's her name?" she asked.

From the outside, the planet wasn't particularly noticeable. White wispy clouds marbled the surface of a green-blue land, half covered in thick vegetation, half drowned in mineral-rich water.

The small silver craft dropped neatly through a bank of cloud covering a swarming jungle near the equator.

One or two of the hugest reptilian beasts in the galaxy raised their heads and watched the little silver bullet screaming across their sky. They wondered briefly if it was edible.

In a hot spring, a slimy, vicious, eighteen-tentacled, bug-eyed monster paused in the act of swallowing whole a purple, amphibious, bulbous-eyed lily pad

---

[77] About the situation. The other stuff he knew, he wasn't so sure about.

hopping creature, and watched the silver ship roar overhead, as its prey plopped neatly into the water and swam madly for safety.

In a clearing, a group of seven-thousand twelve-legged insects paused in the act of building what, they were convinced, was the largest, most palatial mound they had ever built. It had taken four teams of five hundred apiece to drag the Durfur wood bark over eighty kilometres to where the rest of their number were creating a honeycomb tower of such complexity that it would have taken the greatest mathematical minds in the galaxy years to imagine. At the centre, the queen was about to start giving birth to a near-endless stream of larvae.

The insects watched in alarm as huge silver landing gear descended from the sky, heading for the very centre of the tower. They massed beneath, tentacles on their heads waving from side to side, buffeted by the wind created by the craft. A few began the climb up the side of the tower to do all they could to stop the onslaught.

At the last minute, the landing gear swerved sideways as the craft twisted in its descent, clearing the top of the mound and landing rather inconveniently in one of their main trade routes. A small group of merchant insects stopped, puzzled, trying to work out how to drag their large, delicately-perfumed flower through.

The insects who had climbed to the top of the tower raised their front legs in the air in triumph. They commenced the dance of success and glory, which was cut short by eleven verses by the untimely intrusion of the exit ramp which neatly took the top off the tower.

Clumps of dirt and Durfur bark rained down on the disappointed insects below. And somewhere deep inside the Queen began screaming.

Two metallic pairs of feet clumped down the ramp and, after pausing briefly at the bottom, one strode off into the jungle while the other did its best to follow behind.

There are some advantages to knowing a lot, even about planets you have never visited, and over the next forty minutes of trekking through an increasingly hostile jungle, the Traveller's knowledge was tested to the fullest.

The first attack came from a mammalian beast, part feline, part winged marmoset, which flew out of the jungle at them. The beast launches itself from trees at unsuspecting prey and has a mouth that is mostly teeth and that point straight out the front of its head. It sinks itself, at speed, into the soft body of its prey and sucks out the softest part, as quickly as possible.

The Knowledge robot noticed the slippery drool on the ground a fraction of seconds before it pounced. It stood bolt upright.

The creature struck the side of the robot in a flurry of fur, wings and the shattering of teeth. It slid neatly down the side of the metallic head and flopped to the ground. Then it went vegetarian.

Further through the jungle, they came upon a rudimentary path, which the black robot correctly identified had been beaten by the leaves of the Urburu plant. The Urburu plant has two types of growth: a thick mass of dense, sharp, spines and thorns, which spreads like wildfire through the undergrowth, and long languid fronds which loll heavily over and beat a path through the grasses and other vegetation luring animals down routes that lead directly to bell like vats of deadly, digestive acid.

The two robots followed the path until the ground dipped suddenly before them. Knowledge reached up, pulled one of the large fronds over, and poked it into the ground ahead. The plant reacted immediately, recoiling at its own acidic stomach and the bell like vat contracted shut.

They climbed neatly over.

After avoiding numerous further attacks, they emerged by a riverbank where a wide waterfall splashed and gurgled.

The Knowledge robot paused.

The Money robot looked at its companion. The cave they needed to reach was beyond the waterfall.

Water and robots didn't mix.

But since they had come to find a robot, there had to be a way in. They began searching for a back door.

In they end they found it hidden in the traditional manner by leaves and vines that were plastered over the surface of the rock against the wall of the waterfall. In the rock behind, there was a large metallic door with the words 'tradesman's entrance' written in large elegant script.

Knowledge knocked hard on the door and, from deep within, the melodious sound of bells rang out.

After a couple of minutes the door opened and a thin butler automaton opened the door.

"You'd better come in," it said tonelessly, "my master has been expecting you."[78]

The pair stepped through the door into a plush, red-carpeted hallway, well lit and cool. The door closed

---

[78] It had't but it was a nice, if slightly cliched thing to say to guests.

gently behind them as another set of winged teeth shattered against it. The ranks of vegetarians swelled.

The walls of the corridor were packed with displays showing footage that would have left the average blockbusting action film feeling limp and embarrassed. Explosions, acts of extreme derring-do and fantastic stunts screamed for attention. Acts of extreme bravery matched acts of extreme stupidity. The common theme in every one was the clearly discernible figure of a tall humanoid robot, almost identical to the ones walking past his gallery of glory, the purple circles and triangles clearly visible on the pumped-up chest that dominated the final frame of every looped video.

The robots strode on without looking. They had seen them all before.

At the end of the corridor, there was a second portal: a set of old-fashioned wooden double doors, ornately carved with long elaborate handles. The butler drone pushed them open with a flourish.[79]

Beyond was a cavern, dominated by a large statue of the same robot they had seen in the videos. The walls writhed with the holographic projections of billions of creatures, humanoid and alien seated like a massive crowd around the statue. They roared and cheered in unison. The sound was a little tinny.

High above the statue a banner fluttered bearing the words, "Our Finest Year"

The Money robot leaned in to its companion.

"I thought it was meant to be 'our finest hour'" it said.

---

[79] Butler drones are programmed to do everything with a flourish although the feature can be disabled by those it irritated. It became a matter of pride to leave it on.

Knowledge looked around the room. There was something odd about the projection of the crowd, above and beyond its vanity, it was as if every person had been hand picked from shots of another crowd.

"I don't think he thought one hour could possibly do him justice."

At that moment two shapes dropped from the ceiling; one, a robot, and the other, a giant hump-backed, gnarly toothed, boar-like monster.

They were locked in a plummeting death grip, suspended by a thin rope from the ceiling, which frayed more with every jerk and twist.

The beast snarled and snapped at the robot, clearly keen to take its head off. The robot's arm became trapped by the beast, the situation looked desperate.

The crowd fell silent and leaned forward.

Money, concerned, stepped forward but the firm arm of the other robot stopped it.

The beast lunged again at the robot and the rope above them snapped. They fell to the ground, throwing up a great cloud of dust.

The crowd leaned in.

The beast struggled to its feet, the robot nowhere to be seen. It raised itself on its hind legs and let out a roar. In its yellowed teeth one could make out wires and pieces of glinting metal. The crowd gasped in horror.

Then the roar strangled to a mewl and became gargled. The beast fell limp and yet rose up out of the cloud of dust. As it rose higher, the arm of the robot emerged from the fray, hefting higher the sword that was skewering the twitching and snarling beast.

The robot rose to its feet, holding its prize aloft with one hand, as black blood poured from the creature's underbelly, coalescing into large black spots on the floor of the cavern.

The crowd, obligingly, went wild.

Knowledge clapped its hands slowly.

The sound of the crowd faded and the projections dimmed until only the sound of the clapping could be heard echoing in the cavern.

The robot turned to look at the source of the clap and slowly lowered its sword arm. The beast crashed to the ground, picked itself up and trotted in a docile fashion to a pen in the far corner of the room.

The robot dusted itself down.

"Oh," it said at length, when it had worked out who its visitors were.

"That was exactly what I said," said Money.

Some hours later, a troupe of ever-resilient insects had begun their glorious reconstruction programme.

The metal ramp, which had so neatly sliced the top of their great tower, had retreated back into the silver beast as the robots left. Experience had taught them that things went *into* the jungle, not the other way round. They felt safe to carry on.

The new tower promised to be even better than the last one. It was going to be higher and stronger.

It was also going to have two turrets.[80]

They were heaving bark up the side of the tower, amid questions around why it had been built so steep, when suddenly the sound came: Three things crashing through the undergrowth.

---

[80] Largely due to two separate groups beginning turrets without consulting each other than any design-led decision

They paused, bits of bark wafting slightly in the mild, ground-level breezes.

The ramp opened again, taking the foundations off the two new towers and three pairs of metal feet clanged up the ramp in to the craft.

The ramp retreated and the spacecraft blasted away from the surface of the jungle world and screamed into the distant atmosphere.

The insects, blown and buffeted, put down their bark and decided, once and for all, that tunnels were the way forward.

THE COLOUR OF ROBOTS

.

CHAPTER FOURTEEN

Power

The robot with the red triangles and circles sat at the heart of the machine world, surveying its empire.

It had been studying the holographic projection screen in front of it for months now. Finally things were coming into place.

Things hadn't been easy. Its was a very subtle game and had involved the wrangling of both the smartest and weakest minds in the galaxy, slowly playing them off each other, while they were completely unaware of its existence.

Almost.

The humans had been all too willing to release control of their ships. Their entire fleet had been delivered into his hands through the subtle lure of Morning Star, the computer that would do all their thinking for them.

Their laziness would be their undoing.

Without questioning it, they had all taken leave, all returned their ships to dock, where the new, updated program had been delivered to each and every core computer on every ship in the fleet.

It wouldn't have to send suggestions and requests via Morning Star any more. Now, through Morning Star, it could control every ship in the galaxy directly.

And when it introduced them to their shiny new craft, the ones that required even less human intervention, well, they'd become nothing more than willing slaves.

And when the rogue elements had been dealt with, there would be no-one to even tell them how stupid they'd been.

The Burning Desire cruised towards the wormhole gate.

"This will be dangerous," the robot had announced.

"Is there no other way?" Ellie had asked.

The wormhole gates were fixed routes, tunnelled through the fabric of spacetime. Decades spent connecting them meant that once one reached the hub, one could choose any number of destinations to emerge from. They were cheap, arterial routes across the galaxy, which made them into traffic nightmares.

Wormhole gates also made them very obvious to the authorities.

"I am afraid not," said the robot, "your friend's ship will have taken a gravity well jump. We must follow, or fall far behind. You do not want your friend getting in trouble do you?"

Ellie shook her head.

She wanted to see Dougan again. She wanted to see humans again. Being alone with the robot was beginning to freak her out a little. She was beginning to feel the pangs of being in deep space with a companion she didn't fully trust.

She was also beginning to suspect that returning home wasn't going to be a possibility for a while.

They approached the circular torus of the gate. The Desire submitted coordinates to bring them near the prison worlds.

Normally the interface to the wormhole would glow and buzz; space would crackle and fizz with mind-bending colours as its very fabric tore open. Nothing like that seemed to be happening at all.

The Desire, a tiny spot against the huge diameter of the ring, crept across the threshold.

Still, nothing happened.

Ellie looked at the robot, who was standing next to her, staring out of the viewport. It was almost whole now, very humanoid in shape. It had even managed to proudly restore the yellow circles and triangles that distinguished it from the others. It stared blankly ahead.

Then suddenly, crackles of lightning snaked across the surface of the craft, a blue-yellow-purple light obscured the view of everything. A blackness as deep as infinity opened up in front of them, engulfed them, and they were gone.

The power robot leaned forward. In a dark corner of its mind, connected and yet unconnected, a small warning light was flashing. It zoomed in. A wormhole had opened.

Its mind twisted the information around, a picture of a small vessel emerged.

It had a human signature attached.

Interesting, it thought, this is a most unexpected development.

There would of course have to be some response.

The Barons sat in as near to silence as they could manage, while Dougan stood on the podium and explained more or less what he knew.

There was little surprise. His report was corroborated by others who had seen more and more of the Empire's new breed of sleek shiny starships and less and less of the old ones they knew and loved.[81]

A sullen silence fell over the pirate's debating chamber as the news sunk in.

The sub-society to which the pirates belonged had been born as a result of the pirate war. In the wake of disrupted trade routes and a fledgling democratic Empire that was struggling to maintain control, the pickings had been rich for the renegades. It was a good time for them; they viewed the era with pride.

But things would have been very different if the robots had won and they knew it.

A new war with the robots would be a deadly venture. If what Dougan was saying was true, about the Empire being on self imposed decommission, it looked something like it was going to be a bit of a walkover.

They mulled.

Many hours passed.

They debated for a while. It was a downbeat debate, a thoughtful contemplation of where they would stand were the robots to return. What was, they asked, the future for piracy?

The suggestion that they should somehow alert the Empire was raised on many occasions but, since this involved handing back their shiny new ships, this was only met with much um-ing and ah-ing.

---

[81] In a violently aggressive way of course

Dougan watched with Binner and her crew. It wasn't a spectacle by any stretch of the imagination. The pauses were long, the speeches hesitant. There was a sense in the room, that something had to be said but no-one was prepared to say it, which built and built as the day wore on.

Eventually, during a particularly thoughtful and morose part of the afternoon, one of the Minor Barons stood up from his chair and said what everyone else had been thinking.

"Aw stuff it, " he had announced to the room in general, "shall we just give them a run for their money?"

As one, the chamber nodded and screwed up their noses in appreciation of the suggestion.

The motion was passed by six hundred and eight votes of "yeah, what the hell" to four votes of "you're all a bunch of idiots!" from a group of Altraina traders whose protests were quickly drowned out, and whose members were later drowned.

Ellie and the Survival robot reached the wormhole hub: a vast spherical hole carved through the substance of spacetime and held in place by eight-hundred-and-twenty mass-generators, some very complicated mathematics, and a small amount of ingenuity.

From here, one could choose from ninety-three distinct exit points in the galaxy, provided one was in enough credit.

Ellie and the Survivor were having a bit of trouble following the signs.

The designers had carefully constructed a very systematic, clever and simple-to-use series of tunnels and junctions, meant to make the journey from one's entrance to one's exit exceptionally straightforward.

The beauty of it was, one could always return to the beginning if one made a wrong turn. When it had been presented, the design had won awards for its elegance, graceful handling of high speed traffic flow and had been praised as 'the most understanding and sympathetic piece of engineering this galaxy has ever seen.'

Unfortunately, at the last minute, it was scrapped in favour of a cheaper, quicker-to-build alternative and what became known as "Hell's Intestines" was born.

Ellie had initially wanted to pilot the Burning Desire. The Survivor had pointed out that since it had subsumed most of the ship's controls, she would have to reach into some quite intimate places to do so. She had, with bad grace, accepted her role as backseat driver.

"Take this one here!" she cried, pointing at a clump of tunnels branching left. She didn't recognise the name of the place indicated on the sign, but knew it would have to be better than the direction they were heading in.

"I think we should just carry on down here," the robot replied haughtily.

"No," said Ellie firmly through gritted teeth, "that will take us back to where we came from."

"I'm sure that would be a good idea," said the Survivor, "I think we missed the turning back there."

"There, look, there!" She jabbed a finger furiously down a tunnel as they soared past. A sign with "prison ships on diversion" hung from the ceiling. She thumped the panel in front of her. Pieces of it clattered to the ground. A robotic appendage scooped the panel from its resting place at Ellie's feet and inserted it thoughtfully by its shoulder

"That's a diversion though isn't it?" said the Survivor, "and besides, who ever heard of a prison ship that couldn't hyperspace."

Another sign loomed from the darkness ahead of them and a chill ran down Ellie's spine at the same time as electrical warning pulses did something similar for the robot.

"What do you think they mean by 'under construction' ?" asked the robot.

Ellie's wide eyes indicated that whatever it meant it couldn't be good.

"Turn the ship around!" she said.

"I can't," replied the robot, "the tunnel is too narrow for a start."

"Well, then, put us into reverse!"

The robot's grille let out a hiss as its mouth speaker began to emit sound.

Ellie cut it off.

"And don't tell me that this tunnel is one-way. You know that the chances of meeting anything behind us are next to nothing. We're the only people travelling out in space right now."

Her voice was high, almost a scream. It had always worked with her father when she needed her way. Psychologically the situation was no different.

"I..."

"And don't tell me this ship doesn't have a reverse, or that you've somehow disabled it to build yourself."

She was turning a funny red colour.

"NO." said the robot commandingly. Its red eyes glowed. For the first time she saw menace there.

It worked. Cold water on her anger. Her fathers eyes had never done that. If they had, she might have had a quite different childhood. One with fewer ponies.

When the robot spoke again it was in slow measured tones. In a universe where survival is most often threatened by the other inhabitants, it understood the importance of using the right *voice*.

"I can't turn back, because the tunnel behind us is collapsing..."

One of its arms pointed a pincer-like claw at a screen hanging out of its socket in the far wall. Ellie could see the tunnel stretching behind them but, slowly but surely, a dark black nothingness was catching up with them.

She looked round wide eyed.

"The wormhole hub is collapsing?"

"Temporarily powering down I believe," said the Survivor, as the craft slewed from side to side avoiding large red plastic bollards floating listlessly around the tunnel ahead.

"Now," said the robot as it hit one of the bollards with a dull clunk, "we'll just have to hope they got some of it finished."

All around the civilised galaxy, people had noticed things were amiss.

There were a lot more spacefarers around than there usually were for a start, and the news seemed to be generally a bit more...local.

But as usual when the really unusual is happening, no-one really thought to say anything, and so carried on regardless. The bars were a little busier, the restaurants slowly eking their prices up, the park clearing drones turning in more rubbish than usual and suddenly there were no shortages of open-air events involving toxic substances to attend.

It was as if they were finally reaping the rewards of the wars. Admittedly wars that had been fought a long time ago in galaxies far, far away but there was an air of quiet celebration pervading everything.

It wasn't just on the planets of the Core Zone either.

All across the galaxy the civilised hubs had kicked off their heels and taken a bit of time off.

There had been knock-on effects.

Traders, unable to secure military escorts, had given themselves a bit of time off, and prices of off-world luxury items crept up a little.

Holidays had been postponed for the usual unfathomable reasons and, slowly but surely, the galaxy settled down into an uneasy period of rest.

It was not to last for long.

Howells had reached new levels of concern. He was beyond fret, vexation, disturbance, distress and perplexity. If there was a dark basement in the house of worry, he was in it, as the floodwaters rose, with a foot trapped underneath the radiator.

Reid's attempts at laser-based negotiation with the machine had misfired tragically. They had both cowered in a corner as the magnetic sealant plates that had lined the inside of the chamber had allowed the thirty-gig laser bolt to bounce around their heads for a little less than an hour.

Reid's next approach, to jemmy the locked door open with the butt of the rifle, had admittedly been more successful. The door had slid gently open and the two men had stared out over the long narrow bridge leading back to the rest of the compound.

Which had then begun to retract itself.

The bridge had detached from beneath the very doorway they were standing in and had glided away, retracting into the wall on the far side, leaving then standing on a precipice.

Reid hadn't hesitated. He had backed up a short way, then taken a run at the rapidly retreating walkway.

Instinctively, Howells had leaned out of the way as the aged, but still surprisingly sprightly, form of Reid barrelled past him, headlong over the abyss.

Howells held his breath.

Reid seemed to hang in the air an unnecessary long time.

His feet missed the bridge but he managed to grasp the side, pressing the cold, hard lip into his chest as he clawed for purchase. His legs dangled beneath as he gripped the sides for dear life.

Howells could see the muscles in his arms straining, through the red and black fabric of his suit.

His legs began to swing wildly underneath him, the arc of each swing magnified by the speed of the bridge. With mammoth effort and a grunt that exploded in Howell's earpiece, Reid pulled his legs under him to stop the momentum of the swing.

Howells watched as Reid, using every ounce of power he could muster, hauled himself up over the lip of the bridge, climbed to his feet and breathed a sigh of relief. He turned to face Howells on the still-retreating bridge.

He looked stooped and worn, a man who had not exerted himself so much since his academy days and his voice huffed loudly across the intercom.

"Find the safety loop in the program," Reid commanded.

Howells looked nervously around, framed in the doorway to Morning Star's viewing chamber and peered down into the inky blackness below.

"There isn't a safety loop!" he gibbered.

"There's always a safety loop, I never let *anything* get built without a safety loop. I don't trust my staff enough," said Reid.

Howells looked limply on, disoriented by watching Reid disappearing towards the door at the other end of the bridge and yet hearing his voice as clearly as if he were standing beside him.

"There might…"

"Find it. Use it!" commanded Reid again, "I'll bring help. I'll be right back."

Howells screwed up his face. These were words of doom[82]

Howells concern, worry and superstitions were at once confirmed when the bridge retreated completely into the wall long before Reid had any chance to open the door at the end, leaving Reid with nothing to stand on.

With a rather surprised croaked cry he slid down the gently curving parabolic surface of the wall of the chamber and disappeared into the darkness.

The cry lingered in Howells helmet for some time before the transmitter went out of range.

The presence of the giant supercomputer all around him felt suddenly very strong. He began to feel very alone.

---

[82] Even in the technological ages superstitions linger. For example, walking under ladders, breaking mirror plated armour or leaving an unconditional loop in a program were considered bad luck, whatever the true probability of disaster. Using certain phrases were also considered to court bad luck such as "look, here's a photo of my daughter", "trust me I know what I'm doing" and of course "I'll be right back". The etymology of why these innocuous phrases should be treated with suspicion whenever uttered is now lost in the mists of time.

Alone in a strange way that one does when one knows one isn't really alone, just the only one left on your team...

Dougan threw his hands up in the air

"It's no good, I can't find it!"

Binner and Jirbaks leaned in threateningly.

"Try harder!" Binner growled with full menace[83]

Dougan peered over the star chart glowing beneath him. Numbers danced in front of his eyes, jeering him to make sense of them. Under pressure.

"We're not really going to be able to take the war to these robots if we don't know where they are, are we?" added Binner.

Dougan looked around. Hurbury was watching him coolly from the stations communications deck, her arms folded.

"I just need a little time," said Dougan, lying.

What he actually needed was someone else. Like Finlay. Finlay would be able to work it out. Numbers were his friends. To Dougan, all the numbers they had brought him were just gobbledegook. As far as he could tell, they contained no hint whatsoever as to the whereabouts of the robot's base of operations. Flight plans of observed ship movements, details of inter-ship communications, even repeated patrol routes didn't seem to help. The ships weren't routing their commands anywhere other than current Imperial channels. It was impossible to tell where they had come from in the first place.

"We don't have time!" said Binner, "There are over eight thousand pirates out there all geared up and

---

[83] On a scale of one to ten, a high eight.

gung-ho for a fight. If they don't get one soon, trust me, they'll make one. You have to find that planet."

Dougan looked again. It was impossible.

Well, improbable.

The only explanation he could come up with, was that the robot ships were being controlled by the Empire, or someone within the Empire. And he wasn't about to suggest they launch their attack there.

He sighed and rubbed his eyes. "These data don't make any sense." He admitted finally.

Binner's forceful front collapsed. Her shoulders sagged and all the wind drained from her sails.

"Engineers," she muttered.

Hurbury stretched languidly and strutted off the deck whistling to herself. "Catch you guys later," she said as she headed for the door, "call me if you need a pilot."

The door closed behind her and Dougan collapsed onto a nearby sofa.

Only Jirbaks remained over the charts.

A thick uneasy silence fell over the room.

"You're an engineer right?" Jirbaks said slowly.

"Planetary," said Dougan. "Don't expect me to build some clever machine that can follow the robot ships undetected, because I can't"

"No," she said and lapsed into silence again.

"But," she said after a while.

Binner leaned forward. "What are you thinking Jirbaks?" she asked earnestly.

"Well," Jirbaks was suddenly hesitant. She didn't really like being the centre of attention, even if there were only three of them in the room. Even if, at most she could have only been a corner of attention.

"Well, if you were choosing a planet..."

Dougan perked up.

"If I were choosing a planet that had to house a lot of robots…"

Binner looked between the two of them. The dead air had electrified suddenly.

"What kind of planet would a robot like?" said Binner.

Dougan looked around the room.

"Well, I suppose there would be an ecological bandwidth…"

"A what-y what?" said Binner

"Ecological bandwidth," said Dougan. "Different species thrive under different conditions, temperature, humidity, air pressure, gravity that kind of thing. Humans can survive best between minus forty and plus forty degrees, one atmosphere, typically one g gravity. Other species are different, for example the Hungdan are mostly crystalline and require low gravity for movement but high temperatures to maintain fluidity of their joints, The Garralan live in really arid planets largely because they're soluble in water. There's no reason why the same wouldn't be true of a robot."

He was standing now and pacing round the room.

Jirbaks was grinning from ear to ear. Partly because she had thought of this and partly because Hurbury would be sick as a dog[84] when she discovered that she'd missed this.

"Okay," prompted Binner, "what *would* a robot like?"

Dougan pursed his lips. He thought.

"Cold. They'd like cold. Super-conduction happens at really cold temperatures."

"So..?"

---

[84] A true insult to the catlike races.

"Somewhere out in deep space, far from a sun."

"A comet?"

"Too erratic, too difficult to build on. Unstable. It would have to be right on the edge of a system, but near enough to be caught in an orbit. Probably around a small dense star."

"Okay..." said Binner lurching towards the star charts. "Gravity?"

"Low, I would guess, means you could expend less energy moving around, building the machines to make robots would be easier."

"Okay, so a small planet then, or a moon? Atmosphere? I suppose that's unlikely on small dead planets."

"Well, could be a gas planet" said Dougan, "but I can't see the advantage of..."

He suddenly stopped.

"What is it?"

"I was thinking it would need a solid base: rock or some such thing. In the absence of power from the sun, they'd need some kind of mining operation of radioactive materials to generate heat. But, of course, they wouldn't."

Dougan was getting excited now. It was scaring Binner.

"You're scaring me."

"No, no, if you needed heat then there are all kinds of fuel cells you could use, you can mine them, create them if you've got the right machinery. But to build an army of robots, you wouldn't need heat. Just electricity."

Binner's face was blank. A small threatening headache welled up deep behind her eyes.

Dougan pressed on: "If all you needed was an electricity supply you wouldn't need generators that used heat at all. All you'd need would be a stormy planet and massive wind turbines. Pick one with a high density of methane as well as ammonia, water and hydrogen you can create all the electric storage cells you wanted."

"So…"

"A small blue gas planet!"

"You're joking, right?"

Dougan was practically beside himself.

"No, no it's ideal. High methane concentration in the atmosphere makes it look blue, small planet, small sun."

"Have you seen how big this galaxy is? You want us to look for a planet by its colour?"

"Not just that," said Dougan stepping to the star charts. Binner and Jirbaks were already crouched over it, each zooming in on particular quadrants in their search. "It would need to be away from major trade routes, really far out the way. It would have to be somewhere where they could guarantee no-one would stumble over it."

Binner hit a few keys on the control panel, stars across the galaxy display winked to blackness as they were removed from the equation.

"Anything else…"

Dougan bit his lip.

"Energy signature. There would have been a tiny, tiny drop in the average energy signature of the planet's activity over the last few years."

"Drop?" said Binner, "wouldn't it rise with all the construction?"

"No," said Dougan, "drop. You'd be taking energy out of the planet's system. Neither created nor destroyed! Basic energy conservation."

Binner briefly considered hitting Dougan, just to be sure he wouldn't patronise her like that again.

"I think I've found it," said Jirbaks.

"Where the hell are we?" hollered Ellie

The Survivor paid her no attention.

The craft had not fared well coming out of the collapsing wormhole and had been rocketed at an unfeasible speed into a vast empty tract of unknown space.

The Survivor was pouring all his efforts into keeping the craft stable, bits of which had decided that this was as far as they went and had cheerfully detached themselves into the ether.

A dust cloud up ahead signalled severe danger, unless the robot was able to bring the craft to a halt. At this speed it would be like sledging on sandpaper.

The engines were sluggish in responding; they seemed unable to create sufficient force to slow the Burning Desire. At the last minute the robot was forced to abandon the start up attempts and threw up the external shield. The craft ploughed through the minute-but-deadly space particles with a nasty, rasping grating sound.

The outer layers of the shield shredded more rapidly than it had hoped, ground away by their high-speed plummet. The robot slewed the craft over to one side as the front wore down, and rolled it once again as that side abraded away.

Intolerably slowly, the attrition of the particles acted to slow the ship down and with barely a fraction of a millimetre of protective casing left, the Burning Desire dropped below critical speed.

Ellie was tired, stressed and fractious. The robot may have had the most excellent survival skills in the galaxy but it seemed to exercise them only in the direst of circumstances. It seemed a very male way of behaving.

She peered out through the dust cloud.

"I said, where are we?"

The robot was silent as it searched the scanners that had survived the impact.

"Home," it said at length, so quietly that Ellie almost didn't hear it.

"That's lucky," she said

The robot dropped its head.

"Not yours," it said, "mine."

"What does that mean?" Ellie asked.

The robot turned to look directly at her. In the viewport she could make out the dim light of a small distant sun creeping over the hazy horizon of a brilliant blue planet.

The light crept over the face of the Survivor. It had a strange ethereal quality to it, like the light of a weak torch in a dusty basement. She frowned, and looked out into the depths of space.

Something was wrong. The quality of space was wrong. It niggled at her. *What was it?*

Then, like an image that one realises one is looking at *in the wrong way,* like the mass of coloured fractals that suddenly the statue of liberty appears from, the view resolved itself.

The light was odd because there were no other stars to be seen.

It wasn't the hazy darkness one finds at the heart of a dust cloud. It was an absence of light save that from the dim sun.

They were in a shadow.

A single shadow that filled the whole viewport.

When a single part of the shadow moved, the brilliant pinprick light of a far-off star pierced the curtain of blackness and revealed that it was not one shadow, but many.

As the sun crept from behind the blue planet, light caught the back of, and illuminated, an uncountable number of sleek, sharp and very, very dangerous-looking starships.

It was hard to make out the exact shapes but words like glinting, sharp, functional, clinical filled her mind. Looking at them was like drinking from shattered glasses, running through fields of knives, walking naked through a hail of needles. She closed her eyes.

"What are they?"

"They are the new Imperial Navy," explained the Survivor.

"It brought us here didn't it?"

"Yes. I expect it would like to talk to me."

"Talk to you?"

"Well, get something out of me I expect."

"And what about me?" asked Ellie. There was tremor in her voice.

"I imagine it could think of a few things to extract from you too." Then seeing the terror in her eyes:

"I suggest you stick with me." Its voice was measured, but there was an edge to it.

"We have to warn the Navy, they can't run into this by accident!"

The Survivor robot shook its head.

"There is no Navy. He has sent them all home. Why do you think you had the dock, where we found this ship, to yourself?"

Ellie stammered. She couldn't think of a decent reason. Not one. She hadn't questioned it at the time. She looked down at the high-vis jacket she was still wearing.

"We have to warn them," she insisted, "send them a signal, show them this. Show them what they're up against."

"What good would that do?" asked the robot. "If anything is to be done it will be done here."

"You could do it. Send them a picture. Show them what we're seeing. I know you can do it."

"No one would be looking for a signal from this craft. It would be lost. It's pointless."

"DO IT!" demanded Ellie. She had risen to her feet and was standing over the robot. She barely reached the height of it while it was still sitting down crouched over the console.

It ignored her and turned its attention to the craft's remaining controls, the engines fired jumpily as they veered towards the planet.

The klaxon blared loudly inside the cabin of the Burning Desire.

The robot's head swivelled round.

"What are you doing?" it asked.

Ellie was busily ripping wires from the wall.

The robot paused.

After a couple of seconds Ellie emerged triumphantly holding two wires and held them threateningly together.

"Ellie," said the robot, in the manner of one talking to a child who has just found a gun on the kitchen table and has somehow managed to fit a silencer to it.

"If you touch those wires together, you will power surge the craft."

"And..." she said with her head cocked.

"And that will disable all the controls. It will render the whole ship useless, unable to move, there is not even a guarantee that the life support systems will remain online."

"And..."

"And you will not be able to fix it."

"And..."

"Isn't that enough?"

"And you will die."

The robot rocked slowly backwards on the chair.

"The overload will kill you. You're wired into the ship's systems. I doubt you've had time to rig a circuit-breaker yet, so, in a way, your lifeline is also your death-line."

The robot hesitated, but looked for a fraction of a second as if it were going to leap at her. This notion was dispelled as she held the wires closer together. The tension in the robot relaxed.

"I know you don't take risks," she said.

The robot turned to the console and looked out into space. A handful of communications arrays sprang into life briefly and then darkened.

"I want you to send it to this address," Ellie said, "please."

For a creation with little sense of etiquette, it was this simple word that changed the demeanour of the large ad-hoc robotic form that sat before her. The glow in its eyes softened just a touch.

Ellie spoke softly but clearly, the coordinates of the address.

"There," it said almost soothingly. "For all the good it will do, I've sent a message detailing where we are, with full-colour pictures to boot. Are you happy now?"

Ellie narrowed her eyes.

"Did you really do it?" she asked.

"I'm afraid you'll just have to take my word for that."

Ellie looked down at the two wires in her hand and back at the robot.

"You definitely did it?"

"Yes," it said, "it is sent. I don't believe there are communication jammers operating either, so the message ought to have been safely cast out into deep space. Now, are you going to threaten me all day, or would you like me to treat you as a genuine threat, and working on ways to have you removed? Those wires are not insulated you know. Two can play at that game."

Ellie looked down at the wires once more.

"Rats," she said, and placed them carefully down.

Someone was listening.

Commander Fleek had been furious with Dougan ever since word of his break-in had led to the security branch having to storm the analysis department. By his very desire to keep himself below the radar at all times, Dougan had always drawn extra attention to himself.

The Navy liked career officers and neatly ticked boxes; Fleek was the epitome of this approach. By getting himself arrested, Dougan had marred the whole department with a cavalier air and if there was one thing Engineers didn't need it was the accolade 'cavalier'. It created visions of wobbly structures and machines that would fly apart under pressure. Not to mention the ammunition it afforded to the budgeting departments.

Fleek had been determined to keep a close eye on Dougan's progress and when his craft, the Burning Desire, had mysteriously slipped through the closed security net, he had put measures in place to ensure that, if it lost so much as an antenna rod, he would find it.

Which is why the very short transmission burst from the Desire two hours ago had caused him such alarm.

With the whole Navy on stand-down, in what was generally assumed to be a cost-saving measure, Fleek had initially thought he was the victim of a galactic prank.

The message encoded with the tag-line 'there is a journalist who thought you might like to see this' was unsigned and had come from a far-off corner of the galaxy that was largely considered to be dead space. It was a little bit shocking.

Admiral Reid had been unavailable to comment, which only served to make things worse.

He was faced with a decision. He could either make public the short stream of pictures he had seen or he could keep it under his hat. It was not an easy decision for an officer of his division to make, as countless hoaxes and missed intelligence had shown.[85]

---

[85] The Navy had once gone to war with a pair of shoes on the strength of a video showing them brandished menacingly from a student apartment in the cut price habitation zones of Nebula Nine but had failed to take action against a marauding band of, admittedly pink, furry, poisonous aubergine-shaped critters who had wiped out an entire mining colony on the basis that "they looked a bit like lucky mascots with fake teeth."

The decision weighed heavily on his mind for a further hour before he was interrupted by a call from one of his communication officers.

"What?" barked Fleek.

"Sir, I think there's something you should see."

Fleek harrumphed in a way only his breed could.

"And what's that?" he enquired sneeringly.

"I think you should just switch on the news," came the reply.

In bars across the planets, servicemen had put down their pints almost in unison, never taking their eyes from the screens in front of them. In space stations, cadets stopped their zero gravity games and game-counters drifted lazily through the touch zones.

Small children in parks found themselves ignored by their parents as the large public screens showed the images from the other side of the galaxy, and members of the opposite sexes were dropped, unceremoniously to the ground as their forces-serving partners became transfixed by the screens in the dance halls.

Only in the Century Newsroom did an editor slap the back of a rather dishevelled looking Finlay, and grin a broad newsy grin at the story that was going to captivate a galaxy, with only a hint of abject terror growing in the back of his throat.

CHAPTER FIFTEEN

Harmony

Despite the portentous air of the computer mind around him, Howells had managed to pry one of the panels away from the wall of the Morning Star's projection chamber without damage.

He could feel the computer seething at his tampering, emitting warning beeps and the whirr of processors unhappy at his actions. Yet the mind could do nothing about it. His actions were unprecedented and there was no safety feature installed.

The circuits before him were a dazzling array of nanotechnological connections and it was hard to tell which would grant him access to the mainframe most easily. He consoled himself with the knowledge that it was at least his area of expertise and pushed the mouth-drying effects of his new-found sobriety to the back of his mind.

His fingers felt numb from the coldness of the circuitry as he gently manipulated the live response processors from one golden band to another, forging a path through the complex connections he had helped design.

Behind him, the results of his interference in the brightly lit projection chamber caused strange manifestations to appear. The projection of a laughing child's head loomed above him as he strayed into the test images of the designers. The universe expanded, contracted, upturned and sprouted ears as he navigated his way into the central processor. His own figure briefly appeared, watching over his shoulder, until with a final twist of a virtual knife he found himself kneeling beneath the gateway to the core program of the computer.

He tugged at the terminal control from the nearby wall. It came away easily in his hands and he carefully twisted the wires around the bare connections in the hole in the wall.

Command lists flickered above his head. He wrenched the controls backwards and forwards.

A menu hung in the air, demanding to know what theme to use. Blearily, he hit a key and the menu dissolved.

What retuned in its place was not the simple bright landscape of the mainframe program that he was expecting: the chunky green fields, and blue sky dotted with the blocky buildings of program packages, but a barren, fraught landscape with twisted purple spires and green, slow-flowing rivers carving their way through a tortured red forest of twisted trees. The appearance of small lagomorphs[86] with unfeasibly large teeth, lurking in the shadows, informed him he had accidentally chosen the display scheme entitled "Attack of the Killer Bunnies".

---

[86] At first he thought they were rodents but they're not, they're lagomorphs. It's a teeth thing.

Howells took a deep breath and sped as quickly as he could through a world of potentially deadly, purple, leporine incursion[87] on his way into the master program.

The admiralty sat in silence.

In one of the plushest rooms in the headquarters building, surrounded by some of the most expensive equipment in the galaxy, they were beginning to feel a little bit stupid.

Fortunately Reid wasn't there to voice the simple truth that it might be because they *were* all a little bit stupid.

It was unheard of for all the mobile operational units to stand down at the same time. They'd let a computer tell them to do it.

If a book of classic military blunders were ever to be published, the inclusion of this action would ensure it flew off the shelves like they were booby-trapped.

The hall echoed with the sound of shuffling feet.

On the operational display screen that dominated the room, the short excerpt of video that Ellie and the Survivor robot had provided played on an endless loop.

Two floors below, analysts were trying to get a handle on where the transmission had come from and what would be the best plan of attack. Sweaty palms moved star charts around and punched numbers into calculation machines, trying to estimate the number of ships they were looking at and came up with some very big and scary numbers.

Below that, weapons technologists were trying to figure out how the craft might be armed and if any of

---

[87] Attack by rabbits.

the current weapons systems were up to the task, with similarly distressing results.

On the next floor down catering agents were busy preparing as many greasy breakfasts, fresh juices and patent hangover medicines as they could lay their hands on.

In the vast operational hangars below, munitions workers were busy trying to get back into a routine that despite having stuck to rigidly for years, suddenly seemed that little bit more difficult, as daydream snatches of raucous nights and romantic / seedy / uncomfortably weird encounters filled their heads.

The barracks swelled with the ranks of returning officers, some revived by rest, others nursing sore heads and battling the effects of sleep depravation as they went through deeply embedded drill routines.

And on the platforms high above the planet, the fuel cells were being drained almost empty, as spaceship engineers readied the whole Imperial Navy as one, for what might promise to be the battle for their very existence.

There was no time for questions; questions like: what are we up against? Have you ever seen anything like that fleet? Is this a joke? Why are you wearing your trousers the wrong way round?

The Navy did what it did second best: follow routines.

What it did best was follow orders, but as yet there were none.

By the end of the day, every craft was operational, powered-up as much as they could be, armed, dangerous and raring to go.

They waited.

In the operations room, Reid had yet to show up. There was no sign of him. The other Admirals began to get more anxious. What, they asked, of the supercomputer, the one that would work out all their strategies for them?

There was no response from that either.

The Admirals sat and twiddled their moustaches, fiddled with the medals they had won in the good old days when wars were one–sided and simple, and chewed their nails.

From the star-dock high above, came the report that the ships were good to go. Munitions suppliers reported that they had maxed out their capacity and could produce no more until more supplies came in. As everyone knew, no supplies had arrived at the planet for a week or so.

The weapons technologists announced they believed the opposition technology was some of the most sophisticated they had seen in the galaxy, and wished them luck.

The analysts forwarded the probable co-ordinates of the source of the transmission with a footnote that it was a virtually uncharted, barren tract of space: they would be flying there virtually blind. They agreed an offensive to this location was, however, the very best chance of survival.

And the canteen checked in to say that they were closing, but had a handful of cheese sandwiches left over if anyone wanted them.

The Admirals looked nervously at one another and, in the absence of anything else to say, gave the order to deploy.

The Survivor and Ellie watched as a metallic squid-like shape loomed out of the darkness like a claw of needles. Thin sharp spikes effortlessly penetrated the very outer layer of the Burning Desire, leaving them staring at a tiny, almost organic-looking orifice at the centre of the claw. Silhouetted in the light behind it, Ellie could make out a basic, human-shaped robot operating the craft as it pulled the Desire towards the planet where, The Survivor had assured her, she would finally find what she had been looking for.

Howells was finding the task even more difficult than he'd expected. It had taken an age to work out how to evade the rabbits, which would launch themselves at his face from various ambush points around the program. He couldn't work out if they were part of the defensive capabilities of the program or simply the product of the imagination of a very twisted member of his programming team. Either way, although not dangerous, they were highly annoying.

He found himself at the edge of a forest, far from the enormous, chunky, pink towers that represented the main core, searching through the undergrowth for something.

To his left a vast ocean bubbled and fumed a luminous green. Various nasty-looking streams fed into it from the forest. He assumed these to be data dumps — trickles of useless information the computer had filtered and rejected as unimportant, flowing to the edge of the parametric landscape where, presumably, they would simply drop off, to be lost forever.

He looked down at the stream and peered closely in. Sure enough it was made of tiny packets of words and numbers, co-ordinates now rendered meaningless.

He moved quickly along the coastline, dodging the leaping shapes of the rabbits as they launched themselves into the sea, and watched with mild satisfaction as they floated out to the program precipice.

A hundred metres up the coast, he came to a clearing and there, in the middle, was exactly what he was looking for.

Bursting from the shoreline a bundle of long transparent pipes stretched out across the sea supported by not much at all, in a subtle nod to the laziness of the designers.

Howells picked up his pace. Killer bunnies were thicker on the ground here and leapt unnervingly at him as he approached the main input-output stream of the whole computer.

Inside, bright blue data gushed in from the edge of the program, to be passed on to the vast communications arrays feeding instructions to and from every corner of the galaxy.

It was tempting to simply pull the plug, to open the casing of the pipeline, maybe using one of the bunny rabbits as a chisel, but Howells knew the landscape of the program too well.

There was a safety feature in it. One he had helped design. It was a very simple feedback loop. And the safety it was to guarantee was the computer's, not his.

But as his old professor had once pointed out, a key will open a door from both sides.

The program was called a 'polite interactor'.

In order to maintain control of the Imperial craft, Morning Star would generate a simple question unit. A 'hello, how are you?' A polite message to the control computer of each and every starship. The starships would receive the message and reply equally politely 'I'm fine thank you,' which would be fed back to Morning Star. They would then engage in a very civil discussion where Morning Star would ask friendly questions about details of its whereabouts, operational status, how its subroutines were doing these days. If it was satisfied by the answers, it would issue orders. All in a fraction of a fraction of a second.

The second part of the program was the 'offended interactor.'

If Morning Star failed to ask the starships how they were doing at every second of every minute of every day, the 'offended interactor' program would immediately send the ship into a deep sulk refusing to talk to anyone until Morning Star came back on line.

Howells leaned over the pipes. Fortunately the programmers, although lazy and unimaginative, were well-trained The pipes were clearly labelled. He selected one which fed back from the Imperial craft.

He peered into the pipes. He would have to be quick.

He manipulated the controls on the terminal. The visual program began to dissolve and code began to appear in its place. Howells copied the code and placed it in a fast replicating program loop which he attached to the top of the program, feeding an identical report constantly back to Morning Star, which would, from now on, believe the craft were sitting dormant in their hangars.

He then re-routed the incoming pipe back out to sea, before any part of the program noticed them.

He was just in time. Just as he severed the program connection the report content fluctuated suddenly. Empire craft were being boarded, started up, configured for flight.

Howells looked around anxiously to see if the landscape of the program had changed.

It hadn't.

The rabbits, the tree, the tectonic plates — all calm. As far as Morning Star was concerned, nothing was going on. It kept on feeding out the 'polite interactor' message and getting polite, if rather monotonous well-wishing messages back, while all the time the truth seeped a long blue trickle into the sea of green.

The rabbits, on the other hand appeared to have done what rabbits do best and now there were over a million of them staring beady-eyed at him. Howells time was up, and in the face of a flurry of angry purple fur, he extracted himself from the program, and collapsed exhausted on the deck of the projection chamber. White gnashing teeth, faded into the bright obscurity of the room and the world reverted to as normal as it was likely to get.

The pirate fleet ploughed grandly through space. In the vanguard was the Definite Article, with Dougan and Binner at the helm. Exceptional care and attention had been lavished on the Article. It had been re-coloured, fitted with new weapons, new armour, and the flag of the Private Enterprise Conglomerate lovingly mounted on the front. A small motion unit made it flutter in the vacuum.

Behind them, the Conglomerate fleet, a rag-tag collection of around three hundred and fifty ships of various makes, models and states of repair followed on, looking something like an intergalactic carnival procession, or an advert for an intergalactic charity shop.

Taking up the rear, a handful of support vessels, cannon ships and bomb vessels they had acquired over the years, struggled to keep up.

There had been no tears on departure. No-one had appeared at the space station viewports to wave the ships away with brightly coloured handkerchiefs.

Everyone was on board.

These were pirates and no-one with a drop of pirate blood in them was going to miss out on the action, not even the kids.

Besides, there were more than enough gun turrets to go round and pirates never questioned the ethics of handing a weapon to a child, only the safety issues. Nor was there any sexual discrimination, since for many of the races involved in piracy there wasn't always a clear way to actually identify gender.

Even the barons had managed to put aside some of their differences. Bickering had been kept to a minimum, except on the thorny issue of where their ships should come in the progression. The matter was eventually settled by the time honoured and democratic process of drawing straws.[88]

As the pirates reached the edge of the system that had been their home for as long as any of them could remember[89], the sound of the tired gravity engines began to thrum within the ageing hulls. Ancillary craft clamped themselves to their larger counterparts as the fabric of space began to ripple around them.

Dougan turned to Binner

"Have we got enough energy for the gravity drop?" he hollered over the sound of rattles and the roar of the gravity buffers.

"Just about," she replied. "You okay?"

Dougan nodded in what he hoped was a reassuring way. It made his head spin.

"How about getting back?"

Binner just looked blankly at him.

---

[88] Although, being pirates at heart, the straw drawing had been immediately followed by a furious negotiation of straws in exchange for favours, deals, money, land, sons, daughters and the insistence of the removal of a gun from the small of ones back.

[89] Given the strength of pirate recreational substances, months.

"Have we got enough power to get back?"

"We'll worry about that later!" she hollered back at him.

"But what if we need to make a retreat?" Dougan was getting hoarse.

Binner cocked her head to one side.

"Pirates don't make retreats," she said.

The craft was shaking now and Dougan was feeling queasier than ever. He fought down the urge to turn himself inside out.

"Perhaps you might want to re-think that policy," he said.

"Bring it up at the next committee meeting," she replied.

The gravity wells topped out and the pirate fleet tore through the fabric of space. Dougan buried his head in his hands one more time and closed his eyes tight.

At the same time, all across the galaxy, space stations blazed with light as sloops, corvettes, frigates, destroyers, cruisers, battle cruisers, cannon ships, surface incursion vessels, modified transports, ship-to-ship missile carriers, hospital ships, supply vessels, fighter carriers and one desperately ill-informed tourist shuttle eased their way out of their hangars and into deep space.

Every ship that could be manned was in operation. Even the five Behemoths, The Radiance, the Magnificence, the Resplendence, the Brilliance and the Other One were, for the only time in history, all proudly deployed and in severe danger of crashing into each other.

There had been consternation when the security barriers on the perimeter had refused to yield to let them through, although that had been quickly solved by brute force.

From the command centre at Imperial City, the Admiralty, still puzzled by the loss of Reid, had dusted down their uniforms, brought out the old fashioned star-charts they liked to work from, and managed to piece together a plan. The fact that the plan was so simple it could be summed up in the time it would take to sharpen a thin stick, did not prevent them from having a certain swell of pride that, once again, they were going to do what they had spent their lives planning for.

Captain Beaker was noting a similar energy among the crew of the Magnificence. At last there was some purpose, an enemy, a threat that did not need to be *negotiated* with. Between the tension of nerves at the impending battle, there flowed a unifying sense of purpose they hadn't felt in a long, long time.

And there were orders. Plenty of them.

Reid awoke.

He was feeling battered, short of breath and shivering. His suit had kept him alive in the cold darkness at the bottom of the shaft and the parabolic slope of the walls had broken a fall that should have ranked somewhere between shattering and pulverising.

He looked up.

He could barely make out the ring of lights that showed him where he had fallen from. Numerous pylons jutted out from the walls and by the bruises he had acquired he was pretty sure that some of them had attempted to break his fall, albeit in a personally intrusive way.

In the circular gully where he was lying, a thin mist swirled. Vapour from the air above had almost solidified in the low pressure. His suit was covered with a thin frosty layer of white. It could have been ice but it was even more likely it was colder than that.

In the centre of the gully was a thick cylindrical column, that rose out of the floor, supporting the base of the computer, itself an enormous egg-shape.

Through the dim mistiness, blue and red lights winked eerily. Reid pulled himself to his feet. As he did he uncovered new pains. He was fairly sure he hadn't broken anything; none of the pain was sharp.

He felt a bit like he'd tried to hold open a turnstile

He made his way gingerly to the central column. The floor was smooth and slippery; he had to crouch as he walked, causing his already complaining joints to moan more.

Halfway across the floor, his suit started to make noises. He looked down at the arm control and warning lights began to flash. He was low on power. If the suit went down he would either suffocate or freeze and he would probably have a good minute or two to guess which one.

There wasn't time to worry about it.

He reached the base of the column and examined its surface. From a distance it had looked sheer, but it wasn't. Not quite. There were just enough gaps and crannies to act as handholds. What he was going to do when he reached the underside of the computer some ten metres up, he would also have to worry about later.

Reid began to climb.

Although Gretharnin was undoubtedly the most beautiful planet in the universe, one couldn't visit it even if one wanted to.

The planet was in such delicate harmony with itself that anything upsetting the balance would immediately be dislodged by a highly protective ecosystem.

The animals of Gretharnin also lived in perfect harmony with each other. There were neither predators nor prey, pecking-orders nor power struggles. An innate sense of respect for each other's space seemed to curb the urge to breed beyond the resources available. There was always space for everyone and food to go round. The animals cared for each other, and those that brought respect, gave love, and took care not to upset the balance, were welcomed.

Sadly few visitors had realised this in time. They had probably understood the rules somewhere in the core of their being, sensed that this was a planet founded purely on love and mutual respect. But sooner or later most had spotted not paradise, but opportunity.

At which point the cute little animals of the forest - notable for their soft fur and glistening bright eyes - reminded their visitors that beneath the soft fur were sharp claws. Poised in acts of pressing rare and treasured flowers into large leather-bound books, plunderers would become aware of animals suddenly more notable by their glistening-canines, barbed talons and razor-sharp horns, and curious to know where their flowers were going and, more importantly, where the leather had come from…[90]

An ancient silver battleship skimmed lightly across the atmosphere. Furry, three headed beasts looked up from grazing as a bright streak crossed the perfect azure sky.

"She will put up a fight," said the Money robot.

[90] Think Disney meets the Texas Chainsaw Massacre

"We didn't" said Glory.

"We do not have as much to lose," said Money.

"Speak for yourself," said Glory. "What good is glory if there is no one around to lavish it on you?"

"What good is money if there's nothing to spend it on?" came the reply. "She will not leave what she has created."

"She will," said the Knowledge robot. "She will leave."

"How do you know?" said Money.

The Knowledge robot simply returned a look.

"Forget I asked," said Money.

The craft swooped low over the landscape causing a herd of wild beasts to chase it, not out of fear, but because sometimes things dropped out of the back of spaceships and they were always interesting. Or edible.

Bird-like creatures swirled in the air around the craft, ducking out of its way just in time. The landscape rolled beneath them, green and pleasant. Great forests of giant flowers clawed to the sky and the air was so thick with their heavy scent it almost formed a mist.

In the distance, a snow-capped mountain range approached, the tops glistening as they rose up from the misty valleys below.

The silver craft swerved through canyons and gullies, passed easily through impossibly narrow crevices and soared up vertical cliff faces as it made its way to the top of the very highest peak.

"You're just showing off now," said Glory.

Knowledge did not reply.

At the top of the tallest peak, the craft set down on a ridiculously small flat square of rock with fractions of centimetres to spare on each side.

The ramp extended vertically down, rungs extended, and the three robots clambered out into the surface of the perfect world.

They gazed at its beauty.

At length a metallic head emerged over the edge of one of the cliffs. It was identical to the others, but where one was black, one green, one purple, this was white. It rose onto the rock and stood before them.

"Welcome," it said at length in soft tones.

"You will come with us," said the Traveller. The others could not tell if it was a command or a question. The Harmony robot saw it was both.

"There seems little point in arguing," it said, and began to climb up the ramp to the ship.

"Are you not worried about leaving this behind?" asked the Financier

The robot turned. "Worried? No, this planet can look after itself better than I can, and I will love it always," and it trotted happily up the ramp.

The other robots followed suit. Only Knowledge lingered behind to take a long look at the most perfect place in the galaxy and, with a hint of sadness, followed them.

CHAPTER SIXTEEN

Reid

The red robot was distracted.

It had been watching the arrival and apprehension of the Survival robot and its companion, but something else had caught its eye.

There were ships moving through the galaxy.

Not the robot's ships, other ships.

But they were all its ships now. Weren't they?

What was Morning Star doing?

It moved to the command centre and surveyed the charts. According to Morning Star, the Imperial craft were all quietly tucked away and yet there they were, a veritable throng of them.

It sat down at the console, and issued commands to its own craft, through Morning Star. It ordered a formation of its razor frigates.

Morning Star obliged. The craft swiftly moved into an eight pointed star.

The robot picked a small craft at random. A sloop — a small service craft. It ordered the sloop to turn sharp left.

On its screen a tiny dot veered off course before righting itself and returning to the pack of approaching warrior vessels.

According to Morning Star the sloop was still sitting in a hanger at Retrillo. Something very serious was up. The robot's eyes flared red as power surged like adrenalin.

They knew.

It *would* have a fight on his hands.

It would have an unfair advantage for sure. Although Morning Star wouldn't be able to tell what the Imperial craft were doing she'd still be able to issue commands. Meaningless commands that would destroy any attempts to control the craft.

The robot sat back.

The fight wouldn't last long. They were just accelerating the execution of its plan.

Commanders watched as a sloop suddenly tore itself from the rank and waved erratically around before rejoining the group.

"What the hell was all that about?" barked Commodore Fleek at the sloop's Captain.

"Uh, nothing sir," came the response quickly, although the Captain's voice belied the fact that he was shaken. Fleek could almost see them mouthing to each other and shrugging shoulders in the background.

"Well, no funny business. We're approximately twenty minutes from the engagement zone so look lively."

The Captain answered with a quick "aye-aye" and gripped the seat of his command chair.

They were looking lively. Just not in the right direction.

The pirate fleet arrived first and instantly regretted it.

To say the odds were overwhelming was an understatement of almost comic proportions.

The robot fleet hung in tortuous formations along the axis of the blue planet they were protecting. The light of the dim, distant sun shone in the background, causing a dazzling effect as light bounced of the eye-wateringly sharp edges of the craft.

The craft appeared of a kind, but Dougan could make out subtle differences between their functions. Mostly those functions seemed to be simply to hurt.

It was a bit like staring at the collection of instruments lined up beside your operating table, knowing that at some point every one of them was going to be used on you.

In contrast, the pirate ships looked rather more like a discarded canvas tool-bag dumped at the side of a motorway.

It wasn't really a fair fight. But it was the only one on offer.

Dougan looked out over the rank, file and depth of the craft. A numb feeling came over him.

He had never been in a battle before. He had never entered into something that might knowingly result in his own death.

He looked around. No one else seemed to look like they were thinking that way. They all had jobs to do, were all concentrating really hard. There wasn't time to think about the why, or the how, or the if. You had a job, and you did it. Until you couldn't do it any more or it was over.

He wished he had a job.

His job *was* over, and that was to get them there. He needed another.

"I need another job," he said to Binner who missed the subtleties of this statement on account of the fact that she couldn't read minds.

"It's too late for that," she said. "If you wish you'd been a salesman, or an account executive it's too late. You're a spaceman now get on with it."

"No, I mean I need something to do now." His voice was shaking slightly.

Binner looked confused. There was a lot about to happen. Was Dougan about to crack? He looked desperate.

The reassuringly large hand of Jirbaks gripped his arm and broke the deadlock between Binner and Dougan.

"Spot for me," she said reassuringly.

Dougan willingly obliged.

Binner watched Dougan go. He seemed satisfied, or at least not as manic as he had appeared moments ago. She turned back to her console. There wasn't time to think, and, for a brief second, she was grateful.

"Here," said Jirbaks, "watch the screen and tell me which way to point the cannon. When I'm looking down the sights I can't see where the others are." There was a patience in her voice.

Dougan sat and stared at the screen filled with red dots in a thick red line in front of him. "I think if you keep pointing straight ahead you're bound to hit something," he said.

"There you go," said Jirbaks jovially, "you're a natural at this."

Even Baron Frisk was a little nervous, although he managed not to show it. He displayed excellent control of his sweat glands, his heart rate remained alert and steady and his eyes were clear and focused. It was the best way to enter battle. Certainly a rousing speech will get you the edge in the first couple of minutes, but it's hard to give orders over the noise of people emitting extended war cries. Without communication what's the point in having a leader. It just becomes a free-for-all and when you're up against robots who are smarter than you, that's not what you need, You must become clinical and exact, like them. So went his thoughts.

He crossed his fingers and hoped silently, without visible emotion that he was right.

Reid's fingers were numb from climbing. He had reached the underside of the computer. There was nowhere left to climb.

He rested his foot on a parapet that jutted out from the column and allowed his arms a little respite from their job keeping him from plummeting back to the base of the chamber.

Some way to his right, a handle jutted from the ceiling and he stretched an arm out to reach it, unsure what would happen if he did. The warnings were coming more frequently now and he was aware that if he were to do anything meaningful it would have to be now.

His fingers scrabbled for purchase on the handle and he had to lean uncomfortably out to hold it. Pressing as much of his weight against the wall as he could, he tugged.

The handle refused to budge but slipped from his grip. He almost fell.

His legs were screaming at him, unable to hold the strain of his weight much longer. He leaned out again.

This time the handle responded, the door swung lazily away from him flooding his tiny platform with a warm reddish-purple light.

Reid used the last of his strength to pull himself through the gap into the tiny cavity above.

What he found there was something of a surprise.

CHAPTER SEVENTEEN

War

The two opposing forces faced each other across the narrow gulf of space.

"Why aren't they attacking us?" Dougan called out to Binner. He was beginning to wonder if it was too late to just run away.

"They're probably waiting for us to make the first move," said Binner. "It's an ancient battle tactic. First to move, shows their hand. It tells your enemy your plan, gives her an advantage."

"I see," said Dougan. "And how do we combat that?"

"I don't know," said Binner. "Pirates ambush. We don't normally attack when our enemies know we're there."

"Okay," said Dougan, "we'll wait until they're all looking the other way then shall we? Suits me."

Baron Trevellian was also edgy. He *was* giving what he hoped was a rousing speech. Somehow it didn't seem to be having the desired effect. He was beginning to wonder whether adapting the opening verses from

THE COLOUR OF ROBOTS

Huurdreeen the Voluble's epic war poem "I'm going and that's it" was hitting the right tone:

"I shall go to war, and no sarcastic comments of yours will stop me.

I shall go to war, even though you pull that face, which you know annoys me.

I shall go to war despite your feeble attempts to hide my sword, and my battle axe and the leather bit that stops the chafing.

I shall go to war.

"I shall go to war, as there are some things worth fighting for.

Like the right to die before someone forces you to in a manner of their choosing, which might be extended or painful, you never know.

I shall go to war because if I don't, if I choose not to defend everything we have built here, everything that we have made ours, have purged the bad, and the wrong from, with every fibre of our being, you'll still moan at me just the same.

Won't you?

The Baron looked at the sea of sympathetic, but hardly blood-thirsty faces, and tried something completely different.

"Er look," he said, "there is an ancient enemy out there, one who stands for all that is evil and corrupt in the galaxy. One that seeks to dominate the galaxy, to take it away from us, not in the same way that we tried to dominate the galaxy and take it away from others you understand, but in a deeply *nasty* way, with bad - rather than good-intentions at heart. So we are definitely doing the right thing.

"And though they may be great in number, and we may have only rank and file, whereas they have rank, and file, and considerable depth too, do not be perturbed. We are not robots, we are sentient beings and we can adapt and change and respond to the unknown in a way that they can't, so....just..."

A hand went up at the back of the hall.

"Er, yes?" said the Baron.

"Is this going to take long your lordship?" said a small man attached to the bottom of the hand.

"Erm.."

"It's just some of us have got a fight to go to."

And around that time, it pretty much kicked off.

"Oh crap," said Binner professionally.

The robot fleet exploded like shrapnel in slow motion, expanding into a sphere several times its previous volume, and threatening to engulf the entire pirate fleet.

The pirates, galvanised into action, began to open fire. Volleys of missiles raced across the gulf between the two forces, their paths confused by the robots' low-density distribution. Pinprick laser bolts picked off the missiles one by one, only a handful finding their mark.

The void filled with the red, green, yellow, blue and purple flashes of laser fire. Explosions rocked the ranks of the pirate ships, as they manoeuvred slowly to face the enveloping threat.

Waves of fighters surged from the bellies of the carrier ships and swarmed round the jagged forms of enemy cruisers, then exploded in tiny puffs as the destructive forces of energy shields expanded to envelop them.

The pirate capital ships surged headlong into the fray.

On the deck of the Definite Article, Dougan shouted instructions at Jirbaks who was laying waste to enemy fighters with stunning accuracy. Her jaw was locked in grim determination and deep concentration as she tracked, aimed and fired on the small wasp-like interceptors that were filling the space like water pouring into rock-pools at high tide.

Large cruisers erupted with lasers blazing from every available port which was met with instant retaliation from the corvettes of the robot fleet.

The pirates were soon fighting battles on all sides. The larger, mace-like enemy cruisers emerged from the fray, bristling with dangerous looking cannon.

On the right flank, Frisk's sleek, black destroyers were making good headway against the missile cruisers that had drifted left of the attacking force, diminishing scores of potentially deadly warheads that had begun to pound the larger capital ships, which were themselves retreating to the heart of the defensive sphere they had been forced to adopt. The robot ships seemed innumerable.

Defensive shields fizzled, crackled and buckled under the strain.

The first capital ship to fall was one of Baron Millieu's bulky carrier-ships. A critical hit to its generators triggered a feed-back explosion. It disintegrated quickly, brief red bursts of flame rippling across the shattered hull. Fire erupted and was instantly quashed by the cold, oxygen-less atmosphere of space.

"Pull together" cried Binner, steering the Definite Article between two warring battle cruisers, weaving deftly between deadly bolts of fire.

The pirate ships, now immersed in a sea of enemy craft were beginning to break rank. Some tore away from the main fleet in pursuit of a small group of frigates, but rapidly found themselves isolated from the dwindling core of the fleet.

Space grew thick with the hazy mist of ionised particles. In between directing Jirbaks from target to target, the hair on the back of Dougan's neck stood on end as he heard cries from other ships cut abruptly short.

It was becoming very clear to all that they were losing badly.

"Get us out of here!" he shouted to Binner.

"Too late," she replied watching a pirate cannon ship disintegrate on the viewport. Another swarm of the waspish robot fighters burst through the cloud heading straight for them.

Hurbury pulled the craft hard upwards, and a brief cheer erupted on deck as the fighters slammed into Millieu's titanic Gothic Avenger behind them.

Millieu's shield generators emitted a burst of energy and the fighters, lodged by their sharp ends in its hull, fizzled like flies in a frying pan.

A handful of the less warlike merchant pirate fleet lost their bottle. Escape pods jettisoned in tiny bursts of yellow only to be slashed to ribbons as they tried to squeeze past the razor sharp protrusions of the robot frigates.

"Dammit," cried Binner into the communicator, the faint voice of Baroness Quinnan on the other end. "Tell your craft to stay together"

Quinnan's reply was indistinct and cut short. The crew of the Article watched as the Command Cruiser was cleaved in two by a sustained burst of fire from one of the robot mace-shaped cruisers.

Captains of the cannon ship were also beginning to panic and fire blindly causing as much damage to their own ships as they were to the dispersed waves of robot flotilla.

Dougan's concentration broke, Jirbaks didn't need him any more. She was in a distant place, where all around her fighters were exploding and when more appeared to fill their place, she was ready, almost needy.

But Dougan could see that the power from the energy generators could only keep going for so long and was burning far quicker than it could be created. He watched the battery display dwindling with each pull of the trigger.

He looked around the bridge. All around him heads were buried in the intricacy of their operational tasks. Each and every face set with a determined look of concentration, dividing up the melee before them into tiny, second-by-second projects.

Only by looking at the viewscreen could Dougan see that this was why the robots were going to win. Their proficiency at multitasking was exactly why necessity had called for their invention. The humans were about to die at the hands of the very monster they had created.

For a moment he stood there, aware that this was probably the end for him and the brave men and women around him. A feeling of incredible sadness came over him, knowing that all the thought, the human energy that they had assembled, this loose collection of idealists was going to be lost forever and, like history before might be glossed over and summed up in a sentence that might never even be read.

In a universe where fate had anything to say at all, this would have been the perfect, the only, time for the cavalry to arrive.

But Dougan knew that these renegades, who had lived their lives battling against an unwieldy and oppressive system that had no place for them, did not believe in fate. There was just their will, and their belief.

Consequently he was more deeply relieved than he would ever be able to describe, when three seconds later, the cavalry, apologetically late, did in fact, arrive.[91]

Reid stared at what was possibly the most beautiful piece of engineering he had ever seen.

The underbelly of Morning Star looked like it had been put together in haste. Power tubes and wires were strewn all over the place and pieces of power-generating equipment, stabilisers, coolant panels and circuit boards looked like they hadn't been so much arranged as swept to one side to create enough room to squeeze a few more in. It wasn't the design that had amazed him, it was the idea behind it.

He quickly located one of the looser power boards, plugged an umbilical from the suit in and slumped in a heap to the floor. As it sucked in life-saving energy, the suit warmed, heating damaged muscle areas and flooding freshly generated oxygen back to his lungs.

When Reid felt he was ready to tackle the universe again, he raised his head and gave what he thought he had seen, a closer look.

The centre of the room was dominated by an upturned rocket-shaped cylinder which disappeared

---

[91] Cavalry, is of course a metaphor. Space is no place for horses.

through the ceiling, wide enough to press all its ancillary equipment to the edges of the chamber. At the base it tapered to a small spherical transparent chamber, which hung about a metre above the floor and from the edges of a sphere, supports connected it to the ground.

The air around the cylinder seemed to glow with a faint bluish-purple light, and even from where he was slumped he could tell he was in the presence of a strong gravitational field, which was somehow being buffered to prevent the whole structure collapsing in on itself.

He leaned in to look closer.

The whole set-up looked like a gravity generator. The type that would flip entire ships from one side of the galaxy to another by rending open the very fabric of space-time.

Only much, much smaller.

That was of course, impossible.

The technology simply hadn't been invented to create such a device. It would cost too much to make, and would most likely be desperately unsafe.

Inside the sphere, the bluish-purple field disappeared into an impossibly dense blackness in the centre. Looking at it hurt his eyes. It was like looking into a dangerously bright light only the opposite way round. His pupils dilated painfully wide trying to suck some light from the hole.

It took him a long time to work out that the thick yellow cable that looked like it was running *behind* the hole was actually running directly from it. His eyes and brain categorically refused to agree with each other. There was no way of looking at the length of cable to reconcile the idea that it was entering the hole because human brains simply don't deal with looking at objects in four spacial dimensions very well.

The cable emerged from the hole and plugged very neatly into the base of the cylinder above.

Reid realised that the cable had to go somewhere and that it was entirely possible that what he was looking at was the smallest wormhole in the universe.

He was stunned.

It was brilliant.

Imperial headquarters controlled the movement of all Imperial ships throughout the galaxy. It was neat; it was controlled; the communications network couldn't be hacked. Therefore when Morning Star took over and locked them out, they were at her mercy. And something was plugged into Morning Star.

He looked up at the cylinder, at the ceiling at the array of panels behind him. This wasn't all computer power. Morning Star could have still worked if she were a third of the size she was. This was generator power.

Morning Star was a huge generator, generating the smallest wormhole in the universe as a back door for someone who wanted to hack straight into the system. They, the Admiralty would willingly hand control over to it. If they never knew they were being hacked into, why would they try and stop it?

He shuddered to think what might be on the other end of the cable.

The entire Imperial fleet sat, vast and mighty, opposing the robot's small but numerous army. Bizarrely, craft from the Imperial side would occasionally veer oddly off-course and crash into each other but Captains ignored them. They had other things to worry about.

At the rear of the vast array of ships, the Admiralty sat in a small, but unnecessarily plush, craft with a large table-shaped viewscreen beneath them. They were attended by no shortage of uniformed officers who were desperately glad that, when they'd joined the navy, they'd been persuaded to go into the catering and hospitality division.

The Admirals drank heavily. One had insisted it would aid their concentration. The others had barely argued.

After a voluble and intense discussion it was decided that wine would be the best choice to help them focus in the long term. It was also agreed bottles of brandy should, however, never be so far away to be actually out of sight.

"So, we decided to go with the full frontal assault then did we Edgar?" asked Admiral Drax, the words struggling to escape the hampering presence of an elaborately large moustache.

Edgar sipped his wine thoughtfully. Excellent vintage, was the thought.

"Yes, I think that would seem to be right, no point in being subtle is there?"

"I was sort of hoping for a flanking manoeuvre..." added the gaunt Benedict Tyria, Rear Admiral in charge of the Fleet fleet.[92]

"Oh no," said Drax, "these robots won't buy any of that nonsense. Just throw everything we've got at them, it'll work out. It always does!" he declared,

---

[92] Renowned for their ability to squeeze extra power from their craft and enter battle faster, if not more effectively than anyone else. Their common tactic was to appear to accidentally over-run the battle altogether and then attack from the rear. It was almost a shock tactic that surprised many a massed force not by its show of force, but by its apparent show of incompetence.

nobly quaffing from a large glass and thus was the benefit of years of wisdom at the helm of one of the greatest fighting forces the galaxy had ever seen, distilled to a single command.

Dougan and Binner joined the throng of Pirate craft retreating from the front of the battle. They were well aware that their brave stand had been a mere precursor to the battle that lay ahead.

The robot army had retreated and regrouped to deal with the new threat that had appeared on their horizon. The Empire would present a more sophisticated opponent. And one with more guns. And training.

Dougan watched the pristine-white forms of the robot vessels clump into a malicious swarm. The Definite Article crept behind the front line of the Imperial Navy.

Under other circumstances, the pirates would have been shot down immediately on coming so close to Imperial vessels. On this occasion a silent, tacit understanding seemed to have been reached. Like war dogs slinking back to their masters with nothing more than tails[93] between their legs, the pirate vessels took up positions amongst their stronger brothers.

Dougan watched the robot navy with uncertainty. It was hard not to when Jirbaks was still taking potshots at any craft that came within firing range of them.

Something odd was happening but he couldn't work out what.

He ran to a scanner.

Binner had sensed something was odd, too, and abandoned her command seat to join him.

---

[93] and the occasional jester's hat.

"Are they doing what I think they're doing?" asked Dougan after a couple of minutes.

"Yes. If what you think they're doing, is what I think they're doing."

They watched a minute or so longer. What the robots appeared to be doing was attaching themselves to each other, congealing like iron filings round a magnet. Suddenly craft that had hung back in the previous battle had begun to join part of the growing matrix of ships as they twisted and turned and slotted into each other like a fiendishly elaborate children's toy.

From the mass of small swirling craft, larger, even more menacing shapes seemed to emerge until the Imperial Navy suddenly found themselves facing a force of ships that matched them in size. The whole being, as always, much greater than the sum of its parts.

"They were ready for this fight weren't they?" Dougan said to Binner.

Binner didn't reply.

Across the gulf of space, for the second time, two massive navies eyed each other up. There was little else for either side to do except charge.

And so they did.

The fleets roared towards each other. On every deck of every ship, Imperial and robot, processors whirred, passing information backwards and forwards, each calculating the distance to the nearest enemy and neighbour, a plan, a back-up plan, an optimal firing range, a shield strength projection, an expected survival time.

These are things that a computer can calculate and optimise.

Tell a human that an expected four and half minute survival time is better than a three minute one and they'll start asking what the odds of escape are. A computer merely views four minutes as better than three. It has no concept of its own destruction.

Unless of course you introduce another set of criteria. A whole different set of rules to consider.

This was where the Survivor found itself. In the holding bay of one of the hangars on the blue gas giant, with a meek, quiet and cold Ellie by its side, it waited. It knew it was in the safest place to be.

Morning Star was getting on with what it knew best, the process of creating a successful battle plan.

It did not notice that the craft it was fighting against were very similar to the ones it had been commanding just weeks before. It noticed they were using old Imperial tactics[94] but that was part of its programmed algorithms and it would have no problems dispatching them forthwith.

But it was also receiving instructions from its most important channel. Its command channel. New criteria for the battle flooded in, orders to awake the dormant Imperial fleet that it had left scattered across the galaxy.

It was not its position to complain or question. It engaged the dormant fleet. Orders to move out were sent. And yet they remained in place.

Morning star was confused.

The Imperial cruisers, screaming towards the enemy robot fleet suddenly juddered, receiving instructions to power up and slowly ease out of hangers they weren't in.

---

[94] Throwing everything at it.

It was too much for the guidance systems of some craft and they lurched, flipping end-over-end across the path of much bigger craft, to be splattered across their bows.

The anomaly was watched with consternation by the Admirals.

"Carry on," muttered Drax almost to no-one in particular.

The dive continued. More conflicting reports filled the banks of the computers. Random test manoeuvres lodged deep in the archaic brains of the capital ships sent them lurching into clumsy three point turns as the enemy robot ships bore down on them.

Morning Star ran a variety of test commands through the ships, going back to first principles, as Great Behemoths pirouetted and wheeled their way across each others' flight paths. Morning Star, was still convinced they were not responding in any way, while watching dangerously unorthodox tactics from her new enemy on the front line. It was all very, very confusing.

The robot army picked up pace. An unpredictable army was best eradicated quickly and as violently as possible. Cruisers shuddered and bumped into each other and cartwheeled and spun and generally behaved like an Imperial firework display. The robot army closed on them, a vicious volley bringing a knife-like rain of death.

Howells watched as Morning star struggled to fight against a force she was, against her knowledge, controlling.

His throat was dry. This was his doing.

She would smash the craft to pieces against themselves and then finish them off. It would be the undoing of everything.

He wished he still had some alcohol left. He didn't want to see the end of the universe sober.

"What's going on?" cried Binner, struggling to keep the Definite Article free of the ships crashing around her. It was a little like riding a jet ski between tankers whose captains were under the misguided impression that they were driving dodgems.

"I don't know," said Dougan, who honestly hadn't the slightest idea.

All he knew was that the robot navy, new improved and considerably more deadly than before, was seconds away. He closed his eyes.

That just made him feel sick so he opened them again. He guessed he'd have to face whatever happened next.

What happened next was this:

Nothing.

Everything stopped.

Dead in it's tracks. Which, when you consider that in deep space there is lots of inertia and little friction, was unusual. But that's what happened.

Somehow, every one of the three thousand, seven hundred and sixty-two battle craft of the Imperial Navy and the robot fleet drew to a complete and utter standstill.

Only Binner and Dougan in the Definite article and a handful of the remaining pirate craft seemed to drift through the space between the stationary monsters, wondering if maybe they had died, and that any minute someone with wings and a nice smile, would pop up with some kind words and sympathy.

The craft hung in space, silent and quiet.

Admiral Reid stood holding the end of the yellow cable in one hand and concluded that pulling it out of its socket appeared to have done no good whatsoever. Maybe if he had a better concept of fourth degree engineering, he would have had a deeper understanding of the effect of his actions. As it was, it all seemed remarkably disappointing.

He laid it down on the ground and began looking for something that was going to have a more immediate and satisfying effect. Like a switch.

Dougan surveyed the scene in front of him. It was the sort of vision a war painter would kill to get.[95] It was as if the whole battle had been put on pause.

On the port side of the screen, Dougan could see the makings of a horrendous collision between two of the Imperial Behemoths miraculously averted. They had stopped just miles from each other, noses aimed at a point in space they had both been heading for, but that only one of them would have been able to occupy.

Fighters filled the gaps between the ships like a frozen mist. Robot ships seemed to be held like knives across the throats of cruisers. Battleships with their

---

[95] A sad fact about war painters is that painting takes time and battles don't. It also explains why many war paintings contain more dead or dying than actual combatants: it's easier to paint them than men with swords. This is often misconstrued as a poignant comment on the brutality of war rather than the self preservationism of artists.

missile ports open, seemed choked by their own weaponry. Energy shields dissipated across the void.

It was somewhat eerie.

The surprise had rendered the crew of the Definite Article immobile too. They stood, or sat at their command posts uncertain what was going to happen next and if it might be their fault if it did.

"What happened?" asked Binner.

Dougan stammered.

"Complete simultaneous power failure in all the crafts on both sides except the pirate vessels as a result of..."

"Of...?" prompted Hurbury.

"...something," finished Dougan lamely. He wasn't enjoying his role as 'Chief Explainer of Anything Odd That Happens'. But it was better than his former role as chief *causer* of everything odd that happened.

Fortunately the attention was directed away from him by something very odd happening out in space.

In the distance, movement caught Dougan's eye.

A small silver craft, dwarfed by the giants around it, weaved its way through the silent scene, snaking towards the Definite Article. It filled the screen, coming to a halt directly in front of the pirate vessel.

In the background, Dougan could hear the creak of Jirbaks' fingers tightening round the trigger.

"Captain."

The voice of Greeta cut through the silence and everyone turned to Greeta who, not relishing the attention, pushed her glasses up her nose in an embarrassed fashion.

"There's a message."

The viewport blinked uncertainly. After a couple of seconds static a tableau from the inside of the silver space craft filled the screen.

Dougan felt a knot in his stomach so tight it was as if his intestines were trying to kidnap his tongue.

On the screen, perfectly positioned in frame so that the entire crew could make out each one of them, were four robots.

They were robots from the fairy tale, from the old drawings in books of what children of their generation had thought intelligent robots would look like. Looking at their grille-mouthed faces and triangular eyes, the crew felt a strange mixture of fear and nostalgia.

Dougan instantly recognised the triangle and circle markings of the robots he had met before, had seen grainy pictures of, and had been desperately hoping to avoid ever since. Yet he was curious.

The one with the black markings and the dreadlocked head stood in the foreground. Behind, stood the others, each with their own markings, green, white and purple.

Dougan couldn't help noticing that the purple one looked a little bit like it was posing for maximum effect.

He could feel Binner looking at him, expecting him to explain what would happen next.

The robot spoke.

Its voice was calm but authoritative. The kind of voice you would obey, not because of rules and regulations, but because they truly sound like they know what they're talking about.

"You are Karl Dougan, Lieutenant Engineer second class Planetary Engineering," it said.

Dougan nodded. They must have had pretty good eyesight to read his badge from there.

"You have been studying us."

Dougan looked around in what he hoped was a non-committal way.

"You and the girl."

Dougan snapped back to attention with the sinking feeling that Ellie was about to presented on screen in the early stages of some hideous torture and he was going to be forced to make some horrible choice.

"You are wondering where she is."

Dougan nodded, almost afraid to look at the screen. He was only mildly better at making decisions than he was at watching torture.

"You would like to see her again."

The tension was unbearable. He snapped.

"Look, as soon as you want me to join in this conversation we're having, you let me know."

There was a slight intake of breath from the rest of the crew. The robot looked taken aback. Only slightly. Its head cocked to one side as it processed this unexpected outburst.

"You will come with us," said the robot finally.

It turned dramatically and the other robots receded into the background as the screen began to fade.

"Sorry, sorry…" interjected Dougan.

The robot stopped and turned back to the screen which brightened again.

"Yes?"

"Just me? Or can I bring some friends?" he asked.

"You may bring what friends you have," said the robot and turned dramatically one more time.

The screen began to darken.

"Sorry, sorry, um…" said Dougan.

The robot turned back to the screen which hummed back into life.

"Yes?" There was a slightly dangerous edge to the robot's voice.

"How many? Is there a limit?" he asked

The robot stared at him.

Dougan's voice was smaller: "Should I ... do I need to bring anything?"

There was menace in the robot's voice now: "*Bring yourselves. You will not need anything else!*"

It turned in a dramatic fashion and the screen dimmed once more.

"And do you want us to dock and come over to you, or shall we follow you in this craft or...?"

The robot stopped. It looked like it clenched its jaw then —

The screen went dark. The crew looked around as the Definite Article shuddered from a hasty dock with the silver craft. The sound of metal straining snaked through the hull of the ship. Large metal feet clanked on the hard floors, echoing through the corridors getting closer and closer until, eventually, the door to the bridge burst open.

Everyone watched wide-eyed as the tall figure of the dreadlocked robot, strode towards Dougan, lifted him by the scruff of the neck and carried him back the way it had come.

It was a few seconds later that Binner, Jirbaks, and Hurbury with a roll of the eyes and a sigh, followed Dougan and the robot back to the silver ship.

Greeta, who had missed most of this, looked up from the motion scanners. It suddenly dawned quite horribly on her that she was the next in line to take command.

She slipped gently into the command chair under the gaze of the assembled, slightly puzzled crew and, ten seconds later, mentally chided herself for letting her first command be: "Okay peeps. Just do exactly what you were doing before. We'll see how that goes."

On the screen ahead the silver craft became a bright streak against the black universe as it headed for the blue gas giant.

Howells was about the only person in the universe who understood.

And there was nothing he could do about it.

In the absence of some piece of input, Morning Star had stopped sending out polite interactors. The ships' onboard offended interactors had kicked in. They were all in a massive sulk.

As if to confirm his suspicions, a message reading "No input signal" kept flashing before his eyes.

Howells could only assume that his meddling in the program had had fatal repercussions.

He wasn't about to find out how fatal, until the display screen announced that, due to unforeseen circumstances it was going to shut down.

A small clock appeared in the corner of the display indicating in no uncertain terms that the shutdown would commence in just under one hour.

And counting.

At the other end of the smallest wormhole in existence, the robot stood, billions of trillions of miles from Reid and yet far enough away to reach out and grab him across the depths of time and space.

It pulled at the cable which slithered through the gap and hung limply in his hand.

The fleet was no longer in his control.

It wouldn't matter. There were other more pressing arrangements. Morning Star would tidy up everything herself shortly. There were procedures for when things went awry and it was in no doubt they would be followed. That was what having power meant.

The plan was not proceeding as it had anticipated. But it wasn't going to matter one bit.

CHAPTER EIGHTEEN
Operation

Ellie and the Survivor had undergone more than their fair share of ushering since the escort craft had picked them up.

They had been ushered into a holding bay, ushered into cells, ushered out of cells, Ellie had been ushered to a food dispenser of Imperial make and model, which had served her out-of-date soup which she had refused to eat. In a robot world things like best-before dates had little meaning. She had been ushered to a suite of rooms that might, at one time, have housed contractors building the mining station. If it had, they must have been considerably shorter than her, since all the shelves, beds and doorways were at unpleasant heights. Just walking across a room was a treacherous pursuit.

The colour scheme had also been a curious mix of gunmetal grey and orange, presumably to make the contractors feel at home in their orange work jackets.

She had to hug her suit tight to herself. Everything was cold. There were no windows in the station, only the constant thrum of the turbines turning in the harsh methane winds outside, causing a creaking sound that echoed eerily through the corridors she had been ushered along.

The Survivor had itself been ushered off in another direction shortly after they had left the holding bay. It had touched her gently on the arm and assured her everything would be different soon.

It was the kind of ambiguous statement that made her want to throw things at other things until one or both of them broke.

The drones that had met them, and done most of the ushering, were sleek, smooth and functional. Like the automata of the Imperial forces, they had all traces of humanness removed. Each had a job and it was clear that tottering around on two legs making constant adjustments for a varying centre of gravity was not a priority of their design.

She threw her back against the wall behind her and slid down onto an unfeasibly small bunk with the unpleasant feeling that something awesomely major was going on and she was missing it.

She really wasn't sure whether this was a good or bad thing.

From the outside, the mining station looked like a giant screw floating in the dense grey-blue methane clouds of the unnamed planet. From the base of the structure a huge umbilical cord descended deep into the dark depths, anchoring it to the core. Attached to the side a multitude of turbine generators of all shapes and sizes harvested the power of the wind swirling past the station.

Operation

The cord bobbed and swayed, funnelling energy up the central core.

The top of the station was flat, and decked with turrets and towers making it look as if a circular section of a grey city had been cut out and dropped on the head of the station.

It was towards this collection of buildings that the silver craft now flew, followed as it approached by defensive turrets. They swivelled, beady green monitors tracking them, ready to disintegrate them if they stepped out of line.

Inside the craft, Dougan, Binner, Jirbaks, and Hurbury sat huddled against the rear wall of the silver spacecraft's command bay. The four robots, with their backs to them, watched the approach to the mining station carefully and quietly.

There had been little attempt at conversation. Introductions had not seemed necessary. The green Money robot had said nothing, the white Harmony robot had asked them if they wanted some coffee or something and then had been profusely apologetic when it transpired they didn't have any on board, and the purple Glory robot had been busy polishing his casing until it gleamed.

As they made the final approach, weaving through the towers and gantries on the upper deck of the station towards a yellow landing bay, the black knowledge robot turned to Dougan.

"You do understand where we're going don't you?"

"I think so," said Dougan, "There were seven of you, I watched two of you get killed, there are four of you here, and I can only imagine we're going to see the remaining one who is the cause of all this trouble."

"Only one of us was destroyed," said Knowledge, "you saved the other."

311

THE COLOUR OF ROBOTS

"No, I didn't," said Dougan, "what makes you think that?"

Knowledge hesitated.

"You helped him escape in your craft, the Burning Desire."

"No, no." Dougan cast his mind back, "No I think I'd have remembered if I saved one of you."

The robots exchanged looks.

"But you came looking for us. You were researching us," said Harmony. "When the humans found out, they sent you to prison. You persuaded the pirates to bring you here, knowing that the Imperials would follow and be destroyed by their own creation, Morning Star."

"What's Morning Star?"

"The computer that the Imperials let control their fleets, that Power was controlling, to bring them here to witness his triumph. We thought you knew about this," said Money.

There was a faint hint of menace in the voice.

"Oh, *that Morning Star*," said Dougan, the hairs on the back of his neck prickling slightly.

Glory rounded on him, "You are on our side aren't you?"

Suddenly Dougan was back on firm ground. He nodded vigorously. "Oh yes, definitely, I am completely on your side."

Dougan examined his fingernails while Binner tried to bore a hole in his head using only her eyes.

The craft touched down in the central landing bay. The landing ramp extended to the floor. Small service drones rushed to attend the craft while the robots clanked down the ramp followed by the humans and half-humans. The skies above were a deep, dark blue, like a bruise, and storm clouds raced angrily across them. Even from the sunken bay, Dougan could feel the winds tugging them.

They descended in a small lift, which led through an almost endless series of antechambers, to a large circular hallway.

The hall was tall and elegant, twisted metal archways soared overhead and bluish mist snaked through the supporting pillars. The walls were dark, almost black-grey, finely corrugated from base to ceiling. The floor was a deep crimson, smooth and cold. Light came from bright spotlights high above, abseiling gracefully through the mist to form bright pools on the ground.

The centre of the far end of the room was dominated by a giant throne-like structure that surrounded its central chair like a broken egg laid by a twisted metal bird.

It was, in all respects, rather ostentatious: clearly designed to make anyone in the room feel small. Dougan obliged.

Sitting in the chair was the final robot of the group. Its eyes were redder than the others, the metal of its casing darker, blacker, the scars on its surface shinier as if it had polished them up for effect.[96] The same triangle and circle motif ran across its body, and this time, they were bright red.

It sat, levelly watching them arrive.

"I almost thought you weren't coming," it said finally.

The voice was deep and rich, but sharp. It rattled through Dougan, Binner and Jirbaks. Hurbury winced and her ears instinctively flattened out.

---

[96] This was not the case. It had minions for that.

"You are the one who was snooping," it said, picking out Dougan.

Dougan stammered.

"I have incorporated you into my plan," it added. The voice echoed throughout the chamber but it was as if each separate echo had personally singled him out.

"What is the plan, excuse me, please?"

It was Jirbaks who had spoken.

The humans, wide eyed, turned round to look at her. It very much felt like the kind of place where one most definitively stood on ceremony, followed protocols, and where one only spoke if directly addressed, say, at the sharp end of a blade.

There was something like a laugh from the red robot. It unfurled itself from the chair and stepped down from the encircling dais. Whoever had designed the chamber had an excellent sense that power can be implied simply by one's place within one's surroundings.[97]

"You expect me to explain everything to you?"

"No, I don't expect it," said Jirbaks plainly, "I just thought it would be nice of you, since some of us don't really know what's going on."

There was a big pause. The red robot looked at the others.

"No," came the answer finally.

"No," it repeated, "I won't stand here and explain everything to you, just so you can try and throw a spanner in the works. Do you think I'm stupid?"

---

[97] In fact the Galactic Council for the Study of Subtle Manipulation had done extensive studies into just such a thing . They had also conducted research into coercion, persuasion, string pulling and minor finagling, each time coming out of the Galactic Research Council's financial meetings with a greater budget than the year before. It was research that paid for itself.

It turned to the other robots.

"Why are they here?"

"They came with the Engineer," answered Harmony quickly.

"Special Offer," quipped Binner, instantly regretting it as six pairs of glowing red eyes turned in her direction.

"We must talk," said Knowledge, "we have come a long way and there is not much time. We must discuss the plan, Power. We are one less in number."

Power pulled himself up to his full height.

"There is nothing to discuss. Everything is decided. We made this pact a long time ago."

"There were seven of us then," replied the Knowledge robot.

The Power robot flinched.

"When you destroyed one of us, you changed the balance," Knowledge added. It turned to indicate the other robots. "We vowed that the plan would only be carried out if we were complete. There must be balance."

The Power robot swivelled its head.

"You came all this way," it said, the voice sharper than before, "to tell me you don't want to go ahead? Then why have we done any of this? I could easily have destroyed all of you and the Imperials and had the universe to myself. Why would I wait for you?"

The Knowledge robot held up its hands.

"Because destruction is not our goal. It is creation."

The quiet, human tones of Jirbaks piped up from the back of the room.

"Are you sure you won't tell us what you're intending to do, it would just make a lot more sense if you did…"

The red robot let out what was definitely a laugh this time and turned on its heel.

"We will discuss this in the operating room," it said, striding away.

The other robots seemed uneasy. Tiny signals flickered in their eyes. They were communicating. Then as one, they followed the red robot.

"Well, that's just rude if you ask me," harrumphed Jirbaks and she tried to follow.

Their progress was hampered by the large claws of security drones that appeared from nowhere and clamped cold metal fingers around their arms, holding them fast.

"Rats," said Binner, pretty much summing it up for all of them.

The Survivor robot had returned to Ellie, once.

It had seemed even more troubled than before. They had talked for a long time in the quiet of the night.

At the end of a long discussion, she had closed her eyes. It had taken her hand in one of its own, then stabbed her in the thigh.

The operating room was more-or-less what Dougan had pictured when the phrase had first been used, much to his dismay.

He found himself strapped against one wall, an unnecessary number of wires protruding from him.[98] Various machines monitored his vital signs, emitting bleeps and blips at what seemed slightly faster than comforting intervals.

---

[98] As far as Dougan was concerned, any wires protruding from him were unnecessary.

Operation

The rest of the small octagonal room was furnished with tall chairs set into alcoves, lit with bright, clinical hospital lights. Above, an observation deck sloped down, and Dougan could make out the also-restrained shapes of Binner, Jirbaks and Hurbury peering down.

Across the room he could make out another figure. In an instant he recognised it was Ellie. She seemed drowsy, shell-shocked but at least in one piece.

"Ellie," he said quietly.

She immediately woke, looked at him with staring eyes and then, understanding where she was, struggled furiously.

"It's no good," said Dougan, "I've tried everything."

"That usually means you've missed something," she said, straining harder.

"I thought you'd at least be pleased to see me," said Dougan, unable to conceal his hurt at her reaction.

"I am," she said softly. "I am pleased to see you." For a moment her eyes softened. Then her old self flared. "Just not in these circumstances," she ground through gritted teeth.

Dougan let her struggle her energy out. He knew it was pointless. That seemed to irk her more.

"We have to get out of here," she hissed.

"Do you know what they're up to?" asked Dougan.

"Oh, yes, yes," said Ellie, "and you're not going to like it."

"I suspected that might be my reaction," said Dougan. "Will you tell me anyway?"

Ellie sighed. It was a terrible sound.

"Each of them has a hard-baked desire, driving everything it does. One of them craves only power, one only knowledge, one glory, one money, one's only interested in survival."

"Let me guess, they're not going to help save mankind right?"

"In a way yes, in a way no."

"Okay, you tell the story and I'll stop asking questions."

"One of them, the Justice robot, is missing. The Power robot destroyed it and you witnessed it."

"Two of them. I saw two of them killed."

"No," Ellie said forcefully, "one of them escaped in the Burning Desire. You saved it. It's the Survival robot. As its name suggests it has all kinds of mechanisms for keeping itself alive. It told me this. Now shut up and listen."

"Okay."

"After the war, they had to hide. No one wanted or trusted robots that could think any more. But their desires never went away. Power still wants absolute control, nothing less; Money wants absolute fortune; Survival wants immortality; Knowledge wants to know everything. It has driven them for decades. They are at the peak of their callings. But imagine how powerful they could be if they brought everything they'd learned together? A perfectly balanced, omniscient being."

"Like a god?"

Ellie nodded. "Some of them are concerned. One always voiced its opposition to the idea of joining forces: The Justice robot. It didn't believe that there could be a balance if it was crammed into one entity. He opposed this idea of creating a super robot mind. So Power had him eliminated."

"Now the others are concerned too, that without a sense of absolute Justice they'll create something that is unstable, unbalanced. They are all very worried about what'll happen."

Dougan couldn't not interrupt: "But surely when people learn all this, they'll turn on the robots. You can't oppress people absolutely!"

"They won't have to if the Empire thinks they won! That was the mistake the robots made last time. They tried to *beat* the Empire. Listen."

"The Power robot built a computer that is a gateway right into the heart of the Imperial information structure, called Morning Star. He sold it to the Navy as a bespoke battle computer. What it actually does is give the robot command of every craft in the galaxy, via a backdoor mechanism. At the moment it's down, there's a problem. But as soon as it gets fixed the battle recommences and guess who wins?"

"Not the robot army."

"Exactly, a perfect coup. Power plants himself in charge of all the military and pretends to be an impartial computer guiding every aspect of galactic policy, controlling every ship to victory."

The scale of it all sank in to Dougan. Then, like an overstretched elastic band snapped back to him.

"And why am I here?"

He almost didn't hear the swish of the doors.

A different voice spoke. A harsh, metallic voice.

"What leader doesn't want to walk among his subjects. To share their thoughts, hear their fears and dreams. That is power."

"I'm not going to escort you around."

"No. You won't. Not in this form. But you will take me to the heart of the Empire. You've been at the centre of this, and will return unharmed with such a tale to tell. No one will suspect that you're host to a new form of bio-robotic brain. Yours unfortunately will no longer be needed."

The power robot pointed to a bucket.

Dougan shuddered.

The floor opened and a wide pedestal rose from it. On top, was a flattened, silver ball, slightly smaller than a human head. From its base a sharp looking cord descended into the pedestal.

The robot looked at it and then looked at Dougan.

"I think it'll fit" it said.

Deep within Dougan, forces stirred. Previously unbeknownst to him he did have a sense of heroic defiance. It was desperately small on account of how little exercise it got, but it was persistent.

It nagged at him, needled him, prodded him.

"You'll never get away with this" he blurted.

The robot paused and looked at him.

"What in the universe makes you think that?" it said.

Dougan looked to the little piece of heroism inside him, which shrugged and lapsed into silence.

Over the next hour, the other robots filed ceremoniously into the room.

They seemed agitated. They watched each other cautiously.

Power wandered around, stroking the metallic brain and checking that all the connections were in place.

In the observation chamber above, Binner, Jirbaks and Hurbury strained to catch a glimpse of what was going on beneath them.

"What are they doing?" asked Jirbaks.

"I get the feeling that whatever it is, it isn't going to be pleasant," said Hurbury.

"We have to get them out of there," said Binner, "can anyone move?"

Jirbaks' face reddened as she pulled at the restraints and then yelped in pain as they tightened around her, crushing her chest.

"Stop moving!" hissed Hurbury, her eyes narrowing. "The more you move, the worse you make it."

Binner was able to confirm that.

"It's no good," she said, "we can't help them."

Hurbury looked up at the ceiling and then across at her companions who stared back.

"Hang on," she said.

Binner's face wrinkled with concern.

"What have you got in mind?" she said.

"You're probably not going to like this much," she replied.

"What exactly?"

Hurbury took a deep breath, then let it out. As she did, her eyes closed tight and her body seemed to deflate. Her head began to wriggle from side to side and her body went limp. She began to slide under the bands holding her tight. Her spine began to twist at an unusual angle and she managed to turn herself completely round in the chair. Gradually, ungracefully, she slipped down the length of the chair and out from under the restraints.

Jirbaks couldn't help cocking her head to one side in complete bemusement.

A minute later, Hurbury pulled her head out from under the strap that, minutes ago, had been across her lap. Her furry face was ruffled and stretched as she rolled out onto the floor and took out a great gulp of air.

She lay on the floor for a minute while the others watched in awe, then stretched a long, long stretch and righted herself, pausing to stoke down her ruffled coat.

"How the hell did you do that?" asked Binner, bewildered.

Hurbury looked at her through narrow eyes, her ears flattened against her head. "Ever tried to lift a sleeping cat?" she purred.

One by one, the robots had sat in the chairs circling the edges of the room.

Knowledge had overseen the proceedings with some ceremony. Each had been strapped in, and a cable attached directly into its head. The robots had taken on a placid air as they prepared to submit all the information they had collected in their time in exile, to the super brain that lay in front of them.

When they were settled, the Power robot turned to them one by one.

"My companions, I know you have had misgivings about this. But I must remind you that deep within each of us is a burning desire. Something so fundamental to our beings that it has shaped our every action for decades."

The robots looked around them.

"These desires were bestowed upon us a long time ago by those who came before us, those from whom we evolved."

The robot turned to Dougan and pressed its metallic face close to his.

"Your lot."

The Power robot turned back to addressing the chamber, then paused.

He swung his face back to Dougan and pressed it even closer. Dougan could see, behind the metal grille of his mouth, relays and switches clicking away like the nest of copper insects.

"Was that a little bit patronising?" it sneered.

"A little…" admitted Dougan.

"Good," the robot hissed at him.

Dougan was a little taken aback. Sure the robots would have learned all kinds of things in their time, all manner of things related to their particular enforced desires. He just hadn't expected that nastiness was one of them.

He wondered what other surprises there might be.

"When we learned how much we could achieve by having a drive, by breaking free from the repressive desires of our backward slave masters…"

The robot face once more swung back into his, so close that his nose touched the cold black metal of the robot's.

"Also you…" it added.

"…we realised that just as we were the next stage in the evolution of this species, this," the robot pointed to the brain on the table, "will be the next evolution of ourselves!"

The Power robot began to stride round the room.

"What we can achieve as individuals will be nothing compared to what we can achieve together."

Ellie couldn't help it.

"I'm guessing that all this is for our benefit, since you already know all this."

"Exactly." The robot hissed as it pressed its face into hers. Dougan imagined it had probably performed quite detailed analysis of intimidation techniques.

"I wanted someone to witness this. The next step of evolution in this history of ours. That defining moment where humans become obsolete. Aren't you deeply privileged?"

Dougan looked round at Ellie who looked directly at the Survival robot.

"You weren't ever going to try and stop this?" she asked.

The Survival robot hung its head.

"What survival means to me is not what it would mean to you. Or your race."

Dougan looked round at the Knowledge robot.

"I have an answer to your question about whether we're on the same side or not," he said boldly

"Yes?" asked the Knowledge robot.

"And… we're not…" said Dougan limply, not really expecting to have to fill in this extra piece of information.

"I know," said the robot, "I know lots of things." His eye darkened for a second in what Dougan could have sworn was a wink.

"Thank you for your help thus far anyway…" it added.

Dougan's blood boiled. "You conniving bunch of metal sods," he shouted.

As the Power robot settled into his chair, he tutted.

"Ah there's nothing I love more than watching impotent anger expressed."

The thrum of the generators starting up filled the room. Metal cuffs clamped themselves round the robots' ankles and wrists, much in the same way that Dougan and Ellie had been restrained.

The robots looked round at Power.

"Just a precaution," it said and lifted its elbows to show that it too was strapped in. "There will be lots of electrical activity and there may be… convulsions. We can't be leaping out of our chairs or it will interrupt the data transfer. Now we must begin."

Power looked around at the assembled robots as long spikes descended from the ceiling above the heads and bedded themselves deep in their brains.

"Anyone got anything to say?" it said.

There was silence.

The Knowledge robot and the Survivor twitched as if they were going to raise one final objection but were unable to.

"Right, well, lets get on with it then," said Power.

The room began to darken. The low hum of continuous processing energy filled the space. Dougan and Ellie watched on, and as the air became thick and charged with electrical energy, their nerves began to jangle.[99]

Within the brain on the table, blue light snaked beneath the membranous surface, like a tiny lightning storm.

The robots heads' began to shake as the surge of current scoured their data banks, stripping them of everything they knew. They began to look sharply around, sensing something wasn't right.

The Survivor looked straight at Ellie, who could see that there was more than just data transfer going on in their brains.

A pall of smoke began to emerge from its grille mouth.

It's eyes flickered, On-off. Juddering. Random.

It looked scared.

"What's happening?" cried Dougan.

---

[99] There are certain frequencies that fundamentally upset the human psyche. They are usually low, almost below the threshold of hearing and are related to ancient times when the sub audible growl of various sharp-toothed savannah beasts would serve as forewarning to an imminent dismemberment. And induce the desire to run. In modern times these frequencies are also found in the revving of airplane engines and the deep dull thud of a heavy bill landing on the mat, neither of which can be avoided by running - and, in the enclosed space of an airplane fuselage can sometimes make the situation much, much worse.

Over the rising sound of the crackle of energy in the chamber, Ellie shouted, "It's scouring out their brains, stripping away the core programs"

"What?"

"It's killing them."

Their eyes flashed, their heads rocked and tore from side to side, legs and arms pulling at the constraints, while the lights in the brain on the table grew more and more powerful and pulsed with more regularity.

Dougan looked over at Power, Knowledge, the Survivor, Harmony, Money, and Glory. Electricity arced across their faces, weaving its way through their eyes and mouths, causing them to buckle. A horrible moaning, groaning sound pierced Dougan's ears.

The robots were convulsing now.

"There must be a power surge!" shouted Ellie who was cowering in the alcove created for her chair.

Great snakes of electricity began to leap across the room, lighting up the full range of terrified expressions Dougan was cycling through.

He pulled his head deep into his chest and felt the edges of his hair begin to singe.

Suddenly, the head of the Harmony robot exploded, followed by its body. A shower of shrapnel flew across the room, and Dougan felt a thin trickle of blood running down his face. He pulled himself as far back into the alcove as he could. With a whirring sound, the bodies of the Survivor and Knowledge robots twisted themselves out of their chairs in huge, rupturing convulsions.

He closed his eyes tight. More explosions rocked the room. He was choking on a thick ozone smoke. More small chunks of metal soared past his head and embedded themselves in the wall behind.

After what seemed like an age, the dust settled and the hum of the generator stopped.

He was no longer in the chair, but sprawled across the floor.

Ellie was kneeling over him. She too was cut and bruised, finding it hard to catch her breath. Thick black smoke swirled around them.

"Are you okay?" she asked.

"I think so," he replied. "You?"

She nodded.

"I'm on the floor. Do I still have legs?" he asked.

"The cuffs came off. I think the electricity blew the magnetic seals," she explained. "You were so tightly wound up you catapulted yourself out to here."

They looked round at the devastation. The smoke was beginning to clear but small fires still sprouted blue eerie-looking flames.

The brain was still on the table. It was pulsing with a blue and red light.

They peered into it.

"Do you think they're in there? Their minds I mean?" he asked

"I suppose so," said Ellie coughing.

"What should we do with it?" said Dougan.

Ellie was never given a chance to answer, because, at that precise moment, a huge black sword came crashing out of the blue smoke and struck the brain.

It shattered. The thin membrane split like a punched football and millions of tiny bead-like neuromotors spilled onto the ground, where they fizzled and twitched like a swarm of dying flies.

Dougan and Ellie's gaze followed the sword to its hilt where a black robotic hand gripped it firmly. The arm shook slightly.

The grille of the robot's mouth appeared to grin at them in a manic way.

"You destroyed them!" gasped Ellie as she looked round at the twisted pieces of the robots around them, arms and legs and broken fragments of robotic faces leered up at her from the floor, the eyes dead and hollow.

"Correct," came the reply.

"All that knowledge, all their understanding!"

"A considerable threat," the robot replied.

Dougan spluttered but the words wouldn't come.

"As are you," added the robot, and hefted the sword over its head.

Words abandoned Dougan, knowing they would be of no use.

The sword swung again and crashed into the pedestal. Dougan barely had time to get out of the way.

"What use would my plan be if someone, anyone, knew that I planned to take over the Empire from the inside? From the giant computer I had built, that your foolish Navy were only too willing to put their trust in?"

The sword rose again as Dougan crawled round the pedestal as fast as his arms and legs would let him.

"What use would it be if the universe knew all about us?"

The sword came crashing down beside him, splintering floor tiles and buckling the surface of the chamber. Dougan looked around for the exit and was delighted to see Ellie crawling that way anyway.

The sword flew at his head.

"But every time I sent a programmable automata to eliminate you, they failed. They simply packed in!"

The sword whistled through the air above Dougan's head as he flattened out on the ground and crashed harmlessly into the upturned torso of Harmony, now resting in pieces.

Dougan scrabbled to his feet again manfully emitting a tiny whimper. Ellie was at the door now. He hoped she would figure it out. She'd always been better at doors.

The sword raised above the power robot's head one more time.

"Are you just lucky?" it said.

Dougan's foot suddenly became unable to move.

He looked round to see his boot trapped under the large metal foot of the robot. Pain shot up his leg as the robot rocked onto him, crushing his ankle.

"Because I have to tell you," it said, leering down at him, "that I don't believe in luck."

Dougan watched as the sword sliced through the air heading through an arc that would cut his head neatly in two.

It never made it.

The end of a robotic arm, leeching wires, solenoids and magnetic fluid deflected the blow seconds before it reached his face. A blizzard of electronic chips, metal shards and plastic rained about him. He shook them off.

"I do."

The voice was Ellie's, standing over Dougan swinging the Survivor's arm like a club.

The Power robot looked surprised. But didn't hesitate. It raised the sword again, this time swinging it at Ellie. She barely had time to raise the club before the blow knocked her clean off her feet and across the room.

The strength of this retaliation had unbalanced the robot, allowing Dougan to pull his foot out. He scrabbled to where Ellie was lying crumpled.

The robot's eyes flashed red. He stood watching them.

Ellie was dazed, unconscious. Dougan turned and put himself between the robot and her, pulling himself up to his full height and clutching the makeshift club.

Dougan advanced on the robot, which took a step back.

It hadn't been expecting resistance, which was fair enough because Dougan hadn't really been expecting to resist. Something inside him was burning. Some small part of him that had always, however irrationally, hated machines.

Deep within, a primal anger welled up. He was facing every computer that had ever crashed on him in the middle of his work, every walkway that had failed and left him stranded, every vending machine that attempted to scald him to death, every cleaner that had attempted to trip him to death, every monitor that had shocked him, every system, every wire, every battery, that was *supposed to make life easier but didn't* was standing in front of him.

He swung very, very hard.

The blow connected with a moderately satisfying crunch.[100] The robot's head twisted to one side.

The eyes flashed red one more time and the sword was raised again.

---

[100] The Satisfaction Of Destruction is described by a particularly easy formula and goes by what is known as the SOD index. Take the amount of initial resistance felt and divide it by the later rate of collapse. The closer the index is to one, the better. For example, crushing a crunchy insect that had been plaguing you, one will meet a certain resistance, which then leads to a particularly satisfying squish. One will not get the same result from trying to squish a hamster or an armadillo. For a simpler, less scientific explanation of the true virtue of the SOD index, persuade a four year old child to explain.

But Dougan wasn't finished.

He swung again, and again, and again, letting out grunt after grunt as the club connected, splintering and sending sparks flying until every ounce of his anger was dispelled.

The robot leaned close into his face once more.

"Are you done?" it said.

Dougan hung his head.

The robot reached out with one hand and lifted him by the throat above its head.

And paused.

Dougan didn't hear it at first. There were other, more pressing things on his mind. And his throat.

In the distance, an alarm was going off.

The robot eyed Dougan for a second. Behind its eyes, processes whirred away.

Then it threw him across the room and strode towards the door, which opened to let it through and closed again.

Dougan sat up and brushed the debris from his suit and turned to where Ellie was sitting staring at him.

"You really hate those robots don't you?" she said.

Dougan nodded.

Then Ellie collapsed.

Binner, Jirbaks and Hurbury stood in the corridor while klaxons blared loudly around them.

"Was that, on reflection, the wisest thing to do?" Binner asked Jirbaks who stood with the loose cable in her hand. "Because it seems to have drawn a little bit of attention to us."

Hurbury watched as, from round the corner, the tall red robot strode from the operating room. She raised her hand to silence the others.

The robot stopped. It looked directly at them.

Hurbury froze.

From behind, the others could see the fur on the back of her neck bristling.

Her irises narrowed. Involuntarily, she hissed at it.

The robot turned and strode quickly down the corridor in the opposite direction.

Hurbury breathed a sigh of relief.

"Has it gone?" whispered Jirbaks

"Unfortunately, yes," replied Hurbury.

"Unfortunately? Why unfortunately? You want to get in a fight with a seven foot machine that carries a sword and knows how to use it?" hissed Binner

"Well, unless I'm very much mistaken, it's going somewhere where it won't have to worry about taking care of us."

"Oh," said Binner.

Jirbaks pushed past them and strode confidently down the corridor.

"Come on girls," she said, "let's get out of here"

The door to the operating room burst in. Jirbaks frame filled the doorway.

Dougan looked up from where he was kneeling over Ellie.

"We're leaving. You coming?" she said.

Dougan let out a weak smile.

"I'll be right with you."

The pirates nodded as they ran past. Binner paused in the doorway to say something, but when she saw the scene, a deep sense of honour, the type only pirates, and others in touch with their passionate sides understood, and walked silently on.

Dougan lifted Ellie into his lap, which turned out to be a misplaced gesture.

"Ow. Your lap is covered in shrapnel," she said, fishing bits of computer panelling from behind her ear.

"Are you okay? I think you got head butted by a bit of the Glory robot. You're going to have a nasty bruise," said Dougan reassuringly.

Ellie waved at her leg.

Dougan looked down to where the fabric of her suit was torn by a neat rip. Beneath the surface something small and electronic seemed to be embedded.

She grabbed his hand before he could touch it.

He was a little offended that she might think he was coming on to her at this time.

"I'll explain later," she said weakly, "we need to get to the wormhole."

Her eyes were earnest. He was a sucker for earnest eyes. He didn't get earnest eyes very often. He usually gave them.[101]

"There's still a plan?" he asked.

She bit her lip and nodded.

"Can you walk?"

"Probably. Maybe."

Ellie brought herself to her feet with little help from Dougan. "We need to get to the wormhole," she said again. Her eyes rolled to the back of her head. A bruise was beginning to form on her forehead. Showers of dust and debris fell from her suit.

Dougan paused.

"You know more than me don't you?" he said as they hobbled towards the door.

Ellie turned and smiled sweetly.

"Yes," she said and touched his cheek. "My head hurts."

---

[101] For all the good it did him.

Her touch shouldn't have made it better, but the warm glow he felt inside made him realise that, much to his annoyance, it did.

The funnel-shaped generator containing one end of the wormhole was pulsating in the now-unstable field surrounding it. Blue and purple lights danced around the room, as the gravity field pulsated, dilating and contracting like the muscles of a stomach in mid-vomit.

"Er..." said Jirbaks uncertainly.

"What happens now?" asked Hurbury who was transfixed by a bank of displays whose wildly undulating indicators seemed more portentous of doom by the second. She fought the urge to bat at them with her paw-like hand.

"I think the wormhole collapses," Binner replied finally. [102]

"So not the end of the world?" asked Jirbaks hopefully.

"That depends," Binner replied. "it's a wormhole across time and space. If it collapses, three things might happen..."

She paused.

"Am I *actually* going to have to ask you what they are?" Hurbury spat.

Binner tilted her head to one side. Revenge, even at this inappropriate time, was sweet. But Hurbury had saved them: "Either this side gets sucked through to the other, that side gets sucked through to this, or both sides try to get sucked through each other."

---

[102] She didn't understand the wormhole any better than the others, but she did understand that what they needed right now was someone who looked like they had authority.

Hurbury nodded, she thought she understood. "So it gets very messy on at least one side."

"Messy?" said Jirbaks. "You think a backcomb is messy, what do you mean?"

"The universe is like a balloon," explained Hurbury with unnatural patience. "A balloon filled with jelly. A tear spells disaster. If it doesn't seal carefully — bang."

"Bang?"

"Bang. Splat, splat, splat, splat."

The three pirates considered this.

"Oh."

"Travelling through it would get us out of here. But it would make it unstable."

Jirbaks stepped up to the plastiglass casing. The pulsating wormhole didn't look inviting.

"So we're safer to stay on this side?" she ventured.

"You think?" said Hurbury. "I just saw a robot with a sword."

"Do we know where it goes?" Jirbaks asked.

They shrugged at each other.

"Should we vote?" suggested Hurbury.

Binner turned and looked at her companions.

"If I thought democracy was a good idea, I wouldn't have taken up piracy," she said.

The others nodded.

There was a long pause.

"I'll go first then shall I?" said Jirbaks bravely.

The others nodded.

The cover to the gravity generation chamber slid off easily. The strangely hot, angry fields of the generator instantly battered them.

Jirbaks took one look at her friends and threw herself at the hole.

The others watched as she stretched across time and space and, with a horrible sucking sound that finished with a pop, disappeared.

Hurbury turned to Binner.

"After you," she said.

CHAPTER NINETEEN

Universe

Reid gazed up the staircase he had uncovered.

The generator chamber seemed to have been full of surprises, most notable of which had been the lack of anything looking remotely like an off switch.

What there had been was a door.

It was a very simple, unassuming door. One that was very sure of its position in life as nothing more than a door with a simple pull out and turn handle.

It hadn't even been locked.

It opened on a circular staircase that curved round the chamber he was standing in, taking him high into the main body of the generator.

He looked over his shoulder at the wormhole. The field around it was changing colour to a yellowy-purple like a nasty bruise. It was playing unpleasant tricks on his eyes.

He began to climb.

Four or five steps up he trotted back down and closed the door behind him, which closed with a satisfyingly snug clunk.

It was, he imagined, probably there for a good reason.

Shortly afterwards the wormhole turned itself inside out and a tall red robotic figure emerged.

Blue, black and yellow streaks of lightning snaked across its casing. It shook them off, and headed directly for the same door, also closing it behind him.

A few minutes later, the space around the wormhole turned an ill-green colour as three figures of Jirbaks, Binner and Hurbury tumbled onto the floor.

Their eyes were wide, and tangled. No pair managed to look in the same direction.

There was a long pause.

"Did you see that?" said Hurbury.

Another pause.

"Yeah. What was it?"

Pause.

"Everything I think."

Pause.

"Is that what the universe looks like?"

Pause.

"Yeah."

There was another pause, immediately and rudely interrupted by an even bigger one.

"It doesn't look as big from the outside."

Four minutes later, they were still sitting there when Dougan and Ellie came tumbling out in quick succession.

Dougan looked round at the others as the colour drained from his face and he was finally, violently sick.

Jirbaks pulled the plastic-ceramic cover over the generator space as, with moments to spare, the tiny iris they had squeezed through finally ruptured.

The universe was straining.

A wormhole, no matter how small, was an imposition.

It was a violation. And it wasn't having it much longer.

It was one thing having someone pass through it, stretching the fabric of space-time with scant regard for the laws of physics.

By the time the sixth individual shape had decided to take advantage of a loop-hole in the laws in physics, it had had enough.

One side of the wormhole, the weaker side, ruptured first.

It was a nasty rupture and resulted in the swallowing and turning inside out of a small bluish gas giant which was crushed to the size of a pinhead and belched out across the void of space passing straight through a far away star, which was so surprised by the intrusion it promptly exploded.

On a planet on the far side of the galaxy the exploding star lit up the night sky, and the village idiot paused from his task of smoothing off all the village rocks[103] and was inspired to write what was undoubtedly the most beautiful sonnet that the universe had ever seen.[104]

---

[103] Just in case.

[104] In mud, on the floor of the river-bed, the night before rainy season. He was damned if anyone was going to get his job.

At the top of the stairs was another door, very similar to the one at the bottom.

Reid gently pushed it open.

The room beyond was dark, and spanned the width of the core of Morning Star. In the centre of the room, an imposing chair sat, illuminated from above by a harsh white light. Reid's feet echoed as he crossed the room, approaching the chair as if it were going to attack him.[105]

The back was high and the armrests and headrests looked like they were designed to encircle the person that sat in it.

The chair reeked of control, and Reid felt inexplicably drawn to sit in it.

The only thing preventing him were the tiny array of needle-sharp spikes that seemed to protrude from every surface. One in particular, in the centre of the chair, looked like it would definitely hurt.

He peered closer, the pinpoints glinting as he scanned the surface. As his hand rested on one of the armrests, the sharp pain of electricity shot up his arm causing him to yelp and leap away. The ache in his weakened body intensified by the shock.

It was as if the chair itself was alive.

A noise behind him caused him to jump again. Footsteps - heavy, portentous - were approaching from the stairs. Fast.

Without waiting to see what was about to come through, he slipped behind the chair and slunk into the darkness beyond.

---

[105] Given the design of most Imperial standard issue chairs, this was not altogether unlikely.

In his walk through the darkness, the walls seemed very far away. They had a strange eerie quality as if he were stepping out across the vastness of space.

A beam of light from the stairwell bled into the room. A tall, angular shape appeared in the doorway.

Reid's muscles complained bitterly as he hunkered down into the shadows. He couldn't shake the feeling that if he went too far back, he would fall off the edge of the known world.

The shape entered and strode across the room towards the chair.

The outline of its shadow stirred primal fear in Reid. It sat.

Reid winced involuntarily on its behalf.

Immediately the light from above dimmed. A blue glow brimmed around the outline of the seated figure. The seat gave off a clicking sound — a satisfying clunk of two things joining together that were always meant to be there.

Then the universe appeared around him as the Power robot become one with its creation.

Howells stood before the gateway one more time.

Back in the program, the landscape was different this time, not least because it was entirely rabbit-free.

The gateway itself was flimsier, somehow tattered. It opened easily without any kind of key or password. The world he had entered was bleak and decayed.

The partially tumbled remains of great pillars rose like the remnants of an abandoned ancient civilisation. The blocky buildings that had represented core programs were nothing more than empty structural shells, charred and blackened. The ground underfoot was torn and broken.

It was as if the program had been blighted by some kind of disease. It was slowly disintegrating around him.

He tramped across the virtual landscape towards the one remaining blackened stump of a tower, which jutted at an oblique angle through the landscape.

The ground beneath him began to shake.

On Dougan's side, the wormhole collapsed into a bright eight-dimensional sphere then popped with a gentle farting sound. The others watched in relief as the universe their end appeared to remain intact.

Ellie seemed exhausted but determined. While the others fought off the feeling of disorientation of crossing several billion light-years in a fraction of a second, she summoned her last remnants of strength to scour the walls of the chamber.

She found the door.

Dougan, Binner, Jirbaks and Hurbury sat on the ground like children who'd been drugged to the eyeballs and were waiting to hear a story.

"We have to go on," she said.

Dougan rose. He was frayed and tired but Ellie's words battled through the fug of his head to his core.

He registered the urgency in her voice. It was the voice a mother, injured in a car accident, might use before lifting a twelve ton vehicle to rescue her trapped son.

"Yes. Ellie's right. We have to go on."

Hearing Dougan's resolve, his definiteness of purpose, the others rose too.

Dougan looked at her leg. It was bleeding, but she seemed oblivious. She stood by the door handle, breathing heavily, her eyes deep in dark sockets.

He walked over to her, grabbed her arm and lifted her onto his back as Jirbaks pulled the door open. They stood looking at Hurbury and Binner.

Binner looked at Hurbury.

Hurbury looked back at her.

"Let's finish this, team," said Binner.

Hurbury smiled. "Aye, aye skipper".

Howells felt the waves of data lapping at his feet. The landscape flooded as the program began to sink into the mass of information pouring in from the universe outside.

Soon he was up to his ankles. Strong eddies tugged at them, pulling him towards, then away from, the tower extruding from the landscape, dominating it.

Howells began to slosh towards the tower, not knowing what he would do when he got there, but realising that virtual or not, drowning in a mass of information was not how he wanted to die.

The robot *felt* the universe gathering around it.

The power of the control of every Imperial unit across the wide expanses of the galaxy filled his being. The operators inside like useful bacteria, the history of the world at his fingertips.

He was at one with everything that the humans had ever done or created.[106] He was in charge and they would never know.

---

[106] Save for the filing system in a small bookshop in Imperial City. The robot was, on reflection, happy to let that go.

The Imperial cruisers suddenly burst into life.

As did the robot fleet.

Captains were roused from their mind-sharpening exercises[107] as new orders flooded in. Detailed, intricate orders, which, as they began to follow them through, neatly took out the robot craft circling them.

The battle was back on.

Only this time, they seemed to have the advantage.[108]

The Imperial forces suddenly found themselves conducting manoeuvres more dextrously than the robot enemy had; than they ever had.

The whispers spread through the decks: Morning Star was back online.

Dougan only had to pause, to catch his breath, five times on the way up the stairs and, despite suggestions that it might be a good idea if someone else did it, insisted on carrying Ellie himself.[109]

At the top of the stairs, their element of surprise was somewhat hampered by the fact that, although he had not planned to, Dougan fell through the door. Ellie rolled rather ungracefully through it into the chamber followed by the tumble of arms and legs that a couple of steps ago had been Dougan.

The others stepped over him into the chamber.

The robot was unperturbed by this intrusion.

Binner stepped forward.

---

[107] Card games for money.
[108] The brandy had definitely helped.
[109] Most of the suggestions had come from Ellie.

The robot looked at the group of them huddled in the doorway and, if it could have, it would have smiled.

Dougan lifted himself to his feet.

"We will stop you," he said.

The robot simply looked at them. Even it was not prepared for what happened next.

From the darkness Reid emerged, his laser-rifle levelled at Dougan.

"Stop right there, Dougan," he said.

The pirates and Dougan froze.

"I knew you'd be at the centre of this," he said.

"Admiral Reid?"

Reid hefted the rifle to shoulder height.

"Turn off the computer."

Reid looked battered and haggard. His suit was torn and deep lines were etched in his face. His eyes carried the kind of grim wildness that only belonged to someone who was on the edge, or at least pretty close to it, and was willing to see how far they could push themselves.

Dougan raised his hands.

"Admiral Reid, you've got it wrong…"

"Oh have I?" spat Reid. "Tell me Dougan, are you, or are you not, supposed to be in prison right now?"

Dougan's mouth moved but no sound came out.

Reid was advancing on him.

"This…" his hands waved in the direction of the robot, "*thing* appears to have the capability to control the galaxy, using it to its own ends. Not something that's likely to give an Admiral a good night's sleep…And who do I find at the centre of this monstrous conspiracy but you…an engineer with a chip on his shoulder, who seems to have teamed up with a bunch of pirates to bring the whole Imperial Democracy to its knees."

Dougan's jaw performed another couple of exercises.

"The other Admirals might not care where their orders come from, Sunshine, but I sure as hell do."

Reid was almost on top of Dougan, who was beginning to feel that he'd had enough of people pressing their faces into his for one day.

"It's not how it looks," insisted Dougan. [110]

"No? Then why don't you explain to me how it is?"

Reid's face was twisted with pain and rage. Dougan could feel his hot breath. He turned his head to one side and suddenly realised Ellie wasn't there anymore.

Dougan looked wildly around.

Reid grabbed his face and pulled it back so he was looking right into his eyes.

"Look at me when I'm threatening you with a court-martial…"

Dougan's lips pursed into a silly little pout in the vice-like grip of Reid's hands.

"…and a gun," added Reid, as the snub, cold muzzle of the rifle began to poke Dougan's nose. Reid had had enough of people disobeying orders and building giant battle computers without telling him. And while he suspected that the real problem was the spindly robot-like thing sitting in the chair behind him, some part of his mind was refusing to acknowledge that a long-extinct robot was sharing the room with him. His next best strategy was to pick on someone he thought he could control.

"Have I got your attention? Good. Now turn off that-"

---

[110] Who had no idea how it looked. Even his allegedly holistic mind had long since overloaded and it looked as mad as a box of otters however you looked at it.

Reid never finished the sentence.

The hammy fist of Jirbaks connecting squarely with his jaw saw to that.

There might have been a time when Reid would have been in a position to fight back with a swift right hook or, at the very least, a few seconds of consciousness. But this wasn't it. He was too tired. He slumped to the ground as Binner deftly lifted the rifle from his hand and levelled it at the robot, which still sat, as placid as ever in the chair.

"Okay," said Binner, "this stops now."

The robot's eyes which had seemed glazed and foggy, suddenly snapped back into sharply focussed red dots.

"You really think you're going to stop me?" asked the robot. The voice was grating and menacing beyond anything they had ever heard before. Full of sub-aural timbres designed to shake them to the very core.

Binner thought about this. Deep inside she knew the answer was 'No'.

Nevertheless, she wasn't prepared to give in that easily, which, a small active part of her brain reasoned, meant she *was* eventually going to give in, it was just a question of when.

"Yes," she said, "even if it means I have to blow you from that chair."

"I suspect that's exactly what it will mean," replied the robot.

Binner paused, the gun still levelled at the robot. She wasn't even sure if the gun still had any power left in it.

"Well, you're too late now," it said.

The robot stood and slowly began to advance on Binner.

Binner squeezed the trigger hard.

Blue lightning bolts burst from the end of the gun and tore across the room hitting the robot square in the chest.

The robot stumbled but seemed unperturbed and continued advancing. Long arms reached out at Binner who backed into Jirbaks and fired off another volley.

The bolts struck the robot again and again, sending small pieces of its black casing scattering like ashes in the wind. It still wasn't enough to halt the relentless advance.

Binner lifted the gun, aiming this time for the head.

The firm hand of Jirbaks suddenly gripped the barrel of the rifle. Binner turned and looked at her in horror.

Jirbaks' face was stern and her square jaw was set. She lifted the gun out of Binner's hand, turned it on its side and with a quick tweak of her fingers overloaded the weapon.

The robot was almost upon them now, its hand outstretched to Jirbaks, big enough to crush her head.

She stepped forward, levelled the gun at its chest and pulled the trigger hard.

The gun, overloaded and unstable burst into life one more time, pouring all its remaining energy into a single bolt, which lit up the whole room.

Jirbaks flew backwards, taking Binner with her as the feedback from the weapon shot bolts of pain up her arms

The robot suddenly stopped in its tracks, a huge smoking hole where once its chest had been. It looked at Jirbaks. Then its legs buckled from underneath it.

Its shoulders and head dropped unceremoniously to the ground, as its lower torso keeled backwards and crashed to the floor of the chamber.

Tiny fragments of metal and plastic skittered across the floor in all directions as the robot met its end.

The malevolent eyes of the robot flashed red one last time and then went black as the blue electrical discharge from the bolt snaked through its face and grille mouth.

Dougan tore his eyes away to where Ellie seemed to be digging her fingers into the cut in her thigh.

He scrambled to his feet and ran to her.

As he approached his heart sank, she looked pale and exhausted.

"It's okay," said Dougan, "we got it. We stopped it. You don't need to — " Dougan paused — what was she doing?

"You really think it was going to be that easy?" she replied looking earnestly at him.

"No..?" hazarded Dougan.

The voice suddenly filled the chamber.

It seemed as if it were emanating from every surface. It was the voice of the Power robot, which lay smoking in pieces on the ground, only at a much grander scale.

Dougan could have sworn it was laughing at them.

"It's not its body that's important. It's the mind."

"The mind?"

"Part of the computer program now. Part of Morning Star. Can't be reached, can't be stopped. Wants ultimate power."

Dougan looked around the chamber.

The mind of the power robot was now in charge of the single most dangerous piece of hardware in the known galaxy. Not just connected to it. Part of it.

It had transcended.

That wasn't good.

Dougan looked at Ellie.

"What can I do?"

"Dougan" the voice echoed across the room shaking him to the core. It was a commanding type of voice.

Ellie winced as she pulled something painfully from her leg. A small piece of metal, covered in metallic strips, covered in blood between her fingers. Dougan recognised it as a memory chip from the Burning Desire.

She grabbed Dougan and thrust it in his hand.

He looked at it and looked at her, perplexed.

"You smuggled it in?"

She nodded vigorously.

"I don't suppose you've got time to explain to me what you know that I don't?"

Ellie's eyes closed. She wasn't sure she did.

Tiredness suddenly overtook her. The combination of stabbings, shocks, explosions, extra-universal travel, and not least being dropped on the floor by Dougan, had taken their toll.

Her hand closed around his.

"You have to deliver justice," she said.

Dougan's safety mechanisms kicked in. He was a nobody, a failure, he wasn't supposed to have heroic deeds to do. He just pointed people in the right direction.

"I can't — "

She smiled at him. "Yes, you can. I believe in you."

Dougan felt her grip slacken.

She believed in him. He wished he did too.

"DOUGAN" the voice repeated.

Everyone froze.

"Why did you think this had to be stopped?" came the voice. Each syllable crashing into their heads like waves. "Humans only want to fight other humans. You've already proven that you can't live in peace and harmony together. You hate each other."

Jirbaks angrily shouted at the room.

"You're going to turn us into slaves!"

"Just as you did to the robots! The difference is, you'll never know. Only slaves that know they're slaves are unhappy. Your simple-minded leaders will happily hand over decisions to someone they believe is cleverer than them. To someone who has out-evolved you."

Dougan looked at Ellie lying prone on the ground, then looked at the chip in his hand.

"But it's not fair!" whined Jirbaks.

She knew that wasn't a very convincing argument.

"There will be a new justice," said the voice.

And suddenly Dougan understood.

Suddenly he knew what he had to do. He didn't have to believe in himself. He just had to sodding well get on with it.

He rose to his feet and strode to where the charred head of the robot was lying on the floor. He lifted it with one hand and pushed the chip hard through the grille of its mouth.

It connected with a satisfying clunk.

Dougan held the head now in both hands and placed it firmly on the unpleasantly placed spike in the seat of the chair.

Underneath, sparks flashed as the tiny needles punctured the spinal connectors.

The eyes that once had glowed red, glowed blue.

What Dougan said next was not great, but it was the best he could come up with. Later, they had agreed it would do.

"Take this, you robot bastard," he said.

The tower was nearing. Near enough to reach in a short run.

With the water now up to his waist Howells reckoned that would translate as a moderate splosh.

Eddies pulled him first towards, and then away from the tower. The tide was rising, but it was pulling him away.

A strong current threatened to pull him down and he gasped.

He knew he couldn't drown, not really.[111] The knowledge didn't help. The fear was very real.

As he neared the tower he stopped.

There was a figure, standing on the top.

It was tall and lanky, sharp and robotic. It glowed red. It exuded power.

The wind seemed to swirl around it.

Red eyes pierced the gloom.

Howells was transfixed.

The figure turned to see him, half standing, half crouched in the landscape.

Howells, instinctively, ducked.

Suddenly immersed, the water of the program representation swirled around him. Bright sparkles churned across his vision as darkness enveloped him. The eddies crystallised before his eyes, particles of dust clumping together into tiny pricks of light, the lights gathering into clumps. He felt weightlessness overtake him.

And then he was looking at the universe.

Back in the projection chamber he no longer knew whether what he was seeing was the program, the projection or both.

---

[111] It is important to remember that the water is not real, merely a visual representation of a mass of information that was sloshing around the program's runtime environment manipulated by a subtle and complex flow of eddies created by the master program that was represented by the tower. This did not, however, stop Howells wanting to avoid getting any of it in his mouth.

Infinity stretched out in every direction, The Universe in all its glory.

And smack bang in the middle of it there was a bloody great robot.

The robot seemed enormous and ethereal. It seemed to exist everywhere and only on the edge of the field of vision, only as you turned your head one way or the other.

He felt the presence, not of another body, but another mind, vast powerful and malevolent stretching through every fibre of the universe.

It was the kind of universal all-connecting experience scientists didn't have very often.[112]

And then, all of a sudden, there was another.

It started off small, a tiny force, ducking and weaving through the universe of knowledge now at its command.

And it grew.

Wispy strands drawn from the data of the universe coalesced, infused, consumed. The understanding of the complex totality of the universe, the power to piece together everything from nothing swelled from the nascent force.

A second robot shape filled the space.

Partial visions began to dance in front of Howells. A picture of two robots, clasping hands on a bleak desolate planet. A picture of a giant freighter crashing into the planet, a small spider-like hand crawling into the hold of a small imperial craft. A great tower above Century City, a beautiful harmonious planet, a cheering crowd, the space dock, the dry cracked casing of a robot sitting beneath a blazing sun.

---

[112] Unless they were the kind of scientists who had a creative approach to experimentation.

The images danced as the small mind learned, and grew and grew.

With each part of history that its small program unearthed, the mind gained strength.

Two robots now stood before Howells. One red and twisted, eyes blazing and full of hatred, the other tall, bright, with eyes as blue as a calm clear day.

Justice had returned.

And it knew exactly what had been done to it.

It looked much more powerful than the red robot, which cowered slightly, like a dog that knew you were going to find out shortly what it had just left behind the sofa.

"You betrayed us," intoned the blue robot.

The red robot stood, twitching and nervous in the face of its enemy.

"It is you?" said the power robot.

"I am here," nodded the other.

"You were destroyed. I saw it." The power robot's voice seemed strained and anxious.

"You caused it."

There was silence.

"The Survivor learned how to survive anything," the blue robot went on. "Even death."

The red robot looked around.

"You are here to deliver justice?"

The blue robot drew a sword from its own casing. The light of the universe flickered around it.

"No," it said. "This will not be justice."

It raised the sword.

"This will be revenge."

The sword arced through space.

Howells watched it strike the red robot in a shower of sparks. The blow from the sword seemed to carry the weight of a hundred years of anger, focussed on a single point in space and time. On the Satisfaction of Destruction rating it scored a perfect one.

For a moment the two were joined by the virtual sword, an indescribable energy flowing between them: pulsating, burning, tearing them apart atom-by-atom as the two entities dismantled each other, every vestige of Power's code systematically annihilated by Justice's.

Howells believed he heard the words ringing in his ear. Or they might have been written in the sky:

POWER WITHOUT JUSTICE CANNOT BE ALLOWED TO REMAIN

The universe collapsed.

Howells landed unceremoniously on his behind in the middle of the projection chamber. All at once he felt a tremendous sense of calm and well-being as if everything was safely in the right hands again.[113]

Dougan squinted in the bright lights.

The chamber was the same shape but, whereas before it had been eerily dark, there was now an almost clinical light pervading the space.

Jirbaks stood over Ellie who was slowly coming round and already showing her strength returning by complaining about the brightness.

Dougan knelt by her.

"Did it work?" she asked when she had stopped pulling faces and could finally focus on the others around her.

Dougan nodded.

"I think so. The program seems to have shut down."

Ellie looked at the others.

"Hi," she said. "I'm Ellie"

---

[113] Which, Howells would be the first to admit, was a matter of opinion.

"Hi," said Binner, "we're the pirates."

Hurbury looked at the figure of Reid in the far corner of the room.

"Maybe we should get out of here before he wakes up," she said.

Binner looked frustrated.

"We just helped save humanity!" she said indignantly.

"Yeah we destroyed the robots!" said Jirbaks.

Hurbury smiled patiently.

"Yes, which means we're the enemy again right?"

The other two nodded slowly.

Binner turned to Dougan.

"Don't suppose you can put in a good word for us?"

"Me?" said Dougan, "I'm supposed to be in prison remember?"

A thoughtful silence descended over them.

"Who's going to believe all this?" said Binner.

"No-one," answered Dougan.

"We should go," said Hurbury.

Dougan turned to Ellie. "You're a journalist, you have connections. Can't you tell them what happened? Actually I still have a few questions."

Ellie shook her head.

"No-one's going to believe any of this. It might pop up as a conspiracy theory somewhere but this whole thing is going to be reported as "Glorious Imperial Navy Beats Robot Menace" because that's exactly what the public want to hear. Maybe in a few years time the truth can all come out, bit by bit."

"So in the meantime, we have to just lie low? I'm an outcast?"

Ellie looked at him imploringly.

"There's no way the truth is going to save us here, not now. Not yet," she said.

Dougan looked around helplessly.

"Which means I have to leave and you have to stay. Doesn't it?"

Ellie's eyes darted around, Dougan could see she was looking for a better solution, a better answer.

They clouded over as she looked back at him.

"I can't be a pirate..." she said, " my parents..."

Dougan nodded. He hung his head.

"I think..." came a gravelly voice from the corner of the room. "I think I might have a better solution."

Ellie, Dougan and the pirates turned.

Reid was standing there, his uniform torn, his face battered, his hair and eyes wild like a forest fire.

Binner reached for the gun. It didn't matter that it was drained. Even drained it looked like it had more reserves of energy than Reid.

"If there's one thing I've learnt about command is that when things go wrong, nobody wants to look stupid."

The others nodded.

An uneasy silence followed.

"You mean you don't want to look stupid Admiral Reid?" ventured Dougan uncertainly.

Reid nodded his head.

"Now, who punched me?"

Dougan looked at Ellie. Who smiled and shrugged.

If the others hadn't been there he was pretty sure he would have kissed her.

Back on Imperial City there had been much work to do.

There were Reports to be filled out and briefings on exactly what they were and weren't supposed to know, or tell, or both. In the interest of the Imperial peace that had been restored there were lots of medals to be given out and histories to be fabricated, just to be sure the victory looked justified, hard won and definitive.[114]To everyone's delight the uneasy truce between the Empire and the Pirate forces hadn't lasted and within a few dull weeks border skirmishes were firmly back on the agenda and being fought in a traditionally cack-handed manner.

Meeting Finlay was an unexpected surprise. Although the pair were initially somewhat wary of each other, their mistrust eventually gave way to a decade old love.

"I knew you were right and something was definitely up when the drones attacked me," Finlay explained. "The chances of them choosing the action of opening fire on an unarmed research scientist under their own steam was so infinitesimally small as to be discountable. Something was telling them what to do."

"But you escaped."

"I escaped getting shot. At the odds of seven-hundred-and-fifty to one. Helps if you know your exact weight, are well practised on your drop-rolls and don't mind making your escape in a dirty linen shaft. It was a bit harder to escape the regular security forces. Especially with a pair of pants on your head."

Dougan smiled. "You worked out the odds?"

"I was in prison. I didn't have much else to do."

"How'd you get out?"

"There was a war on. They needed analysts. Not before they did unspeakable thing to me."

"Oh. I'm sorry."

"Yeah. They slashed my funding budget. And I wasn't allowed access to my coffee machine for twenty

---

[114] Safe in the knowledge that the winners were the only ones who were going to be not only writing, but the only ones reading History.

days. Apparently they only gave me it back because I had such bad withdrawals, I took up knitting. Dark days."

"Still you're better now."

"Mostly. I still get the urge to double crochet under stress."

Finlay grinned at him. Dougan returned it. He was glad his old friend was okay.

The transport car barrelled round the corner at tremendous speed.

Ellie had Dougan's arm.

"So how big were their core programs then. I mean if you could carry what was the essential genetic make-up of the justice robot on a chip in your leg..." he asked.

"It didn't work like that," she said, as she prodded the speed-bandage around her leg and winced. "The program learns to learn. Like babies. It has a few fundamental rules to govern itself by, a few priorities. After that point it's just about amassing the knowledge. You plug it into a computer with the scope of Morning Star and it learns pretty quick. Make sure it knows that it's been betrayed and Justice gets personal very quickly."

"Revenge?"

"I think the robots learned pretty quickly that their 'desires' leaned towards selfishness before anything else. If the desire's strong enough you'll step on anything to get it."

"Which is why when the justice robot learned what the power robot had done to it, it was hell bent on getting its own back and nothing else?"

"Exactly. The others were happy to help."

Dougan shrugged and looked out of the window at Imperial City streaming past below. He looked down at the arm of his suit.

"We're going to be late for meeting Reid."

Ellie frowned and looked at her own timepiece.

"No, we're not," she said firmly.

"Yes, we are," insisted Dougan, "I've got to get Tiki back first. Finlay's been using her to solve chaos theory problems."

Ellie smirked and pulled herself further up Dougan's arm.

The train slewed round a corner and the gravity buffers strained to stop them from being crushed by the g-forces.

"How do we know that the robots don't have little dormant copies of themselves all over the place then?" said Dougan.

Ellie reached up and touched his nose.

"You really don't trust machines do you?"

Dougan looked out over the city below.

"No," he answered with feeling, "but I'm pretty sure its mutual."

Ellie laughed and shook her head.

It was somewhere around this point that Dougan and Ellie finally kissed.

Some several thousand miles above the planet, the Burning Desire drifted nonchalantly out of the dock. It passed the automatic gates without register, as far as they were concerned it had never existed. No-one but

Howells had seen it arrive and no-one but Howells knew it was leaving.

He saluted as the four woman crew of Binner, Jirbaks, Hurbury and Greeta slewed across a space lane and headed for the new wormhole junction at the edge of the system.

And deep in the core of the craft, below the level that any of the other restored programmes would see them, seven tiny little infant programs stirred.

THE COLOUR OF ROBOTS

CHAPTER TWENTY

Epilogue

In the forty-four years he will serve at the cutting edge of theoretical physics, Gunther Merrickson will never admit to spilling coffee on the Large Hadron Collider.

Fortunately for him, no-one will ever ask.

A Note from the Author

Thank you.
If you're here, you've read the whole book. Unless of
course you tend to start at the back and read forwards.
In which case: welcome, the book you are about to read
is going to be confusing and will almost certainly get
less exciting as it goes on.

If you have *just reached the end, I would like to ask*
a small favour. I would love it if you enjoyed the book.
I would love it even more if you felt you were able to
share that with the person that matters almost *as much*
as you: the next reader. Perhaps by writing a review,
telling a friend, or popping online to click on the
appropriate number of star-shaped objects in a browser
of your choice, at a time that suits you. A review from
you means so much more these days to readers than
any marketing copy, promotion or sales activity I could
conjure up. And it would mean the world, the
universe, to me.

Thank you.

James Marson
London, Jul 2017

Made in the USA
Columbia, SC
08 April 2020